Charles Vivian was born in London in 1959. He worked in the fine art and antiques trade for twenty years in both England and Australia before devoting his time to writing about the subject for a number of magazines and journals. He moved to Ireland in 1997 where he lives with his wife and four children.

The Ballingaddy Find

Ringrone Books

Published in 2008
by
Ringrone Books
www.ringronebooks.com

Copyright © Charles Vivian 2008
All rights reserved

ISBN: 978-0-9558500-0-4

This book is sold subject to the condition that it shall not, by way of trade or otherwise, be lent, resold, hired out, or otherwise circulated without the publisher's prior consent in any form of binding or cover other than that in which it is published and without a similar condition including this condition being imposed on the subsequent purchaser.

To A, T, O and A

Prologue – 945 AD

The unending chant of the sea meeting land told Orri Sigrifsson that he was alive. In which world he had awoken he couldn't confirm but if it was the underworld, it had, so far as he could ascertain, all the qualities of the seashore on earth.

His eyes were glued shut by a crusty film of something he couldn't identify, but imagined it to be blood. However, even when his numbed fingers rubbed them open, he was enveloped in a darkness only weakly penetrated by a grey line denoting the ocean's edge. His return to consciousness also awakened sensations all over his body, from frayed finger tips to bruised and battered limbs whose muscles and ligaments were reacting violently against the ordeal that they had been put through. He had lost his boots and his trousers and remembered discarding his cloak whilst in the water so that he was clad only in his shirt which seemed to be intact, held on to his torso by his cloth belt.

He felt around him and realised that he was on smoothed rock, a stark contrast to those towards the water which were like blades of iron, thin layers of slate set at right angles to the sea and eroded to create an efficient shredder of flesh. The salt water working its way into his many cuts was evidence of just how efficient a combination of rock, wind and ocean could be at ridding a helpless animal of its skin.

He sat up with some difficulty, a sharp twinge telling him that all was not well with his ribs. He had broken his ribs before whilst misbehaving on the turf roof of the long house at home as a child, losing his footing and falling onto a rail set up beside the house to which animals were tethered. Carelessly touching his left side was a mistake he only committed once as the resultant pain jolted him so that his whole body ached and groaned with complaint.

It had stopped raining but the wind was still whipping up from the south west and occasionally treating him to a spray of sea water as another wave crashed against the shore. The absence of the moon concealed any indication above of moving clouds, all sound and movement came from the sea and the wind, and both sounded angry.

Orri and the sea were friends, they had conversed all their lives, and he had no reason to fear it, for he had long thought that it was only man's indifference to the sea that made him vulnerable to its power. It was a theory he kept well to himself for his family and village paid great deference to their God of all fears, Thor. Everything they did, they laid in the lap of one of their Gods whereas Orri had heretically suggested that a lot of their undoings and almost all of their good works were due entirely to themselves. If they feared the sea, he once told them, then they had no place to be on it. No God had the power of nature, he argued; but God was nature, they replied, and he must not challenge the Gods, otherwise he and the rest of them, no doubt, would be struck down by the might of those he chose to taunt.

And now, the men of the village and their crop of gold, fourteen thralls to be sold in Jorvik or at home, were shattered on the south coast of Ireland; their boat, a knarr built by Thureil himself, the finest of boatbuilders on their coast, disintegrated into more pieces than it took to build. No doubt, in the morning, he, Orri, son of Sigrif, and heretic, would be blamed for his lack of deference and, if they had any blood-letting to do, it would be Orri's, offered to a God in whom he did not believe.

If they wanted blame then they had no further to look than Olaf Imarsson, the village leader who took them from home to the bountiful shores of Ireland, rich with food and human commodities which were taken across to England and sold as slaves to the more adventurous traders who took them on to the hot lands in the South and the East.

They had first gone to Ireland because they had been told of the wonderful treasures, pots of coins, gold fashioned into jewellery, items with which they could persuade their women to sleep with them and cook for them. There wasn't any gold or pots of coins, at least not where they went, but there were young men to be sold as labourers and young women to be sold as whores, cooks and cleaners, but not until the men of the village had sampled their wares, making sure there was no sign of resistance; damaged goods were hard to sell in an increasingly fickle market.

Orri, Eric and Harald had all told Olaf that to sail whilst all the signs of a southerly gale were waiting over the horizon was madness but he paid no heed and set sail on an easterly course anyway. Eric could read the clouds like Orri could read the sea and Harald could read the faces of the two he knew he could trust in these matters, and he did not like what he saw. Orri, he reckoned, knew about nature and didn't fear the Gods but he was now visibly afraid and you cannot beat what nature has to offer if all you have is a construction of frail timbers that was no match for a surging sea and a windward shore of pitiless rocks.

They were undermanned anyway, after the fight with Olaf's half brother at sea two days previously, and even then, some at the oars were in no condition to row for any more than a few minutes before they started to miss strokes and clutch at wounds. The cargo of ten girls and four boys were of little help as the boys were merely that, although they would fetch good money in Jorvik, and the girls could be sold anywhere for a handsome return, but none could handle an oar.

Olaf would not be told and he hoisted the striped sail, a sight that had terrorised the west coasts of Britain and Ireland for two years now. It was faded and much repaired since the day it was dedicated to their God, Tyr, and was first unfurled before the people of the village who had, after all, paid for it to be made so that a select thirty-eight of their men could search for the riches to be had in the west.

It had also been agreed that a part of Olaf's mission was to find a place for them to settle in a warmer and more hospitable climate. It was their last throw of the dice; there was nothing else to spare from their stored funds, not since they had dispatched Karl, Olaf's half-brother, in a similar knarr but had heard nothing of him since. It was supposed that he had angered Odin and that He had taken His revenge whilst, in the same summer, they gave offerings to Thor for their bumper crops and fair weather. The old men of the village knew, however, that Karl was a malevolent waster and once he had been given command, ignored the needs of his village in bringing them their bounty in the autumn. He was rumoured to have joined a renegade mob of unsavoury characters and to have wintered over in an estuary on the west coast of Ireland and to have struck further inland to a large lake, but when a survivor of that winter returned he could not recall a Karl Redblade.

Orri shifted his weight to his right hand side to alleviate the pain in his ribcage. He would move to a more comfortable spot if only he could see anything but he was afraid of falling down a deep crevice, a feature of these rocks that he had observed when they had passed them many times before. He hoped and prayed that he was above the high water mark as another battering on the rocks would be the end of him, of that he was quite sure. In his muddled state, he wondered whether a few choice words to Thor would help but if he were to believe in Him then presumably he was where Thor thought he should be. He drifted in and out of consciousness, each time his thoughts returning to the ship and where they had gone wrong.

Having established that setting sail was their first mistake, their second was in not overpowering Olaf once the storm clouds showed themselves to the south-west. The wind had propelled them well on their way across the south coast towards the east but despite Harald's best efforts at the rudder oar, they were being forced towards the coast. There was little use in working at the oars, the wind was doing its job, the sail at full stretch, so much so that Harald, the sail master, feared for the strain put on the mast fork. He had heard of rotten uppermost strakes being pulled right off by over-burdened sheets in a high wind, resulting in loss of the use of the sail, until the rigging could be adapted by putting it through oarposts.

Orri kept to his thwart in order to maintain the balance of the boat. In front of him was one of the girl slaves sobbing at her plight for she had never been to sea before and she knew that there was little, if any, chance of ever seeing her home again. Orri's intended reassuring hand on her shoulder brought the adverse effect as she jumped with fear, cringing forward to be out of his reach but looking back at him as she did so. He recognised her to be the pretty one that the men liked and used rather too often in a rare fit of preference amongst them.

Above her cowered head, the black-based clouds towered into the sky, the sides facing the sun billowing walls of white contrasted by the dirty grey of the shaded side and all the time, the blackness at the base growing in size as it neared them. The clouds were such that no sun penetrated them, the blackness touched the horizon and as they got closer, the sky and sea melded into one dense mass.

Orri could feel the hull slewing through the rising waters as sail, rudder and ocean current fought it out. Harald shouted for help to hold the rudder and ordered the spar to be lowered, the strain on the mast and mast fork was going to rip the keel out of the boa. Jjust as two men approached the relevant sheet, the metal ring attached to the uppermost strake came away, the sail whipped forward carrying the sheet with it, armed this time with an iron tip which cracked like a leather whip when it reached its most forward point, a few feet beyond the prow. How it didn't kill anybody was a source of wonderment but those in the know, those that had faced a sea at its most contrary, knew that they were in trouble.

Olaf, upon advice from Harald, ordered the oarports to be opened and oars to be put out. Twenty-two men, eleven each side, manned the oars, just over half the usual complement of thirty-six oarsmen, and started to pull to bring the ship back to an easterly course but it was an impossible task. Water was beginning to burst over the gunwales and Harald and Olaf were beginning to argue with each other as to what was the best thing to do.

Olaf wanted to find shelter, Harald laughed at the suggestion pointing to the curtain of black cloud and asking Olaf where one was to find shelter from that and suggesting an alternative of finding somewhere to beach the boat, even if there was a chance that it might be broken up in the subsequent storm, at least they would be on dry land and they could, if necessary, walk to Dublin.

Olaf pondered this for a short while and looked over the prow at the coastline which, the sun having disappeared behind the storm, looked dark and bleak. He said that they must go on, round the head and shelter in the Pill to the east, they would be alright there, surely? Harald and Orri knew of the place, it would be a fine refuge from a south westerly but they had to get around the headland which would mean rowing with the wind on the starboard quarter, a task made impossible with so few men at the oars. Orri knew that they had to go with Harald's idea and find somewhere to beach and find it very soon before the full gale force wind was upon them.

The darkness overcame them quickly, the rain added to their discomfort and diminished their visibility. Their work at the oars was of little benefit as they felt the running surf pick them up and bring them closer to the shore, now only made known to them by the spume that delineated land from sea. Harald and Olaf held the rudder but they were only just managing to keep their precious knarr upright and stern on to the wind, all the time aware that they were headed for the coast. Distance was meaningless then, the white line could be a thousand paces or a fraction of that away, horizons were obliterated except thin lines of lighter sky still apparent through the veils of rain; the sky they had enjoyed a few hours previously.

Orri raised his oar and prepared to ship it when it struck something and shot his end at a frightening speed towards his head but he managed to duck under it before it slid into the sea. Eric, stood, looked behind him to see the coast a few boat lengths off and decided that it was time he put his trust in his God and dived overboard.

Olaf, upon seeing this desertion, reached for his sword stowed under his thwart and shouted something, audible but the words indistinguishable, to the remaining crew who, sensing that all was not right, looked in terror over their shoulders, Orri included. Anybody trying to get ashore past that boiling surf were beyond their senses but two more jumped overboard and when Orri glimpsed the slash of a sword blade before it sank deep into the shoulder of one of their captives also trying to jump, he knew that there was now only one thing to do, so put his left foot onto the gunwale and propelled himself deep into the sea.

Thereafter, his recollection was hazy. There were oars and timber in the water and a girl floating with her head bowed as if to purposefully drown herself.

His first contact with the shore was a knee striking a rock and then he was washed out again. Losing his sense of direction completely he swam back out to sea only to be dumped on the rocks, winded, and the endless succession of rollers pounding him, each time he caught smaller gulps of air between the unrelenting walls of water and he told himself that if he didn't move then he was going to die. Saving himself was now all on his mind, he had gambled and won, he gave no thought to the others, at least he was still alive and now he must get out of the influence of the waves, strike higher ground and wait for the storm to end. He slid on his bottom, pushed by his aching legs away from the ocean but the further he went the sea still pursued him. He slipped a few times and the rocks were razor sharp as though they had landed on a part of the coast with man-made defences of sword blades.

There was no respite, no seaweed to cushion the rocks' adversity, no grass knolls to reassure him that he was getting any higher and no slackening of the rain to aid his visibility. He didn't know how long he shuffled inland, he was only just aware that he was headed in that direction, but by the end he was resigned to die there, he could do no more than wait for daylight to return. His lips were covered in salt, and then he could taste something else and realised that it, too, was salty but more substantial than sea water, it must be blood but the salty invasion of his mouth from the minute he jumped from the knarr had dulled his sense of taste.

His legs could straighten no more, his fingers ached with numbness, his neck was beginning to tell him his head was too heavy to support any more and his heart was beating so hard that he could hear it in his throat, a nervous exhaustion that had only visited him once before, after his first real fight, and a feeling that, as on the previous occasion, he had survived the ordeal.

That night's journey, a journey entirely through his imagination, evoked the stories of the skalds of the Hall of Warriors and underworlds of immeasurable pain, stories that he had previously laughed at, internally of course, but which now seemed to have some meaning in life, now that he had experienced everything any man would need to experience.

The first softening of the darkness revealed a partly cloudy sky, the dark smudges still propelled by a south westerly but with no sign of rain. Orri moved his head so that he could check on the sea but it appeared that he was a long distance from the breakers. His feet were bruised and cut but there was little blood, the sea water having washed and sealed each gash, leaving jagged lines criss-crossing his pallid skin as in some barbaric inscription. His hands, too, were washed pale, the fingers were blue with cold, the upper skin weathered like dried fish skin. He had lost the nail on his left thumb and it was this, with its exposure to the elements that was giving him so much pain. It seemed curious to him now that he had not noticed the loss of the nail during the night.

It was only when he tried to move his upper body did he understand the severity of his injuries to his ribs. He carefully undid his belt, raised his shirt to his shoulders and looked down at his chest. One rib had a bone pointing outwards although the broken point had not penetrated the skin. Another seemed to have collapsed inwards and it was this that was so sore; the bone was jabbing into his lungs making movement painful and breathing uncomfortable. There was nothing he could do about those.

The rest of his body ached like it had never felt before, as it would feel if it had been tumbled down a steep hillside, not once but several times and then trampled on by a cow for good measure. He slowly made his way to his feet, the light was sufficient for him to find his way across the perpendicular blades of rock towards a gently sloping bank of grass above which was some cropped grass. Obviously the area was grazed and he could not be far from habitation but this was a foreign land and he could speak very little of the language. What hope had he, barely able to stand, let alone fight, if he was recognised as one of the feared invaders?

He settled into a sheltered spot in the grass, largely out of the wind and facing the south east, just the place to catch any morning sun if the clouds dispersed. On the horizon a yellow streak told him that the chances of getting some sun were high and he was glad of it for his constant shivering was driving his broken rib harder into his lung. Out of the wind and with a soft straw-like bed his demeanour brightened and from his vantage point he started to search for any sign of survivors or wreckage. Seagulls swooped up into the southerly air stream and dived down onto a prey unseen by Orri, he suspected it to be somebody who was on board the knarr, possibly the poor girl who had given herself up to the sea, denied her family and freedom and now cheated of life.

Curiously, there was nothing to be seen, no timber nor bodies, no flotsam that marked the passing of a proud vessel, admired and feared by the same eyes. He watched the strip of turquoise water approach the land knowing that it was the sun's rays that coloured the sea like that and when just off the breaking surf it appeared to stand still whilst the clouds flew across his ceiling revealing an unbroken roof of pale blue and a sun low on the horizon. The first touch of warmth, albeit feeble, cheered him enormously and took his mind off both his ribs and his situation.

His stomach growled in demand, he hadn't eaten since they had set sail at midday but to eat, and eat well, he would require fire, and whilst he was capable of lighting one, the resultant smoke would betray his presence to whoever tended the livestock that grazed the land behind his position. Food, however, was going to be a necessity to build up his depleted strength and he was luckily one who had watched his elders as they searched for food at low tide near his village. Whelks and winkles were bound to be amongst the seaweed washed up between low and high tide and that would involve him moving about and crouching over in search for his meal. There had been a small amount of food on the knarr which, being stored in barrels, might have floated free when she went down.

Struggling to his feet once more, he moved gingerly down the bank and back onto the rocks. It was a low tide and a small sandy beach rested between two sharp points sticking out to the sea. He got onto the beach, no more than a boat's length wide, but found no whelk-bearing seaweed, nor any signs of the shipwreck. Perhaps, he thought, the knarr did not sink after all and he had chanced his life prematurely.

To the west was a plateau of jagged rock interspersed with the deep crevices that he had seen from the sea, passable for a fit man but too jarring for him to contemplate tackling. Looking to the east he could see the big headland that they had tried to round the previous evening, and smaller headlands between, against which the sea dashed itself into thin wisps of spray carried high on the wind. The east looked a more favourable direction to head; there would be caves in which to shelter along that coast and that was where he was likely to find the remnants of the knarr and any other survivors if it proved to have foundered.

He had walked for a short while before a larger cove opened up before him. One hundred and fifty paces wide, the shallow bank of sand sloped up to more grazed ground about four hundred paces from the ocean's edge. Further inland, on top of a gently sloped hill there were unnatural hummocks, grass-roofed dwellings from which two plumes of smoke were blown horizontal as they emerged from the roofs. Lying at the high water mark were tell-tale signs of the fate of the knarr; a body stripped of its clothing, a few planks of wood, an oar and one or two unidentifiable pieces amongst the dark coloured weed lying in a line of clumps amongst the grass slope that bordered the stretch of sand.

Orri walked, painfully, in a northerly direction along the western shore of the cove, mindful of the fact that movement betrayed his whereabouts to anybody watching from the settlement but if he stood still whilst still in view then he would blend into the colours and shapes of the seashore from that distance. Once near the northern-most slope, the hovels were hidden from his position by a hillock covered in vegetation and he could move more freely.

The body was that of one of the girl thralls, a pale blue torso with few signs of injury, her matted hair covering her face which, when Orri pulled the hair back, was a grotesque mask of agony and terror; no gentle drowning for her, she had fought her way to shore but the sea had won the unequal battle. He was relieved to see that she thought her life was worth saving after what she must have endured over the past two weeks; the destruction of her home and family, the rounding up of her kith and kin, the arbitrary choosing of who was saleable in the market and who was not and the driving into the sea of the useless ones until they sank beneath the waves or under the swords and axes of his shipmates if they turned for the sanctuary of the land.

Then there was the voyage around the south west coast and the chance meeting whilst just in sight of land of another ship, one familiar to all the crew, the ship they had watched leaving the jetty of their village four years previously. The ship entrusted to Karl Redblade, Olaf's half brother, the murderous brute who had apparently seen to the demise of his own mother when she gave birth to Olaf, fathered by the revered Imar the Bold and born whilst he died in the great battle in the Thames against the South Saxons.

At first the older ship tried to run but theirs was faster and under the mastership of Harald had little trouble in overhauling them. Olaf expressed a wish that they had bows, just the right weapon for this sort of fight but largely useless for their day to day existence as harvesters of Ireland's youth. They were uncertain if Karl's crew would be so armed but as they got closer, the lack of airborne steel tips capable of penetrating their coats of mail told them that they did not. They opted *not to wear their armour; they could survive a sword cut but a slip or stumble over the gunwale and they would sink like a stone. They anxiously looked across to their foe to see their preparations but there were no signs of readying for the fight to come. Olaf champed to settle a score with his half brother, nothing to do with their mother, but more a matter of honour. Karl had betrayed his own people and was in possession of a stolen knarr, something that belonged to his village.*

When they were two boat lengths away they recognised the face of Karl standing by the stern, a lot fatter than he had left the village and smirking at the prospect of another victory. The smirk disappeared when Olaf called out to him and reminded him of his obligations to his people. The battle had become personal although to both crews the prospect of victory and, hopefully, the victor's spoils, was more incentive than grudges against individuals.

Remarkably for two ships coming from the same village, only Olaf and Karl were related closely, there were a few cousins that had slipped a generation or two and some who were friends with brothers or sisters but it wasn't considered by anybody, other than the two leaders, as an internecine battle.

Harald manoeuvred their boat by sail and rudder alone whilst Karl's helmsman asked his crew to man the oars to gain position. Thus, when Harald was able to put the prow of his boat alongside, his crew were ready to jump from one ship to the other and start their dreadful business whilst their enemy were still fumbling around for their weapons. Olaf led, swinging his axe with such ease that it might have been a piece of rope, and the forward oarsmen retreated under the onslaught, tripping over the thwarts behind them and lying helplessly as they were overrun. Karl arranged a last defence at the stern, about twenty of his men stood between the mast and the rudder, the rest dead or dying in the forepart of the boat.

Orri watched from his own boat, he had been detailed along with ten others to ensure that there was not a counter attack on their vessel whilst the fighting took place on the other. He saw the two sides square each other off as much as they could within the confines of the bulwarks and then Karl's men knew that they had to break out of their predicament and, five or six abreast, advanced upon Olaf and his men.

Orri had been in fights, he had seen his sword cut into flesh and sever limbs with a lucky strike but whilst in a battle there were other things to look out for than the spectacle that unfolded before his eyes. It was soon made obvious those who could fight and those who just shut their eyes and defended, hoping upon all hopes that a colleague would rescue them. There was also the extraordinary noise of clashing swords, swords hitting wooden shields as an axe splits a piece of firewood, grunts and the occasional groan as the recipient of a blow submitted to death's call.

It occurred to Orri that there were no shrieks or wailing as one heard when civilians were trying to defend their homes, just men going about their daily business as if toiling in the fields or boatyards. Men were falling on both sides and there was a great deal of slipping, the reason for which, at first, Orri could not understand, but Harald reminded him that blood and entrails did not provide a good footing when lying on wood.

Karl's men seemed to be getting the better of Olaf's and the latter was looking to see if they could escape back to their own ship and be able to cast off without his half-brother's crew following on. He had already lost eight men and several others were badly hurt, it was they that would have to form a rearguard and be sacrificed. Whilst Olaf had been in the thick of it for most of the action, Karl stood back directing his men to any perceived weak points and his unused sword belied his name, Redblade.

Suddenly two of Karl's men fell on Olaf's right and he rushed forward to get behind the first line of defence. This brought two or three men against him but in the cramped beam of the ship they could not all wield their weapons at the same time. Olaf's first swing of the axe bit deep into the shield of one of his attackers who remained upright, but the other two, in an effort to avoid the heavy weapon's arc, slipped backwards between two thwarts and the man behind Olaf was on to them in a flash before they could recover.

Olaf could not prise his axe from the shield of his opponent and only just managed to avoid a thrust of his sword that appeared from one side before he placed his left foot on the shield and, with all his weight, which was not insubstantial, he pushed shield and defender over and was able to lever the axe head free whilst defending a sword blow from another quarter with his own shield.

It was that charge from Olaf that won the day for his crew. The remaining defenders either sat awaiting their fate, nursing cuts and broken limbs, or jumped overboard preferring to drown than suffer the ignominy of being put to the sword by their so-called betters. Karl was one of those that deserted his ship and his crew and it appeared that he had gone straight down as he was not seen amongst those whose heads still bobbed up and down with the swell and were drifting away from their one chance of life; their ship.

The victors tipped the bodies and bits of bodies overboard but they had no desire to slaughter their countrymen any more and let the living alone once they had purloined or discarded their weapons. Harald boarded the enemy knarr and inspected the timbers which, he declared, had not been well looked after and he doubted the boat would last the voyage home, especially if they met a storm in the channel. There was little to salvage other than the weapons and some salted beef and grain to add to their own stocks.

Olaf recovered his half-brother's shield, not painted with concentric circles or geometric designs as were most of his crew's, but a distinct white background with a vertical sword depicted in red, Karl Redblade's shield, Olaf's proof that he had brought him to justice the way his people would expect. Attached to the back of the shield was a waxed cloth bag, which Orri noticed once it was stored amongst their own shields along the bulwarks of the knarr. Nobody pried into the contents of the parcel and it was Olaf, some days later, who disclosed that it contained some personal objects that belonged to Karl and that they were to be returned to his family.

Orri traversed the cove across the north side to the eastern wall of the inlet of which he was able to walk the length unseen from the settlement further inland. Up on the rocks were other bits of wood that would have formed some part of the knarr but nothing recognisable. There was, however, a small stream of fresh water with which he washed the salt from his wounds and slaked his thirst.

He reached the eastern headland and saw that the coast went back inland, possibly to another cove so he braved the jolting journey over the uneven rocks to round the small promontory. The coast opened up to a long stretch of cliff, a masthead high at the most but vertical, below which was another plateau of vertically stratered slate, covered in brown weed and rock pools but not so badly cut by deep fissures. Two dark stripes running down the cliffs some distance to the east promised caves and he could see one or two gaps between the rocks allowing sand to settle to form small beaches.

He knelt gently beside a rock pool and ran his fingers through the seaweed scoring five whelks, one of which he dropped and moved too quickly to recover as his ribs reminded him of their broken state. He soon had a reasonable pile of molluscs which, at home, they would boil in sea water and then extract the animal from its shell by means of a pin, but he couldn't risk a fire, easily enough started using the dried tuft grass on the cliff above him, and he didn't have a pin. He tried to crush two of the shells together but they were remarkably strong and it was only by smashing them between two rocks that he could get at his breakfast, picking off bits of shattered shell as he went. It was a most unsatisfactory meal with too much preparation for too small a return and the salty slugs only exacerbated his thirst and he sought another source of fresh water. He soon found a stream cascading down the cliff but the wind was blowing it over a body's length wide by the time it reached his mouth so he had to cup his hands to get a good mouthful.

The sea was still colliding with the foreshore propelled by the slowly abating wind, the percussion of the waves reverberating in his ears. In amongst those waves, that were almost translucent whilst suspended in the air and with the sun behind them, Orri could see bodies and oars but when the waves transformed into opaque froth, they were not to be seen. There were bits and pieces at the high water mark but nothing of any use. What he was looking for was a body, the previous owner of which, prior to jumping or being thrown out of the knarr, had the presence of mind, unlike himself, to have put on his sword belt. At least with a sword he could defend himself of sorts and he could slaughter a beast for food which he could cook once away from inquisitive eyes.

He ventured further east to one of the small beaches and there he found another body; that of Eric, who, whilst still clothed, was not carrying any weapons. Orri became squeamish about these dead, they seemed to be bodies that nobody wanted, pale flaps of skin pealed off the bone and showing sinews in their limbs, all blood having long been washed away. Having been quite used to the sight of carcasses hanging in the cool rooms at home he thought that he was inured to such a hideosity but a human carcass was quite different, a pathetic lump like a beached boat without its strakes.

Beyond Eric was the body of the boy that Olaf had struck with his sword, his right arm virtually severed and the cut extending well into his chest, and another of the girls, her long light brown hair spread from her head like a stain in the water. There were also more pieces of the knarr but nothing substantial until he came across a small barrel, one that was usually lashed to the mast and contained dried meat to chew on whilst at sea. His hopes were to remain just that when he reached the barrel to find the top had come away and the contents dispersed.

He went further east and the cliffs got higher until he came to the first of the caves where even the low water lapped at the mouth. Here he found six more bodies but none armed, he chuckled to himself to note that another of the boy slaves had, literally, lost one of his upper limbs, and there were more shattered pieces of oak and pine, testimony to the strength of the sea when provoked by such a wind.

Half submerged was a larger piece of wreckage which Orri waded out to retrieve and only when he was above it did he recognise it to be a shield. He hauled it to the shore and when held upright, the bottom still on the sand, he recognised the waxed cloth panel nailed to the back and the distinctive image on the front, now a bit battered after its encounter with the shoreline. "Personal items", he recalled Olaf telling them, perhaps something that he could use in his present situation, but try as he might, he could not separate the parcel from the reverse of the shield and being waxed cloth, there was no possibility of it being ripped open. He could feel something dishlike and hard, more than a hand's width in diameter, a flat, oblong object behind that, with a smaller lump in front.

He dragged the shield up the beach using his right arm whilst clutching his complaining left ribcage with his free hand, it seemed to help putting pressure on his side. In the cove were other items from the knarr, some cordage which he gathered up, timbers he could recognise as thwarts by the wear to the places that his shipmates had sat for days on end and part of the rudder tiller, over the end of which he had watched Harald curl his long fingers for two years, as any warrior would rest his hand on the pommel of a sword.

As he went further into the cove he found more objects that were familiar to him but nothing with a sharp edge. Disappointed, he emerged from the cove and decided to return to the larger beach to the west. He stopped at the waterfall to quench his seemingly insatiable thirst and whilst there he noticed a cloth caught up in some seaweed on the rocks between him and the sea.

He trod carefully over the slippery seaweed and eventually reached a cloak which he instantly recognised as being Olaf's, a mantle of authority worn over his sheepskin, the two edges joined by a gold coloured brooch set with coloured stones that was much admired by all those that saw it, and, by some miracle, still attached. He untangled the material from the seaweed and took off the brooch which had a thick iron pin with a point sufficient to pierce the thick cloth of the cloak.

Almost running back to where he had left the shield he soon managed to breach the cloth around each of the nails by using the iron point, and the parcel came away from the sodden wood. He then ran the point under the stitching that had been face down on the shield, and which must have been undone by Olaf at some stage as the stitches did not conform with the other holes in the cloth. Once undone, the parcel became a small bag inside which were three individually wrapped objects, again in waxed cloth but not stitched.

He took the smallest out first and rolled it out of its protective pouch. It was a gold cross covered in gold beaded decoration on one side and quite plain on the other with a small gold ring on the upper arm from which, Orri presumed, one suspended the cross as a pendant around the neck. It wasn't of his people's workmanship but he had seen things like it both at home and in England and Ireland, and was aware that it was a symbol of the Gods of these islands, that it was in gold was unusual and it would command a good price amongst the money traders.

He next extracted the oblong treasure, a leather covered board with gold mounts in each corner of voided and engraved decoration depicting people, seated and with different objects in their left hands. He did not understand what this was, he had certainly never seen anything like it but, coupled with the cross, he surmised that it must be something to do with their religion.

The last item was the round dish that, once uncovered, even Orri's uneducated eye could see was a very special plate indeed, made of silver, the rim was made up of gold beads within which were eight sections of differing gold decoration, forming a band, each section separated by a raised square knob, enamelled in red and blue, then another small band of beading before a shallow fall to the flat dish, quite plain and in which Orri could see his face and the cuts it had endured. He turned it over to find it plain again but not as finished as the surface.

It was the sort of object Orri would ascribe to a great king, although modest in size and hardly fit to carry any meal, its intricacy told of beauty ahead of necessity or perhaps its intended function above the basic needs of man such as food.

He packed the objects back into their bag, threw Olaf's comparatively cheap and vulgar brooch in with them, picked up the cloak which he hoped would soon be dry if he laid it out onto the rocks and retraced his steps to the large cove. The tide had come in a bit and he had to stick to the higher rocks making sure that on the few occasions that he could see the settlement his movements were short and sharp, a lesson taught him by his father, the hunter Sigrif.

He passed the naked girl and was beginning to make his way south along the western wall when he heard a dog barking. As the wind was full in his face and the noise came from behind him he couldn't judge how far away the beast was but he hurried along to his clump of grass from which he could observe anything coming from the north or east, the west approach being made impossible by a jagged cliff face.

He hadn't heard the dog again and was beginning to think that perhaps it was a trick of the wind when he saw three men emerge from behind some shrubs at the northern end of the cove, the same shrubs that had hidden, or so he thought, his progress to the other side of the beach. One man held a large grey dog on a lead and a spear in his spare hand whilst the other two had spears and swords, it looked as though they were out hunting for something slow on its feet. The dog soon led them to the girl and whilst they stood looking at her ghastly expression, the dog started along the footprints that led to and away from the recumbent body. Orri's footprints.

The hunters turned their attentions to the prints and discussed their origin and likely direction with much pointing from one headland to the other, eventually agreeing to walk down the middle of the beach looking in each fold of the rocks and in the crevices that could conceal a human. They stopped every now and then as the dog scratched away at a spot in the sand for an imaginary bone or a rock and they appeared to be in little hurry.

Orri stayed transfixed, he was certain that he would be impaled on the spear points once found and he had the choice of jumping up to disclose his position or to stay where he was until one of them approached and he could surprise him, disarm him and get the means by which to defend himself. On the other hand, he could plead to be a seaman trader captured by the murderous pirates whose ship had foundered off the rocks to the east and was seeking food and water so that he could journey on to a port to find a passage home. He was unarmed, obviously in distress and had no outward signs of being one of the country's invaders. His language could be one of many of the eastern trading nations, whose main trade happened to be the saleable youth in the slave markets but these simple farmers weren't to know that.

His one problem was Karl Redblade's "personal items", these were worth killing him to own and were undoubtedly plundered from one of their religious houses or settlements. He looked around and thought of burying them there and then but wasn't sure if they would be washed away during a high tide. He worked out that he could make his way round the grass knoll and to the top of the cliff without being seen but couldn't go too far along the cliff before it fell into view from the beach.

Orri rolled over and crept slowly upwards hidden by the fold in the cliff and once on top he backed further inland so that he was three body lengths from the cliff face. He tore at the tufts of grass and succeeded in ripping a gash in the web of dead grass beneath uncovering a dark soil containing many small stones, not good soil for tilling, he thought.

He dug with his hands until the hole was at least two hand's deep and was just about to throw in the bag when he remembered the few silver coins he had sewn into the back of his belt. Despite being able to raise himself to no more than a few inches off the ground he relatively simply retrieved the pennies and added them to Karl's bounty, folded the cloth back into the shape of a flat parcel and bedded it into his hole. He scraped the soil back, put the turf on top so that even he had trouble to see that the area had been disturbed and noted the spot in relation to three reference points and its distance in from the cliff. It would only be a few weeks before he had recovered and would be able to return to collect his treasure before making his way to the east coast and thence to home.

He slid down to the knoll and saw that the three men were combing the seaweed being brought in with the tide, every now and then holding aloft a piece of wood or rope. The dog was busy gnawing at a piece of timber and they had laid down their weapons to make their sifting easier. Now was the time, he thought, just as he had when he decided to leap from the knarr at, what turned out, it seemed, the prescient moment, the night before.

He rose from his hiding place and was able to walk a full fifteen paces before the dog noticed him, abandoned his stick and sought meatier quarry. He hailed and waved the three hunters who at first made for their weapons and then seeing that the blond haired man was unarmed and obviously in no condition to be a threat they made towards him and one of them whistled at the dog who was in full stride flicking great divots of sand behind him as he went, suddenly stopping ten paces from Orri upon his master's command and assuming a benign face and countenance as Orri kept walking.

He reached the sitting dog and extended an upturned palm to his muzzle at which the formerly ferocious beast lifted a paw, a sign, he felt, that these were peaceful and tender people. The three men approached without saying anything to each other but looking over Orri with curiosity and suspicion.

They came to within an arm's length of each other and Orri instinctively held his two hands shoulder high to show that he came as they saw him. He then pointed to the sea and holding his right palm parallel to the ground made a wavy motion at which they all nodded, said something in their own language and pointed out to sea. They still eyed him suspiciously and expected him to explain a bit more about himself. He knelt on the sand and drew a merchant ship, the sort that plied the waters up and down the coast at home and that he had seen in ports such as Dublin and Jorvik. The picture started another conversation amongst the three hunters who plainly couldn't agree what it represented and they started to ask Orri questions which he could obviously not answer, he couldn't even imagine to what they referred.

One then pointed up the beach towards the girl and then at the ship. Presumably he wanted to know if the girl came from the ship so he nodded, pointed to the girl, himself and then the ship. This incited another discussion between the three men and caused one of them to draw a row of shields along the bulwark of his merchant ship, thus converting the gesture of friendly peace to one of brutal invasion.

At this Orri vehemently shook his head, pointed to the girl and himself and held his hands out, crossed at the wrist as though tied and then pointed to inside the ship. One of them nodded to indicate that they understood and translated his gesturing into their language and the other two acknowledged that they now understood what he was trying to say.

Orri chanced his luck by putting his fingers to his mouth and rubbing his stomach and one of the men mimicked a person drinking and then swaying at which the other two laughed. They walked over to where they had lain their weapons, picked them up, leashed the now pliant dog, and made their way back up the beach, making allowances for the slowness of Orri.

When they reached the sprawled body of the girl two of the men and Orri stared at her wasted form without comment whilst the third man bent down, closed her startled eyes and tried to shut her jaw, but it was frozen open. His clumsy attempts at treating her gently whilst simultaneously having to use force to close her mouth seemed ridiculous to Orri who instinctively and unknowingly smiled.

He never felt the first sword blow to the back of his neck as it severed his spinal cord, nor the subsequent blows and spear wounds that punctured his body as the three suspicious farmers, wary of intruders at the best of times, took his inexplicable amusement as a callousness not to be tolerated in their ancient and reverent society.

1

It had been a long journey for the Armstrong family from Shropshire to Cork, something they mentioned every time they got out of their car when they arrived and promised themselves the luxury of breaking the trip the next time. In the fifteen years that they had taken their holidays in Ireland, sometimes twice a year, their eagerness to get there and their reluctance to return, resulting in the ubiquitous five o'clock in the morning dash to catch the ferry, had precluded the option of an overnight stop en route. They tore past the famous castles of North Wales, spent as little time as possible in Dublin, flew along the motorway past Kildare, bypassed Portlaois, Cashel and Fermoy, invariably got lost in Cork itself and got to their holiday home exhausted and bloated from having eaten on the ferry and then again in Abbeyleix without having taken any exercise in between.

They had crossed the Tipperary-Cork border an hour and a half previously and could have driven another hour before they reached the south western tip of the county but where they were to spend the next four weeks was still considered to be West Cork.

Whilst they blithely called Ballingaddy their "holiday home" it was not theirs at all but belonged to a Dublin family who had bought the farmhouse as an investment and never used it as they failed to see the attraction of having a half hour round journey to buy a newspaper or a pint of milk and an hour's drive to Cork to visit the cinema or theatre. The Armstrongs treated the house as their own in that they left their seaside equipment in the garage and had planted a few roses and shrubs to brighten up the neglected garden. It was they who had installed an aerial and had purchased a small television just so that they could keep up with the news and have some sort of entertainment for the children when they tired of endless card games during an inevitable wet day.

Other than that, the entertainment was all outside the house and beyond its garden. Ballingaddy was the last house on the western bluff of a three mile long north - south valley before it jutted out into the

Atlantic. The line of hills that ran either side of the valley were about two hundred feet high and were host to a number of small farm houses and cottages, mainly raised above the valley floor to afford a view to the south or as a precaution against severe southerly storms that could result in seaweed being found some quarter of a mile inland.

Access to the valley was by a narrow lane that tapered into a single track as it served fewer houses until it stopped at the driveway to Ballingaddy. It was, however, also the lane to Nisbet's Cove; at high tide, an inlet about five hundred yards long and a hundred yards wide, its sides being twenty foot high climbable rocks that gave way to grazing pasture. The gentle slope of the beach gave a large stretch of sand at low tide, perhaps four hundred yards long, interrupted only by the stream that had cut the valley in the first place and which flowed down one side of the strand, and a few islands of rock protruding through the sand.

Ballingaddy was fifty feet above the beach and all the windows in the century old farmhouse were devoted to the view to the south and east. The house itself was never going to get an artist racing for his easel and palette, being a utilitarian three bedroom dwelling with small rooms and low ceilings, the tiny windows letting in a modicum of light and set low to the floor so that the best view upstairs was obtained by lying on the beds. There were two fireplaces and a kitchen flue, testimony to the difficulty in pre-electric times of keeping the damp and cold out of the house and, even when the electricity line did make it all the way down the lane, the owner installed only one electric light and a single socket to each room. It had remained so ever since.

Outside was the garage in which the Armstrongs stored their surf boards, kites, beach balls, buckets, spades, fishing rods and tackle, various apparel to assist with swimming and snorkelling and a free standing barbeque on which most of their cooked meals were prepared during their stay. Octavia couldn't cope with an electric oven and anyway she refused to cook whilst on holiday. Eating out for the two of them wasn't too ruinous but the expense and anxiety of entertaining three young children between the ages of ten and fourteen in pubs or restaurants was such that Jonathan, her husband, not only purchased the barbeque but learnt how to use it properly so that there was little he couldn't cook outdoors. There were a few other outbuildings which had lost their roofs, and thus purpose, and a greenhouse that once boasted a proud vine but which now provided a sheltered sun trap for those all too frequent cloudless days when the temperature barely made it to double figures due to the cooling influence of an arctic wind.

The gate to the drive had been opened and the front door was ajar when they pulled up in the small yard. A smiling face appeared at the door, sparkling dentures glinting in the gloom behind her and her milk white hair freshly coiffured as though she were receiving dignitaries. Mary Hassett had been looking after the cottage for more than two decades and she and her husband, Brendan, had watched the Armstrong family grow and multiply as if they were their own grandchildren. Whilst they looked after many holiday cottages in the valley, and a few beyond, it was the Armstrong's visits to Ballingaddy that provided their yearly highlight. Not content to limit their contact to a few weeks a year, each child received a birthday card from the Hassetts and the Armstrong family Christmas pudding was the work of Mary. This was accompanied by a Christmas card of pressed and dried flowers and leaves, Brendan's speciality which sold for a great deal of money in the tourist shops in the summer, inside of which was a message of hope and thanksgiving in a copperplate script which couldn't be bettered by any amount of computer wizardry.

'You're very welcome', she announced emerging from the doorway and holding her arms out to the children who reluctantly allowed themselves to be hugged, inspected and their heights compared against their Easter standings only four months before, and she declared that they had all put on at least an inch. The children all blushed whilst Mary fussed over the unloading of the car and beseeched them all inside where she had put the pot on and announced "I've cakes" as though their spare frames needed nourishing.

The children followed her into the kitchen looking longingly at the beach and the thin white ribbons delineating the poor excuses for waves on the calmness of the water as it rolled up the sand. They had set off at ten o'clock in the morning and now, nine hours later they had finally been able to escape the confines of their transport, be it car or ferry, only to be ushered inside once more. It was the oldest, Augustus, who, in defiance of Mary, pleaded to be allowed on the strand and the instant Octavia demurred they were off, paying scant regard to their mother's appeal for them to be back in half an hour.

Mary made them some tea and, ever the one to know when to depart, declared herself to be happy now that "her family" was back. Jonathan and Octavia drank their tea sitting in the garden watching the children swing at each other with branches of seaweed and run the length of a beach as would a colt newly released into a field. The strand was a sight of which neither grew bored, indeed, when tense, Jonathan could close his eyes and picture every rock, every indentation and watch the ripples of the stream as it trickled down to the ocean's edge, all from his office desk in central Birmingham. What provoked most discussion between them about the valley was how little change had taken place in the fifteen years. There were one or two new houses and some of the existing buildings had been restored, largely sensitively, and the introduction of aluminium gates was no improvement, but the road from the main coast road remained unsignposted whereas most others that led to the ocean had an all too obvious finger sign "To the Beach", which drew tourists to any stretch of sand as flies to jam.

The land at the southern most end of the valley was still in the hands of the Nisbet family, albeit a vastly reduced holding from their eighteenth century heyday. The responsibility of running the farm was the domain of the only Nisbet son, Seton, who had recently moved into the family seat, grandiosely called Castle Nisbet, although it incorporated no castellation in its 18th century and earlier building. It also did not overlook the cove but was on the reverse slope of the eastern bluff, protected from the predominantly south and south-westerly winds.

Seton Nisbet was only twenty-five, had recently married Jane, whose family owned a large farm near Mallow, and, the Armstrongs had learned at Easter, was expecting their first child in November. Seton had introduced himself to Jonathan and Octavia on their first visit, when he was ten years old, as Ballingaddy was surrounded by Nisbet land; the parcel on which the house stood having been sold during one of the many crises land owners had had to overcome in rural Ireland. His parents had recently retired to a house further west, just outside Skibbereen, where his father could indulge in his hitherto neglected pursuit of fishing, free from the shackles of farming life and content that he had perpetuated the Nisbet family name and that he had been able to leave something to the next generation.

The sun streamed through the east window of Ballingaddy's main bedroom the following morning but Jonathan was on holiday and in no mood to hurry, whereas in Shropshire it would have made him leap out of bed and start his assault on the day. This would involve the twice daily battle on concrete slabbed or tarmacadamed ribbons laughingly called motorways, which, whilst they were indeed thoroughfares for motorised vehicles, the speed limit signs of seventy miles an hour mocked those that were crawling past them at one tenth that speed. He worked in the centre of Birmingham as an accountant for an advertising agency and had long thought that the bright minds that devised nationally famous campaigns should at least be given a more conducive environment in which to work than a soulless glass and concrete box. It was not to be and his battles were rejoined each day remorselessly grinding him down until he could recharge his ebbing resolve with a dose of West Cork.

He could hear the children arguing downstairs as to the ownership of a piece of toast and Octavia's never hurried or unduly raised voice awarding the trophy to her daughter, Livia, whilst her elder brothers were promised a piece each from the next batch and the ensuing silence told Jonathan that the compromise had been accepted, sulkily he imagined, but accepted all the same. He reached over and pulled the curtains further back and from his position he could see that the tide was receding and that Seton was inspecting his 'big beasts', as he called his cattle, on the eastern bluff. Above him was a blue sky with veils of sirrus cloud and a series of crazily angled jet trails headed for the New World.

He rolled out of bed, made his way to the bathroom and indulged in a decadently long bath, both in the amount of water and the time spent therein. When he eventually arrived in the kitchen, Octavia had left his place laid and his breakfast requirements, meagre as they were, on the table. He boiled the kettle and added the water to a lukewarm pot of coffee and made himself some toast which he took outside to the garden. Below him he could see the children kicking a football around on the beach whilst their mother talked to Seton who had walked down to greet them. He was about to join them when he saw that they were headed in his direction so he put the kettle on again in order to make something more appetising than the weak brew that he habitually made for himself.

'Welcome home', Seton boomed whilst he was still twenty yards away from Jonathan.

'One day perhaps, Seton, when the lottery cheque comes,' he replied.

'Come off it, that house in Shropshire will buy you a comfortable place here and some money to live off besides. You needn't run a car like that either,' he said, pointing to the Range Rover.

'The company runs a car like that, ask Octavia what sort of car we run.'

Seton turned to look at Octavia.

'Rusty, slips out of third gear, has done more miles than your average comet and was built in the same year as Ballingaddy,' she replied.

'Just feel the air,' Seton continued, 'like freshly ironed sheets, crisp and clean.'

'Can't argue with you there, I could get drunk on air like this but it's too early for that, cup of coffee?'

'Well, I shouldn't really, but Janie can't see me from here. I've a major holiday project for you all,' Seton announced as though it was a substantial first prize. 'The storms after Christmas have made the far end of the cliff field too dangerous so I'm going to bring the fence in. It's not hard work, we've got a machine to bore the fence holes but it's just a lot more fun doing it with somebody else.'

'Yes, of course we'll help, when do you want to do it?' Jonathan replied, trying to sound enthusiastic.

'I've got the auger for today and tomorrow only so we'd better get cracking. You didn't have anything planned?'

'No,' Jonathan said truthfully but could have added that four weeks without plans and timetables was his idea of a holiday.

They drank their coffee in the garden and Seton filled them in about the development that had plagued the coastline with caravan parks springing up along the larger beaches and Bed and Breakfasts opening in every direction. The once charming fishing villages and even the coastal towns were under pressure from developers who wanted to construct totally unsuitable buildings for the holiday trade with no reference to existing historical buildings. It was a blight that was spreading across Ireland and although the area had escaped the worst so far, the pressure was growing.

'Take the beach field,' Seton said, pointing to the five acre field directly behind the strand which was on two levels, the lower containing the stream and being the flood plain, the higher, larger portion, out of risk of being washed away but scarcely protected by the southerly wind. 'A man approached me a week ago and wanted to buy it, just the five acres. Well, I'm not adverse to flogging off bits of land that are more trouble than they're worth but I asked him what he wanted it for first and he was sheepish about it but he admitted that he wanted to develop it a bit. Well, I pressed him and he right there and then offered me one hundred thousand per acre – I know prices are getting ridiculous around here at the moment but half a million for a soggy field!'

'Is it still yours?' Octavia asked.

'Yes. He wanted to make it into a caravan park, he said that there was enough room for a hundred sites, imagine a hundred caravans on your doorstep! Each caravan with three or four people in it and you've got two to three hundred sharing your beach at any given time.'

'Doesn't bear contemplation, but I'm sure you could have done with the money?' Jonathan asked.

'Half a mill! We could do everything we need to do to keep the place running for twenty or thirty years: new roof on the house for a start and then some machinery and a general clean up. Don't think I haven't thought about it, not selling it, but doing the same thing myself.'

'But they wouldn't give you planning permission, surely?' said Octavia.

'Well, no. There is apparently a big, black line drawn around the coast which excludes developments. However, there are ways, I'm told, not illegal, you understand, but ways of gilding the lily, making the whole thing a great boon to the rural community, local employment, tourism benefits, bringing Ireland to the Continent, that sort of stuff.'

'What would everybody else in the valley think?'

'A caravan park there could be shielded from virtually every house apart from this one. Now you can see how much I've thought about it. Only two or three things would have to be done; one, widen the road, two, you would have to bring in new power lines, and thirdly, you would have to build some sort of mini sewerage plant for that many people, and that's the snag, the capital outlay.'

'What's the sort of annual return per acre on a field like that? asked Jonathan, always the accountant.

'Hundred, hundred and twenty an acre.'

'Say six hundred a year, at a cost of what?'

'You've got me there, say twenty per acre for fertiliser, the fence maintenance is minimal.'

'I wonder what you'd get for one hundred caravans?' Jonathan mused.

'Oh, it's not just the sites that you sell or lease or rent, it's your local shop, electricity and water supply, tent sites, parking charges for the beach, and then there'll be the terraced holiday cottages up that hill and more behind you, I think I could squeeze in about two hundred and fifty and that would be without them encroaching on my side of the bluff.'

The Armstrongs fell for the tease and it was only when they saw the broad grin on Seton's face did they realise that he was pulling their legs but it had set them both thinking just how these ideas germinated.

Seton set off across his "caravan park" to get his auger and fencing tools, having arranged to meet them in the field above a small cove they called the Cowrie Beach because it was where they sourced that particular commodity, vital for use as counters when playing vingt-et-un, their pre-television holiday evening entertainment. They lay on the cliff's edge, twenty feet above the cove and they could see how much had fallen further west from them so that the concrete fence posts, the only sort viable so close to the sea, were almost on an overhang and if given a hefty nudge by a cow itching its hind quarters would plummet to the beach below. The storm damage was still apparent more than six months after the event such was the devastation. Even when they were there at Easter, power lines were still lying along the hedgerows, their presence made known with yellow plastic tape being tied around them. Everywhere one went trees that had been blown down, roots and all, across roads were truncated in line with the hedges, sometimes the tops still lying beyond the hedge on the other side of the road. In the pine plantations, whole avenues of trees had been snapped off, ten feet above the ground as the trunks proved themselves to be too inflexible. It had been "awful fierce", Brendan Hassett admitted, but not as bad as the storm of '89.

Seton appeared with the requisite tools and a foot diameter auger attached to the rear of the tractor. He did a rudimentary amount of surveying with a great deal of looking down his outstretched arm and using a shovel as a plumb line, very much as a golfer lines up for a putt. Jonathan was bemused because the line beyond the intended adjustment followed the cliff face and contours of the hills with no effort to being in a straight line at all and when he pointed it out, Seton complained that it had been done by his father who maintained that cattle couldn't walk in a straight line anyway. In the end they tied a bit of wire to the post furthest from them that they were not going to move and brought it down to the corner from which they were beginning the adjustment. Seton then paced out the distance at which he required each of the eleven posts, marking each spot by digging away a bit of turf. They were going to use the existing posts so he thought it better to dig the holes first and drop each one in as they loosened them.

Seton lined up the auger for the first hole and set it spinning, sinking the hole to about two and half feet and bringing the screw up every now and then so that the earth would be deposited in a neat pile around the hole, ready for filling in around the post. Octavia, in the meantime, cut the wire from the existing fence, every now and then looking over the beach to make sure that the children were not up to mischief.

The eleven holes were drilled well within an hour and Seton turned his attention to loosening and extracting the posts from their previous line. He used his front end claw bucket for this but had to be careful not to break the posts, nor to be so reckless to collapse the cliff too much. As each post was pulled out, Octavia and Jonathan carried it to its new position but it was slow work and Octavia signalled to Seton that she would have to take a break to feed the children. He stopped the tractor and agreed that it was time for lunch and rather badly feigned surprise when she asked him to join them.

'Janie's gone to pre-natal breathing exercises in Cork, so I don't mind if I do,' he declared and they walked back the few hundred yards to

Ballingaddy, calling to the children to follow them.

Jonathan produced cold beers, Octavia cold meats and they sat around the table in the garden remembering that twenty-four hours ago they were sitting in the queue for the ferry at Holyhead contemplating a restful four weeks.

'You don't want to vegetate,' Seton offered helpfully.

'When was the last time you went on a holiday Seton?' Octavia asked.

'Our honeymoon last year.'

'And before that?'

'The year between school and ag. college. I went to Australia and New Zealand, if you remember.'

'Ah yes,' recalled Jonathan, 'the Crocodile Dundee accent.'

'Didn't last!' Seton said defending the appalling accent he had developed in the Antipodes, a mixture of Paul Hogan and Dennis Lillee with a West Cork seasoning.

After lunch, the children went to go and see what they had been up to and were suitably impressed with the machinery and amount of work that had been done. Octavia was overly worried about their proximity to the cliff face and kept telling them to move back but they were transfixed by Seton's manoeuvring with his bucket and the dexterity with which he eventually pulled out each post with his machine. Not able to watch the children any further, she ordered them down onto the beach, away from the cliff, and to look for cowries as it appeared that other visitors to Ballingaddy had relieved them of their supply.

The children slothfully ambled around the cliff end and down onto the beach where they pretended to search for shells but kept their eyes firmly on Seton and his antics. The penultimate post broke off at ground level and although the iron reinforcing kept the two halves together it was obviously useless. Seton left it where it stood, a forlorn relic looking sorry for itself as though its defiance in not coming out of the ground was a regrettable mistake.

Seton moved onto the last post which gave way easily and having expected a tougher battle he had pulled too hard so that the ten feet long overhang on the cliff peeled off like a strip of paper and landed in a cloud of dust at the bottom. Octavia ran to the edge to check there were no children under the fall but she could see all three standing back and, even over the noise of the tractor, hear Marcus and Augustus express delight at the sight. Seton had expected the fall; it was, after all, the reason he was moving the fence inland in the first place, but he didn't expect so much of it to go and an inspection told him that a good five feet in width had gone down with it so that the cliff face, once vertical was now a climbable slope.

The children started towards the pile of grass, earth and small stones before Octavia screamed at them to stop as more might give way and engulf them. Seton corrected her in a manner so as not to give offence to her authority but he had seen many such falls and they remained like that until another storm swept the loose stuff away and one had a precipitous cliff once again. Reassured, the children clambered up the slope, slipping on the scree as they went. It wasn't easy and their attempts were amusing to the adults watching above them as well as to themselves as the harder they tried the further back they slid.

'Hey, look at this,' Livia cried, and held up a circular dish, much encrusted with the light brown soil in which it had been buried.

'What is it?' her father asked from the top of the cliff.

'A plate, I found it here,' she said pointing to the spot she had pulled it from and realised that she was pointing to something else. She threw the plate like a frisbee to Marcus who started to rub off the dirt, and dug further, extracting a triangular golden coloured object, a brooch, she thought, and put it on her left shoulder to see if it suited her. Her parents and Seton had all gingerly descended the slope well away from her so that they didn't disturb the soil around her. By the time they had got to her she had found another triangular piece, matching the last but one could make out the seated figure of a man, and from that Seton deduced that the other one was the same. Jonathan took over the search, careful not to dig away too much and cause further collapse to the cliff. He sifted through the soil but couldn't find anything, if indeed there was anything else to find.

'It's got gold on it,' Marcus exclaimed, as he rubbed the dirt off the plate. Octavia examined the find and announced that it was made of silver and gold, with small amounts of blue and red enamel and that the decoration was Celtic or Anglo-Saxon. Seton had cleaned up one of the triangular pieces and had concluded that it, too, was gold and had a religious significance.

'We aren't doing this very scientifically,' suggested Jonathan, 'what we need is a sieve, or a couple of them, there's one in our kitchen but it's not very big.'

'We've got earth sieves in the greenhouse, about three or four of them but do you think there's anything more to find?' Seton asked.

'Off you go and get them,' urged Jonathan, 'and some spades and trowels and paint brushes.'

'Paint brushes?' Octavia and Seton chorused.

'I've seen it done on archaeological digs, they brush everything with paint brushes,' Jonathan explained.

'Yeh, sure Dad,' Augustus chipped in, 'when was the last time you went on an archaeological dig?'

'On the television, surely you've seen them, Tavie?'

'Only unearthing dinosaurs,' she replied, 'but the sieves would be a good idea, do you want a hand Seton?'

'Not really, oh, I suppose you could give me a lift, it would be quicker than taking the tractor.'

Octavia and Seton set off for the house whilst Jonathan and the children took the two gold pieces and the plate to the sea to wash them. The plate was definitely silver and had gold decoration in an interrupted band around the rim with eight raised knobs into which were set blue and red coloured stones or glass and Jonathan agreed with his wife that it was either Celtic or Anglo Saxon, like something from Sutton Hoo but it and the two gold brooches, or whatever, were in such good condition he rather doubted their antiquity and began to suspect that Seton had staged the whole thing as a joke.

They returned with the sieves; wood-sided circular drums with layers of the ply coming away but still holding onto the rusty meshes.

'Gardening is not my or Janie's priority in life,' Seton explained whilst Jonathan unconsciously looked with disdain at the deplorable condition of the sieves.

They returned to the spot on the cliff and, forever conscious of not disturbing the line of soil below that point, started to dig with a trowel and put the earth in the sieve with the larger mesh which they then placed on the sieve with the next size mesh and so on. An hour of this painstaking work yielded nothing but earth and rock and only about a cubic foot of that.

Whilst everybody else thought that anything more to be found would be below their initial hole, Jonathan had convinced himself that he had to go further up and as he was the man with the trowel, Seton and Octavia followed him. The children's attention span for the project had lapsed and they had returned to the beach for a swim. Livia and Augustus were dismissive of the find anyway considering an old plate and some costume jewellery to be of little consequence. Marcus was not so sure about the pieces being insignificant and was convinced that they were part of some treasure off a Spanish galleon forced ashore during the Armada's demise in 1588.

Jonathan's hunch, or 'reasoned calculus' as he later called it, paid off when they found a third triangular plaque and a small silver coin, the like of which none of them had seen and both of which had been caught by the first sieve so they collectively decided to abandon the thought of finding anything less than half an inch wide. Jonathan went further up the cliff face so that he was only five feet from the top and where there were a lot more grassy tufts to combat before getting to the earth. Here Octavia found three more silver coins, similar to the first in size but two with a stylised bird on one side and a small cross in the centre of the other, both with unreadable inscriptions running around the images on both sides. The third had a trefoil device within an inscription on one side and what looked like a pennant on the other. There was no further clue as to where these coins came from, they were made from thin silver discs about three quarters of an inch in diameter and appeared to be in very good condition although none of them could decipher any of the inscriptions.

They dug for another hour before all admitted exhaustion and agreed to continue their work the next day, Jonathan and Octavia meant sifting the cliff face, Seton meant erecting his fence which had remained neglected. They carried the sieves and trowel back to Ballingaddy, Octavia was given the finds to nurture which she did by putting the coins in one shirt pocket, the mounts in the other and carried the plate. Back at the house she put all eight pieces on the kitchen table and offered Seton a cup of tea, or a drink. His hesitation was enough to signal that he would surely like to celebrate their find but he declined explaining that there was a lot to be done before the day was out. As he parted he suggested that they didn't mention anything of the find to anybody as it would only lead to people clambering all over the cliff and if they came to any grief then they could sue him, especially as the fence was down. Jonathan and Octavia had absolutely no intention of mentioning it to anybody else but for a quite different reason; both were convinced that there was more to be found and that, on the evidence sitting on the table in front of them, it was worth finding.

2

Everybody assisted Seton in putting his fence up from first thing. Jonathan hadn't time to shave and the children were still eating their toast as they walked along the edge of the beach to the cliff. Seton had found a replacement post for the one he had broken and they set all eleven up in their holes, Seton measuring their height and adjusting the depth of a few so that the fence was not only ramrod straight but horizontal to the ground. It was, Octavia observed, a compulsive neatness and attention to detail that was usually lacking in any farmer she had encountered previously.

Once all the posts were in place, he started to unroll the wire, four strands of it and when Jonathan stooped to help, Seton assured him that he was much better off doing it himself as he only had equipment for one person to handle. Thus excused, he and Octavia returned to the cliff where they dug for an hour and a half yielding nothing. Resting from their labours they started to discuss how the bits and pieces got there in the first place and what sort of date the deposit had been made. Octavia plumped for a Christian monk escaping from somebody and that the pieces found were parts of his trappings of office, a theory upon which Jonathan poured scorn, reminding her that monks weren't allowed to have money at which she countered that they didn't know if the small silver discs were money, they could quite possibly have been intended as earrings or a component part of a necklace or bracelet.

They then discussed where else they should look as it was quite possible that they had exhausted that particular spot but there could be more further along the cliff. The thought depressed them both, there were weeks of digging if they were to do the job thoroughly and they were rather glumly looking at the slope when Seton joined them, the fence completed.

'What you need is a metal detector,' he suggested cheerfully.

Octavia and Jonathan looked at each other, their demeanour visibly improved and it was Jonathan who asked if Seton knew of anybody with one.

'Oh, there's a nuisance of a man who travels around in a blue van scouring the beaches for dropped coins and things. The gardai are never very far behind him, he's always being charged with trespass but gets away with it by saying that he thought he was on public land. He's pretty brazen about it too, my father caught him above the high water mark on the beach, technically - no, there is no doubt about it - our land, and when Dad suggested that they share the spoils he just laughed and told him to get his own detector and learn how to use it. I don't think that he is the sort of person we need to assist us, far too sharp.'

'I suppose we could buy one,' Jonathan proposed.

'Where from, Cork?' Octavia asked.

Seton shrugged his shoulders.

'Never needed one before. I'll ask Jimmy at the Co-op when I go this afternoon, he's bound to know, he can lay his hands on virtually everything I've ever needed.'

'We don't want to alert anybody though, wouldn't it look a bit odd you wanting a metal detector all of a sudden?'

Seton thought for a moment.

'I've just bought my yearly stock of weedkiller from them so I'll say that I was spraying the brambles along the lane and lost my watch.'

'That's cunning,' complimented Jonathan.

'I'll just have to remember to take my watch off before I go. Right,' he said, struggling to his feet, 'I've got a herd to drench, don't suppose you want something to do?' he asked laughing.

'What, drenching cattle? No thanks, I'm on holiday,' Jonathan replied.

'Wasn't asking you, I was asking Tavie. She's better looking than you.'

'I'm on holidays too,' Octavia answered, 'and number 44 is particularly good looking.'

'44? What do you know about 44? She's a brute, she was nearly topside last week when she trod on my foot. I haven't enough drench anyway. I'll go into the Co-op now, do you want anything else whilst I'm there?'

Both Jonathan and Octavia had all they needed. Seton left them on the cliff lying in the sun, protected from the mild northerly pushing cold air from the arctic circle. The Atlantic was calm, a merest ripple at the water's edge in which the children were playing. Water and sand were the cheapest entertainment devised for children, and adults for that matter, dependent, of course, what particular stretch of sand and reach of water one chose in the world. Nisbet's Cove happened to be one of the cheaper destinations and the sand and tides were such that not only was it safe but when the water rolled in over the hot sand, especially if the high tide was at about four in the afternoon, it was noticeably warmer than the sea off the rocks. It would be a full week before the children would be looking further afield for something to do, perhaps a trip to the cinema, or a picnic at some ancient monument, of which there was no shortage in Cork.

Jonathan was impatient to find out what it was, exactly, they had found in the cliff fall. Even as he lay on the slope his hands dug around just in case they had missed something. The coins or silver discs were so small and they had found those but perhaps there were hundreds more to be unearthed. He couldn't imagine that any of it was worth a great deal, they were interesting but hardly set the heart beating harder. The three triangular pieces, when he had laid them out on the table, were obviously the corners of an oblong or square tablet with small holes through which one would put the holding pins, four to each piece. They were missing the lower right hand corner piece, if he was correct in his assumption as to their function and then one would have the set of four, the three that they did have were each decorated with a seated man, right hand held across their chest with their ring finger bent towards their palm and a symbol above their heads. If there were four then surely the images must be of the Evangelists and he and Octavia were stretched out above the missing one.

This set him to more, ultimately fruitless, work until the children declared their hunger and reminded him that he had promised them sausages cooked on the barbeque for lunch. His impatience to find the fourth corner would have to wait and he started to pack up the sieves and trowel when Octavia suggested that they leave them there, they hadn't seen anybody on the beach all day and the northerly was bringing a fair amount of cloud, always a deterrent to visitors to Nisbet's Cove. Jonathan relented and they walked back empty handed.

Before they had finished their meal and resumed their digging, Seton returned, armed with the knowledge that only Paddy Hearn had a metal detector that anybody knew and that, yes, he did drive a blue van. The lost watch ruse had worked well he thought and everybody at the Co-op had commiserated with him on his loss, 'such a handsome watch, too,' the girl behind the till had commented revealing a hitherto concealed interest in Seton.

They went into the kitchen and looked at the pieces again, now referred to as "The Ballingaddy Find" by Seton. Jonathan explained his theory on the mounts which was accepted by Octavia and Seton in the absence of any other explanation and Seton recalled seeing coins like those before, perhaps in Dublin. Jonathan's frustration grew, fuelled entirely by wanting to know what they were looking at rather than how much they were looking at, the primary concern of both Octavia and Seton. However, the consensus was that there was another gold mount, at least, to be found and that they ought to set about searching for it. Octavia had flicked through the Golden Pages to find that a metal detector supplier listed himself in Co. Kildare, but none of them had an eight hour round trip in them when they might find the missing piece in a couple of hours.

As they walked out of the house and down the drive, Octavia noticed the roof of a blue van peering over the hedge. Seton saw it too and swore under his breath.

'Where the hell is he?' he asked himself, scanning the beach.

'I bet you he's at the cliff already,' Octavia said.

'Ah, but that's my land, he can't touch it,' Seton replied and hastened his step so that he could prevent Paddy Hearn from finding anything, 'somebody must have told him about the fall, he hasn't been here for months.'

When they got to the bottom of the drive, they found Mr Hearn changing into his gum boots, his metal detector leaning up against the side of the van.

'Just the man I want to see,' Seton said, rounding the open door of the vehicle.

Paddy Hearn looked up at Seton and once seeing who it was looked back down to guide his foot to the top of his boot.

'And why would that be, Mr Nisbet?' he mumbled.

'You see that patch of bramble over there?' Seton said, pointing to a vast stretch of blackberry canes in the field above the cove opposite them, 'I lost my wrist watch in it and I was wondering if you could lend me your machine to help me find it?'

Paddy Hearn stared at him with bewilderment.

'Lend it to ye? Oh no, Mr Nisbet, 'tis an awful lot of money and a precious machine, not for the untrained, ye know? Now, if I were to go over the ground meself, that's an idea, but there'd have to be something in it, ye know, for me.'

'Well, I suppose, would a tenner do it?'

Paddy Hearn looked at the size of the ground he was to cover and nodded his head.

'There's mebbee an hour's worth of work there and how d'ye know ye dropped your watch in't?'

'Because I had it before I went in and didn't have it when I left,' Seton explained.

'Is it waterproof?'

'Yes, but what's that got to do with it?'

'Well, Mr Nisbet, my times are scarce and I'd be after suggesting that I come back anudder day and have a look?'

'Oh, alright,' said Seton, trying to sound dejected, 'another day, but I don't want you going over the patch without me knowing. The watch isn't worth much in itself but it was given to me by my wife just before we got married so that I'd get to the church on time and I'm going to be in trouble having lost it.'

'And only ten euros worth of trouble?'

'I suppose I could wait until the bramble has all died but she might notice before that happens. Where are you searching today, Mr Hearn?'

''tween the tides, of course, wouldn't want to trespass now. I'll try round the rocks there,' he said pointing directly at the cliff that had come down.

'Rather you didn't, unless you keep strictly to the rocks. We've had a fall and I think it is too dangerous for people to walk over it.'

'That's up to me, I can look after meself,' Hearn said.

'It's not up to you, in fact. It is my land and, as such, I have a responsibility towards the people who cross it. I haven't had the time to put up notices but I am giving you a verbal warning, please do not trespass on that section of the cliff and the beach immediately below it, do you understand?'

Hearn rose to his feet and without acknowledging whether he had understood or not, picked up the detector, rested the wand on his foot, put his headphones over his ears, and played with the controls near his right hand. Satisfied that all was well he set off across the beach without once looking back at Seton or the Armstrongs.

'I've left the sieves and trowel at the site,' Jonathan admitted to Seton.

'It's alright. I'll go over there and pretend to play with the wire until he's gone. He wouldn't dare do anything if I'm there but I wouldn't trust him if I wasn't. Either somebody has told him about the fall or he has a sixth sense, I suspect the first, don't you?'

Neither Jonathan nor Octavia had a clue what to think but coincidences like that were rarely without reason. Seton set off for the cliff taking a pair of fencing pliers and a shovel with which he intended to bury the sieves temporarily and hide any evidence of excavation that would draw Hearn onto the spot. The weather was closing in with darker clouds getting lower in the sky to the north but were moving slowly. The children had not taken themselves to the beach but were playing some sort of hiding game in the garden that usually pit eldest brother and younger sister on Marcus, the middle child, who was independent enough to withstand being a victim.

Jonathan returned to the kitchen and played with the pieces again.

'I wonder what the law is about finding things in the ground,' he commented to Octavia who was folding yet more washing, the first of a regenerating crop that lasted all holidays.

'Treasure Trove you mean?'

'Yes, that sort of thing. Who owns these?'

'Seton, I expect,' she said.

'Well, Livia found the first things, doesn't she get a say in the matter?'

'I'm sure Seton will give her something if he wants to sell them. Perhaps he'll give her the coins.'

'But are they Seton's to give?' Jonathan continued.

'How on earth would I know?'

Jonathan walked through to the small sitting room where he found the telephone book and looked up Government Departments to see if there was a Heritage Department. Under the Department of the Arts, Culture and Gaeltacht he found the number for the National Museum in Dublin.

'Oh, good morning,' he said to the third person he had been connected to by the Museum's operator, 'I'm devising an advertising campaign for Securelock in both Ireland and the U.K. and I wish to check out the legal obligations of somebody who finds something in the ground, can you help?'

'Yes. Put basically, under the National Monuments Act of 1930 with subsequent amendments, all archaeological objects, that's anything dug out of the ground with a cultural interest to Ireland, belongs to the State.'

'Regardless of who owns the land?'

'Yes, anything found in the ground belongs to the State. I assume you are talking of an archaeological item. There are further laws about palaeontology finds but you'd have to talk to the Natural History Museum to get an accurate account of those.'

'Does the land owner get anything at all?' Jonathan asked.

'Not necessarily. It isn't like the English or Scottish laws of Treasure Trove. Here the State can reward a finder but it is done under individual review, there is no set percentage reward for recovery. Does that answer your question?'

'Er, yes, I think. Is there a license system for taking items out of the country?'

'Archaeological items?'

'Those first.'

'If the item is of interest to the State then we will retain it for our collection and, as I have said, there may be some remuneration to the finder or on whose land it was found. If the State finds that there is already sufficient like-material in their collections then they may permit export but honestly, so little comes out of the ground in which we are not interested that it hasn't really been tested. Other items such as silver, paintings, furniture, etcetera, have their own criteria and you'd best talk to the gallery if you want to know what they are.'

'Right, I think I've got all that. One last thing, what are the penalties for taking protected items out of the country?'

'I don't have the amended act in front of me, but confiscations of the items, a fine and/or a jail sentence, the amount and length of which I can't immediately give you but they're quite severe. I must say, that I'm intrigued about the direction of the advertising campaign.'

'It's a sort of "Need Somewhere to Store your Valuables?" campaign for safes but it's very much in its infancy, ideas flying in all directions you know.'

'Yes, I see. If you want chapter and verse I suggest you get the 1930 Act with the amendments and you might, perhaps, find something in the Cultural Institutions Act of 1997, that should cover everything you need.'

'I must thank you, you've been of immense help and I'll get the two acts you have mentioned. Goodbye.'

Jonathan turned off his phone and relayed everything he had been told by the helpful man in Dublin to Octavia who was equally taken aback by the rather stingy attitude that everything belonged to the State who may, or may not, give anything in return for finding it. They both, however, admitted to having jumped the gun by assuming they were entitled to any share of what they recognised as Seton's perceived property. It would be kind of him to give Livia something and perhaps something for themselves as a 'thank you' but all that had changed now that the State owned all the pieces.

Seton returned later in the afternoon, after Hearn had left the beach and had heeded Seton's warnings of trespassing on the cliff. They, sheepishly at first, told him about the law of the land and that the items were the property of the State. He took it in good humour initially but when Octavia reminded him of the possible returns, not as much as selling the five acre caravan park perhaps, but it could still be a substantial amount, he began to ask questions.

Jonathan busied himself by getting them all a drink.

'Don't they give me anything?' Seton asked for the third time.

'They might, but by the time you've surrendered them to the Museum you are never going to be able to find out what they are worth and thereby know whether the sum they do give you has anything to do with the value of the find. You also can't get them independently valued because you can be arrested for not turning them into the State in the first place,' Octavia said, having obviously thought it through.

'What date was that Act?' Seton asked.

'1930,' Jonathan replied, straining at the corkscrew.

'Well, it's obvious, isn't it, they were dug out of the ground before that, sometime last century and have been hanging around in the house and now I want to sell them.'

'Wouldn't it come as a surprise to your parents?' Jonathan offered.

'Oh yes. They wouldn't be happy, would they? Alright, I've got it now but only if you agree. You take them back to England with you, get them valued as your property, you don't have parents to worry about, and when we find out what they're worth, we offer them to the Nation at, say, half the valuation and we split the profits fifty-fifty, what do you say?'

They both silently weighed up the enormity of what had been proposed.

'My great-grandfather was based in Ireland at the turn of the century, we could say that he took them back to England then, having bought them in a shop, and that they have been lying around our house since then. We couldn't possibly think of taking fifty per cent from you,' Jonathan said.

'No, I insist on the equal split, if it weren't for your children, Hearn would have the lot by now. Also, you are doing the really hard work, getting the things out of the country, you are putting your neck on the block, not me.'

'I appreciate that bit, but you need the money more than us, although God knows a few thousand quid would be very welcome to knock a few bills to pieces.'

'And how would you explain your sudden wealth?' Octavia asked, accepting her drink from Jonathan.

'Lottery win?' Seton suggested.

'They can check that.'

'Who can check what?' Seton replied.

'Officials or whoever, they can ask the Lottery people if you had won.'

'I don't think that the Cultural Heritage people and the Lottery people have cross linked computers,' he said sarcastically.

'Don't you believe it,' Jonathan replied, 'but we're getting off the point. They could be worth fifty or a hundred thousand or more. You could re-roof and do all you need around the farm for that. You take what you need for your repairs and we'll split the rest.'

Seton drained his glass of wine in one gulp.

'Let's leave it at a straight fifty-fifty split. I don't think for a minute that they are worthless, but they might not be worth anything like six figures, that's why I like Tavie's idea, we only act once we have some idea of what they are worth. In the meantime, we've got to find the fourth bit of those,' he said, pointing at the gold mounts.

'We've got four weeks to do it casually, we don't have to work at the coalface every waking hour, besides which, I'm on holiday,' Jonathan said, refilling Seton's glass.

3

It was only after the Armstrongs were prepared to admit to themselves that their holiday plans had been disrupted by events that they could settle down and try to make it more fun for the children. The temptation was there for them to leave the children on the beach whilst they sifted through the rubble and earth on the cliff face and Jonathan more than once suggested he drive to Dublin to buy a metal detector. He had already ventured into Cork to buy books on Celtic art and coins but the coins they had found were unlike anything featured and the Celtic art books concentrated on earlier times than the Christian Celts, the period Jonathan had presumed the pieces originated. He did, however, notice that a cup in the National Museum of Ireland was quite like the plate they had found although the reproduction was not sufficient for him to make a detailed comparison.

They did the tourist routes to the Ring of Kerry and Mizen Head, spent days on beaches that they had not previously visited, kissed the Blarney Stone for the fifth time, toured Kinsale and its forts, had three days of torrential rain when trips to the cinema were the only alternative to card games and fed the children ice creams and packets of crisps. They both knew, however, that there was a pervading gloom over the horizon, the time when they were to break the law and take the items out of the country.

They had managed to avoid the question of the find with the children. Livia mentioned it once and Octavia palmed it off by saying that Seton was looking into the law relating to finds and that they may have to be sent to Dublin. That seemed to satisfy her whilst the two boys seemed to have forgotten about it altogether or, if it was on their minds, they failed to let either of their parents know. Seton was like a cat on a hot tin roof and had taken elaborate measures to prevent anybody going onto the find site with fences and notices regarding trespass and the denial of land owners' responsibility if anybody did go onto the area. It appeared to successfully put people off as they stuck to the beach or the rocks to the east which, as far as rock pools and caves were concerned, were the more interesting anyway.

After the three days' downpour, the first sunny day was a Saturday and the children took themselves off for a swim before anybody else turned up, an inevitable invasion after the bad weather. Jonathan and Octavia promised to follow after they had tidied the house up but five minutes after they had left, a puffing Augustus stood at the front door begging them to "come and see". He related that Seton's good work had been for nothing as the cliff had either been dug over with an excavator or had collapsed even further.

The three returned to the cliff to find another huge section had fallen down, taking with it half of Seton's new fence and two of his notices. The children had been wise enough to stand back from the slide and were staring in awe at the power of nature. Jonathan was thanking his lucky stars that he wasn't digging away at the slope when it gave way; he would have been crushed without doubt. Now the elusive fourth corner was gone from them, not only had the area in which they found the other three been swallowed up but the instability of the slope prevented any but the most foolhardy from venturing onto it.

In a way he was pleased that he no longer had to think of the last piece; he hoped they had enough to see that Seton no longer entertained thoughts of turning the valley into a caravan park and that there might be some pocket money for them all at the final account. They fiddled with the fence and resurrected the warning signs that had turned out to be providential, but they would have to get Seton down with his fencing equipment to do the job properly.

They meandered back to the beach, Jonathan looking wistfully at the pile of dirt and rocks; what other treasures lie within, he thought? The first of the day's visitors had parked their car so that it partially blocked the driveway to Ballingaddy. It didn't matter normally, if there were a premium of car parking spaces, but as it was the only car there it seemed a bit rich. Jonathan walked up to the car to find it empty and he searched the beach for its occupants but couldn't see anybody. It all served to get him into a poor temper, a condition initiated by his disappointment about the cliff face and now to be unleashed upon unsuspecting tourists from, the numberplate told him, Co. Cavan.

He strode up the drive, got to the kitchen and wrote as forceful a note he could, without the use of profanity, about the poor choice of parking space and stormed back down the drive to find an elderly couple sitting in the car preparing to leave. They were full of cheer and apologised profusely if they had inconvenienced him in any way, which Jonathan had to admit they had not, or not yet at any rate, and when they left he felt ridiculous and deflated.

When he turned round Livia was standing between him and the beach with her hands behind her back.

'What have you got there?' he asked.

'Nothing,' she replied which wasn't what she meant to say.

'Nothing at all, or nothing important?'

'Well, I don't know if it's important but it is pretty.'

'An intrigue! Let's have a look,' he said holding out his hand. Livia slowly approached, her hands still behind her back.

'You promise not to tell anybody, not Mummy or Augustus or Marcus, and especially not Seton?'

'No, I can't promise that, I don't know what it is, they may have to know.'

Livia stopped, shot her right hand up to his eye level and between her thumb and forefinger was a gold coloured cross, still with some soil attached, the decoration consisting of gold beads in patterns all over one face, the reverse being quite plain. The weight told him that it was made of gold but the decoration was the most noticeable aspect of the decoration, there must have been hundreds of beads and seemingly, to the naked eye, all still there.

'Did you find this on the fall?'

'No, I didn't go onto the fall, it was on the beach,' she explained.

'What, just lying there?'

'Yes, on the shells.'

Jonathan had no reason to disbelieve her.

'Why can't we tell anybody about it?' he asked.

'Because I found the plate and one of those gold triangles and Seton's taken them away from me and I want to keep this, it's pretty.'

'Well, sweetie, let me tell you how it is,' Jonathan started.

'I knew I shouldn't of told you.'

'Shouldn't have,' he corrected.

'You always take things away from me,' she complained and was about to cry but she never cried in front of her father, she was made of stronger stuff than that.

'Like what?'

'Scissors, that's one!'

'That's for your own protection. Now, this is different, we don't know who these things belong to and Seton is trying to find out. They could be very important to the nation and they might give you a reward for finding them, we don't know. Just if you find something on the street, you can't pick it up and say 'that's mine!'

'The boys do.'

'Then they need a little talk about it. If you give me the cross, we'll wait until Seton finds out about the law and if they say we've got to hand them in, that is what we'll do but everybody will know that Livia Armstrong found most of it and if they want to give you any money then you have to give Seton half and I'll put some in a special account for you, which you can have when you are older.'

'But Dad, I'm old enough to spend money!'

'Yes,' he replied smiling, 'but not old enough not to.'

This left Livia completely bewildered and she looked at her cross, rubbing her thumb gently over the beads.

'So, I can't keep it?'

'It's not yours to keep.'

'It's not fair!' she protested.

'I agree, I agree entirely but it's the rules and we have to live by the rules.'

'Who made up the rules?'

'The Government.'

'So they want everything and we're allowed nothing?'

Jonathan thought it would make an excellent political slogan.

'It seems that way but it's a bit different. If you give it to me then I promise, listen, promise, you will get some of the money if we are given any.'

'And the boys get none of it?' she asked hopefully.

'They can share in the money for the other bits, provided there is some money but this cross is your find.'

Livia dangled the cross by holding the suspension ring between her thumb and finger. Jonathan's outstretched hand was beneath it and she laid the piece on his palm but held onto it for a few seconds as though she was having second thoughts as to whether she was doing the right thing for herself. When she let go, Jonathan left his hand there to show her that she could take it back if she wanted but Livia turned her back and, slowly at first, returned to the beach. Once upon the sand she seemed to forget the whole thing and started to skip towards her mother and brothers.

Her father felt more than a little wretched about taking the cross from her but it was obviously a part of the hoard and confirmed the religious nature of the find. He also considered it to be the most valuable, although only two inches or so wide, the workmanship was such that if intricacy translated to worth then it was by far the superior object. Did this now mean he should get on his hands and knees and go over the ground again or was this the last thing, other than the fourth corner piece, to find? Fleetingly, he thought of keeping the find of the cross between himself and Livia as she had wanted. After all, it was found above ground on the beach between high and low tide mark and was presumably the property of the finder, a salvage rather than excavation.

Then the good in him floated to the top before he could entertain any more such thoughts. Cheating on authority was one thing, cheating on friends was quite another. Whilst his conscience was troubled with the thought of breaking the law by taking the finds out of the country it was placated by his measured opinion that the law was quite wrong. As an accountant, senior company director, and citizen, he had never broken a law other than drinking in the pub before he was eighteen and, on the rare occasion that traffic conditions allowed, exceeded the speed limit on motorways. He paid every penny of tax that was his due, he was scrupulous about expense accounts and logging the correct private use mileage for his company car. He didn't see why he should have to break the law to save a few pounds here or there but had met many upstanding people who habitually did do so and thought none the less of themselves.

The National Monuments Act of 1930, was a bullying Act, was contrary to the purpose of a democratic government to protect its people rather than fetter them and was counter-productive, in their case certainly, and probably in a lot more situations as well. Reward systems had been in place in most civilisations for several millennia whereby somebody doing a good deed received promotion in rank or a more tangible prize but the Act said that this 'could' happen and did not guarantee it. Thus the government enacted that it must have the objects first and then it would start to bargain, from an unassailable position of course. Jonathan had little problem in recognising why the law was there, to stop the entire country being dug up by an army of metal detecting fortune hunters with their propensity to wreck archaeological sites, but the law failed to account for the chance find, as theirs had largely been, and he was happy to punish the law for its shortcomings.

Seton presently joined him on the beach and took the news of the further cliff fall with an air of resignation until he was shown the cross. When Jonathan explained where it was found, Seton was insistent that it belonged to Livia, she had found it on public land but Jonathan stuck to their agreement that they would split the proceeds. They wandered round to what used to be a cliff and Seton declared it to be outside his responsibility now as most of it was below the high water mark and that he would remove the fence and notices so that there could be no question that it was his land any more.

'There's more rain coming,' Seton commented as he struggled with a wooden fence post.

Jonathan looked up at the cloudless sky.

'According to the weather forecast,' Seton explained, 'so it's more than likely that more will come down, I can't see any use in trying to contain it. It must have been a hell of a lot of water that brought this lot down.'

'Quite astonishing really. Lucky, though, we found the bits and pieces in the interim.'

'That's just the point, isn't it? You wonder how many thousands of hoards lie under the ground all over the globe and ours is but one. I'm never going to find another so I may as well get what I can when I can. It's not as though we're going to destroy the things, now is it? I just want my fair share and if that lot in Dublin think I'm going to accept any old figure they pull out of the air then they can think again. Who will you go and see in England to value them?'

'I haven't a clue. There's a chap in the company who collects antiques, I'll ask him who the best people are. Why don't you come with me? I'd be much happier if you could be sure ...'

'That you don't run away with the loot, eh?'

'No, well, yes, I mean, you are being tremendously trusting.'

'Jonathan, if I can't trust you, who can I trust in this world? Besides which, I know where you live. I think it's best to avoid the involvement of an Irishman in all this, don't you? I don't think for a minute that they'll doubt your story that they've been in your family for a few generations and there's bugger all the government can do about the things once they're in England. I'm the one who should be feeling shamed by being a traitor to my country but I have long believed that patriotism should remain on the rugby field; too many people have died for this country in the name of patriotism.'

'Goodness, this from a farmer.'

'A poor farmer, who is willing to screw his country for all it's worth. You only have to ask where my lucky break is to be, what government contract can I get, where's my free ride on the gravy train? Some members of parliament are currently asking for a review of the tax breaks given to farmers! I'd love to pay tax if I earned enough but they take away quite enough with bloody VAT.'

'What you want,' Jonathan said, warming to a theme of his, 'is value for money. You don't mind paying for something if it's worthwhile.'

'Quite, and that mob in Dublin aren't worth a cracker, not as far as

I'm concerned. Now I have to contend with Brussels as well. I do rather wish that they'd leave me well alone, have a mutual parting and we can all get on with it.'

'No man is an island, Seton,' reminded Jonathan.

'Oh, I know, don't I know it! This is our break though Jonathan, the one and only chance to slip the leash, it could set us both up for good, they could be worth millions for all we know but I'll be buggered if I have to surrender my good fortune to some bloody bureaucrats.'

August passed too quickly for the Armstrongs and the last few days were occupied with the depressing tasks of cleaning up, storing away and packing. Jonathan had been contacted by his company to return a few days early but he had refused and did a bit of what was required on his constant companion, his laptop. They farewelled the Hassetts who pressed sweets onto the children and Mary demanded another hug from them all, they called in on Seton and Janie, wishing them luck for the arrival of their first child and promised to be in touch at Christmas time. Nobody mentioned anything about coins or gold trinkets or plates which Jonathan had casually packed in their luggage without any attempt to conceal them so that he could profess ignorance of the law, in the extremely unlikely event of being stopped and searched.

The following morning they left at five, the first two hours taking them into Tipperary with hardly a car passed, thence to the Portlaois bypass and the quicker part of the journey through Kildare and into Dublin. Jonathan only got lost once in the capital, something of a record Octavia maintained, and they arrived at Dun Laoghaire just after ten o'clock, an hour before the fast ferry was to leave. However, they were informed that there was no ten past eleven sailing and that they had the option of driving away and returning for the four o'clock sailing or driving into the terminal and staying there for six hours. It was the sort of thing that drove Jonathan to despair as he had telephoned and confirmed the eleven o'clock ferry but the unapologetic man in his booth said that it was out of their control. They opted to turn around, receiving absolutely no assurance that they could actually get on the four o'clock sailing.

They discussed what to do whilst driving towards the centre of Dublin and each had a different idea but Jonathan, without explaining his reason, said that he wasn't going to leave the car unattended. They chose to go to St. Stephen's Green to do some shopping whilst Jonathan sat in the car and then Augustus suggested a visit to the National Museum. Octavia volunteered to stay in the car whilst Jonathan took the children to the Museum. He wasn't, he admitted, a great Museum buff, but he was particularly keen to see just one thing, the cup that had been badly depicted in the Celtic art book.

They wandered around looking at a variety of displays and it was only when Jonathan consulted a floor plan did he find the relevant gallery. A bored looking guard sat on a chair at the door, barely acknowledging their presence and it took no time for Jonathan to find the cup, The Ardagh Chalice, Celtic, 8th century A.D. He was without the slightest doubt, even to his untrained eye, that the Ardagh Chalice and their plate began their life together and were made by the same craftsman. He compared the Derrynaflan paten exhibited nearby and could see differences in style of decoration and it was significantly larger than theirs but the idea was the same. Their plate however was a lot more sophisticated in execution.

Telling the children that he would be in the bookshop, he went in search of the purpose of a paten, having never heard the word before. It took him several books to find what he was looking for, every book mentioned patens but they did not expand to say what their function was until, finally, a general book on silver told him that a paten was the plate from which the bread was served during the Eucharist and was accompanied by a chalice.

They had, therefore, found the missing half to one of Ireland's principal late Celtic treasures, the paten that was originally with the Ardagh Chalice.

4

The area around the reception desk of Messrs. Lonergan's, Fine Art Auctioneers of Regent Street, London, was bustling. Jonathan had telephoned their antiquities expert, a Peter Grier, to ensure that he would be in on that particular morning and was free to look at something that might be of interest. Grier was courteous but short and confirmed that he would be in his office on Thursday although he had a number of appointments and his time might be limited.

Jonathan introduced himself to the hurried young man behind the counter and said he had a tentative appointment with Mr. Grier. The man reached for the telephone and had a brief discussion with whoever was on the other end.

'I'm afraid Mr Grier will be tied up for at least fifteen minutes. He suggested I race upstairs with the item you have so that he can see if it is worth your while to wait.'

Jonathan was unprepared for this sort of treatment.

'Please relate to Mr Grier that I am perfectly at ease with the thought of waiting but perhaps he can 'race' downstairs to see if it is worth his while to keep me interested in so doing. It is, after all, only three minutes' diversion to call upon Trotman's whom, I'm informed, have a particularly good antiquities department.'

Without a word the young man picked up the telephone again and flicked his centre-parted hair back with his free hand in an ill-disguised gesture of impatience. There followed another discussion, the content of which Jonathan was not privy as the young man, his hand still upon his head, had turned his back.

'Mr Grier apologises but he did warn you that this could be the case and he is really sorry that he can not slip out of his meeting. However, we have an internal video system and if I place your item under the camera he can give you an idea of its value in the meantime.'

Jonathan looked, and felt, stunned.

'I see,' he said, placed his briefcase on the counter and extracted the gold cross from a soft cloth pouch, made for it by Octavia, and positioned it beneath the camera. The young man was awaiting a reply from his interlocutor and then fiddled with the camera, obviously on orders from above. He turned the cross around and then over and after fifteen seconds or so he put the telephone down and gave the cross back to Jonathan.

'He'll be down in five minutes,' he said and showed Jonathan a row of chairs lined up against a wall, 'if you'd like to take a seat.'

Jonathan looked at the less than welcoming waiting area surrounded by posters of paintings and valuable objects that Lonergans had managed to sell over the years.

'I'll thank you for your obviously busy time and please pass my good wishes on to Mr Grier, at least he has now seen what he is missing out on, or rather part of it, and I will be suggesting to your Chief Executive Officer that a quick course in civility would be a far wiser investment than more publicity about how great your organisation has become. Good day.'

Jonathan walked out of the reception area without trying to subdue any of his anger, but returning the nod and smile from the Commissionaire on the door. Regent Street was still full of tourists although it was half way into September and their habit of stopping every five feet or so to consult a map slowed the pedestrian traffic to a confused scrum where there was a lot of pavement dancing to avoid oncoming globe-trotters. He walked, hopped and slid his way up Regent Street, managed to cross whilst there was no traffic, walked down a calmer Conduit Street and turned left into Savile Row, somewhere he had never trod before, in search of Trotman's, a much smaller firm than Lonergan's, who specialised in antiquities and numismatics and whom everybody he had consulted named as the people to use. He had chosen Lonergan's because of their international reputation and that the wife of their north-west Midlands representative played tennis with Octavia, although they were not particularly close chums.

A modest brass plaque beside the opened door informed Jonathan that he had found Trotman's and he walked up the short staircase to the entrance. The building was identical to every other in the Row but once inside it was apparent that it had not seen the attentions of an interior decorator for many decades and did not suffer as a consequence. This, Jonathan thought, was a place of scholarship not market or shop, there were no posters with prices or the word SOLD superimposed over masterpieces like a real estate agent's window, no bustle like a train station or crass commercialism like a department store.

A young lady sat at a mahogany desk with a bank of telephones and a computer between her and the reception area so she stood up and walked around her desk to greet her visitor.

'How may I help you, sir?'

'I'm not sure, I have to admit that I have arrived without an appointment but I was interested in getting the opinion of one of your experts in some coins and some artefacts I have.'

'Of what origin?'

Jonathan became flustered, why would they want to know that already?

'I'm sorry? They belonged to my grandfather, my great-grandfather in fact ...'

'No sir, where are the artefacts from, Greece, Egypt, India?'

'Oh, I see,' he said with some relief and then smiling, 'I'm new at this, please forgive my stupidity. I'm led to believe that they are Celtic, some coins and jewellery.'

'One second, sir.' The lady returned to her telephones and summoned some help.

'In the meantime, would you like to follow me to the client room?' she said leading him to a small office with chairs either side of a table and a small bookcase containing some well-thumbed reference books, mainly on coins, it seemed.

A few minutes later a man in his early thirties entered the room. He wore a bold, pin-striped, double-breasted suit which was not buttoned up, a blue and white striped shirt with a primrose yellow tie on which were red emblems of some sort and a pair of scarlet braces. A white handkerchief flamboyantly flopped from his suit breast pocket and was, to Jonathan, the epitome of a yuppie city banker, down to the brogues and oversized signet ring.

'Morning!' he greeted Jonathan, as though they met on a daily basis, 'I'm Drew Gatacre, English Hammered.'

'That's quite a mouthful, you'll have to say it a bit slower,' Jonathan replied.

'Sorry, Drew Gatacre, my area is English hammered coinage, I believe you have some Celtic coins? My colleague, Harry Knox, will be down soon to look at the bits and pieces but I'm your coin man. Here, take a seat, it's quite warm out today,' Drew said, at which Jonathan automatically wiped his perspiring brow.

They sat at the desk and Jonathan produced the coins, each separated in small brown envelopes bearing the legend 'Department of Environment', a legacy from his father who seemed to have purloined a great deal of stationary from his employer.

'Not from Defra are you?' Drew asked before he gently rolled the first coin out of its packet onto a felt covered tray, 'ooh, look at that, marvellous condition,' he enthused.

'Yes?'

'Umm, don't often get them like this. Are you a collector?'

'No, perhaps I should explain. I've only got four coins, they were left to me by my father and, as far as I know, have been in our family for generations, certainly since my great-grandfather's day. It is family tradition that they were found with the artefacts in Ireland at the turn of the century, my great-grandfather was stationed there after the Boer War.'

'It's a bit unusual finding a coin of Edmund in Ireland, he was the king of Wessex in the mid 900s, but it was minted in Norwich so may have been taken over there by traders. Are they all like that?'

'Not exactly, that's the only one with a head on it. These are the other three,' Jonathan said handing over the other coins. Drew flicked the next one out of its envelope onto his hand, picked it up between his finger and thumb by the edge and flicked it round with his middle finger.

'Boy, that's a beauty, it's worth coming into work each morning if I can see something like that. It's a coin of Olaf Guthfrithsson, struck in York during the Viking occupation, around 940, I think.'

He repeated his trick with handling the next coin and this time emitted an appreciative whistle.

'Not one, but two! Both with Athelferd as the moneyer and probably the same die. You know nothing about coins?'

''Fraid not.'

'I'll explain then. In fourteen years of cataloguing coins, specifically English coins, I have only handled a Raven type Olaf penny once and even then it wasn't all there. We got £2,500 for it about five years ago. These two knock spots off any example that has come up for sale.'

'Why a raven?' Jonathan asked.

'The raven was the symbol of the Danish Vikings, in their mythology they were messengers for Odin.'

'Nothing to do with the Viking's raven desire to plunder?'

'Oh, very good, yes, I like it. A visual pun?'

'It seems so obvious,' Jonathan explained.

'In hindsight. I wonder if the word came after the event: it was the men under the sign of the raven that undertook all the plundering and hence it became the verb? One for the OED to sort out.'

Drew rolled the fourth coin out of its envelope.

'Ah, a triquetra type, another corker,' he enthused and Jonathan winced at the expression, it was a bit close to home.

'Hello, it's a Sihtric, not a Regnald or Olaf, moneyer Ascolv. You've made my day now Mr Armstrong, I've never handled one of these, in fact I'm really not sure how many are known for Sihtric, hold on.'

Drew rummaged around in the bookshelf, pulled out a catalogue of British coins and flicked over the pages.

'Says it's "unique" here, not any more it isn't. The funny thing is that Ascolv is a Germanic name and Athelferd is English, so we've got a German and an Englishman striking coins for Vikings in York and three of them end up in Ireland. If only they could talk! It does, however, date your find to having been deposited in about 942 - 943 as these were never circulated and were presumably hidden or lost soon after they were minted.'

'I see,' said Jonathan, who was utterly lost, 'and presumably if they are so rare they are valuable?'

'Lord yes! The Edmund portrait type is worth a thousand to twelve hundred pounds in that sort of condition, perhaps a touch more, but you don't want to overdo it. The Viking coins are something of an unknown quantity. I would suggest five thousand each for the Olaf raven types and eight to ten thousand for the Sihtric penny although that may take off. The last three are guesstimates as the trade likes to term them. There are only four coins in the hoard?'

'Yes,' Jonathan confirmed.

'Do you mind if I have a look at the artefacts?'

'Not at all.'

Jonathan unwrapped each of the gold mounts, the paten and finally the gold cross and put them on the felt lined tray beside the coins.

'I think Harry's going to die and go to heaven after this lot. It's not really my area but any fool can see how exquisite these are. They look remarkably clean.'

'I washed them, they were in an attic and pigeons had got in,' Jonathan said, his days of rehearsal paying dividends.

'Glad you didn't wash the coins.'

'I was an amateur coin collector in my youth, you know, saving the loose change from uncles who had come back from a trip abroad, nothing too serious, penny and halfpenny collections in those blue fold out albums. I learnt more about how to handle coins than the geography or history of the countries my collection ever represented.'

'We all start somewhere.'

'And you, where did you get your start?' Jonathan asked, trying to satisfy his curiosity fed by the incongruity of a city type enthusing over foil thin discs with such passion.

'I had a fascination for Roman Britain and a friend of the family knew John Orman, then the chairman of Trotman's, now retired, and he gave me a job here. I was eighteen, eager to learn and please people and I'm still here. It can be repetitive and a bit mundane but then you have a day like today and all's right with the world. It's now a long wait between drinks to handle something I have never handled before but now I can tick another one off the list. Are those the sorts of prices you were hoping for?'

'I hadn't a clue what they were worth. I'm not the only beneficiary to my father's estate, so I'll have to discuss the matter with the others, this is a bit of a preliminary fact-finding mission.'

There was a knock at the door and another thirtyish year-old man came in and introduced himself as Harry Knox, North European Antiquities. Drew Gatacre excused himself to go and find some further references for the coins and promised to be back within ten minutes.

Harry sat in Gatacre's chair and examined the paten, finally using his jewellers' loop to examine the detail of the gilt decoration.

'Tell me about these,' he asked whilst still squinting into the magnifying glass.

Jonathan repeated the story about his great-grandfather and how these were now left to him and others and that it was the intention of the beneficiaries of his father's will to sell them and split the proceeds. They thought it best that they sold them together as they were apparently found together. In the five minutes it took in the telling, Harry examined the paten minutely and didn't say a word, even when Jonathan had finished his story, he continued his examination. Finally he lowered the paten and put it on the tray.

'Found in 1900?'

'Around that, but it's family tradition and could have lost accuracy over the generations.'

'Umm. You see, Mr Armstrong, the paten and cross and these mounts were made in Ireland in the 8th and 9th centuries and Ireland is very particular about its tangible history, they have very strict laws about taking things out of the country.'

Jonathan was about to say that he knew all about the Irish laws but managed to stay in character and professed no knowledge of Irish laws.

'You see,' Harry continued, 'if these were taken out of Ireland after a certain date, Ireland can seize them and enforce their return. If, on the other hand, we can prove that they have been in this country or anywhere outside Ireland since before that date then we are free to do as we like. Do you understand?'

'Yes, I don't think that there will be any trouble on that score,' reassured Jonathan.

'Good, it's more than my job's worth to sell something when ownership is in doubt, I'm being cautious because our market is under scrutiny all the time and our fellow competitors in the trade are eager to seek out any chink in the armour, as it were, and do us in.'

'You can have my guarantee.'

'Only if we require it but it's as well to get the legal side over as soon as we can. I hope I haven't alarmed you?'

'Not at all, I can imagine that it's an area fraught with danger, aren't Greece still claiming the Elgin Marbles?'

'Probably the most famous case but there are hundreds of smaller claims, most of which can't be proven either way. Ireland has largely managed to stay out of it but it doesn't mean that they won't try. Anyway, enough of that,' he concluded and picked up the cross, examining it with as much attention to detail as he had with the paten.

'It's a most remarkable piece of work. If it were not found with the paten I would declare it to be a fake because it is too good. I say that because the person who made this paten made something else that was also found in a hoard.'

'Oh yes?'

'It is a famous cup, the Ardagh Chalice, which is now in the National Museum in Dublin. Unless I am very much mistaken, this is the paten to go with the cup or at the worst, by the same goldsmith. The cross is just the most remarkable thing I've seen in years but the paten is where the money is; you see, one has a ready buyer, it would be criminal if Ireland did not reunite the pair. These mounts are desirable as well, only the three?'

'Yes, how many should there be?'

'Four definitely, well, let's see what we've got,' he said picking up each one, 'here's St. Luke with his calf, Mark with his lion and Matthew and his winged man so we are missing John and his eagle which would have been the mount on the lower right corner of a book cover, presumably containing the gospels.'

'And those are Irish as well?'

'Yes, but earlier than the cross and paten. What did Drew say about the coins, they're English?'

'Viking occupation of York, but one's English.'

'So about 950.'

'942-943 to be precise.'

Harry allowed himself a smile.

'So precise, these coin people. What you have, I would guess, is a Viking treasure hoard, albeit a modest one, stolen from a Christian Celtic community in Ireland, probably on the west coast to which the owner added his own few coins and then either perished or couldn't remember where he had put it! It isn't unusual to have such hoards, perhaps the most famous was the Cuerdale Hoard found in Lancashire and there was another found in a mine shaft in Cornwall and quite a few have been found in Ireland. Some are obviously to do with a burial but I don't think this is, if this is all there was, it's so frustrating when these things are dug up without proper care and attention.'

'Not only do I not know whether they were dug up with care and attention but I don't know where they were found or if this is everything that was found. Obviously my antecedents were not exactly over-excited by the things.'

'So you don't know that these came from Ireland, might they have been found in England?'

'I don't know,' Jonathan replied, aware that he was liable to make a mistake if they got into too much detail, 'is that a possibility?'

'Yes, a very real one; whilst the earlier things were obviously made in Ireland, the Viking coinage, and this English one, are pointers to a Viking who plied his trade between the two countries and who may have had a base in York or in the Danelaw, centred on East Anglia.'

'The English coin comes from Norwich.'

'Does it? Does it, indeed? Well, that could be a talking point. You say that it is only family tradition which links the find to Ireland?'

'Yes.'

Harry hesitated.

'Can I ask you why you cleaned the artefacts?'

Jonathan spun his line about the pigeons and the attic and as he finished Drew Gatacre rejoined them with the news that the rarer of the coins, called "unique" in the catalogue was now the third known and by far the most superior. He and Harry discussed the hoard and the possibility that it may have been found in England after all.

Jonathan did not like to dampen their enthusiasm at all but he was due in a meeting in half an hour so he had to hurry them along.

'What value would you put on the artefacts?'

'Er, you've got me there,' Harry started.

'That's what I said,' Drew commented.

'Roughly, very roughly, half a million for the paten, quarter of a million for the cross and perhaps the same for the mounts, no, not that much for the mounts, they would exceed that if the fourth one was with it, but let's be conservative, say one hundred thousand for the mounts and what were the coins worth, Drew?'

'Twenty thousand the four but we'll have to play it well and assure everybody that this is it, we can't have raven and triquetra types flooding the market.'

'This is all that I've got,' Jonathan assured him.

'I suspect you'll nett about a million pounds in total,' Harry said, taking another look at the cross, 'perhaps more if we can get a certain institution in the fray.'

'Would it be best for me to offer them to the Museum directly?' Jonathan asked naively.

'Not as far as we are concerned,' Harry replied dryly, 'are these the sorts of prices you had in mind?'

'As I said to Mr Gatacre, I haven't a clue what any of it is worth and you have been honest enough to say the same thing in light of their rarity. I imagine it is difficult to value things that rarely appear on the market. If we were to sell by auction and we obviously have a buyer in Dublin, if I gauge your thoughts correctly, who is to provide the opposition?'

'We'd reserve each piece of course, so there is a minimum price at which we would sell, but there is no upper limit, that's the beauty of the auction trade, Mr Armstrong, especially when they are one-off lots. Items such as the paten and the cross are an unknown quantity because there's nothing to compare them with, whereas a Picasso measuring this by that and from his blue rose period (I am no art expert) can reasonably expect to sell between x and y, the limits set by the reserve, 'x', and the cut-off figure of 'y' which would be the price of a similar work on the market.

'The auctioneer's job is to shield the 'y' figure from our buyers by promoting ourselves as the business end of the market whereas the galleries and antique shops are a rich man's play thing, somewhere where they get their freshly brewed coffee and a chance to feel their wealth. Hundreds of business school students have analysed the fine art trade but hardly any of them get it right; oh, they get the prices and the annual percentage gains right, that's a matter of maths, the real business is getting people to believe that they cannot do without a certain lot.'

'That's just selling, that is what we do, I'm in the advertising game, not the creative side but as a number cruncher,' Jonathan said.

'It's all very well selling toothpaste or shoes, they have a retail price but this junk doesn't,' Harry said pointing at the items on the table.

'Junk?' Jonathan queried.

'Just a term we use so that we don't get carried away, it's all junk, tat, the worldly possessions of dead people. I'd like to do a bit of work on the paten, a private thing, of course, that will be of benefit to its selling price if you want to eventually sell it. Would you mind if I took some snap shots?'

'No, go ahead, I just have to be in the city pretty soon.'

Harry disappeared and soon returned with a camera with which he took photographs of all the pieces and then, upon a request from Gatacre, some close-ups of the coins for 'his reference'. They then helped to pack them all up, both gave Jonathan their cards and urged him to call them at any stage should he be keen to sell and that their commission rates were considered to be amongst the most competitive in the trade. As they escorted him through the reception area, the secretary gave Jonathan a catalogue from a previous sale and a leaflet about Trotman's and their standing in the antiquities world.

Jonathan, concerned that he was going to be late and feeling pressured by Messrs. Gatacre and Knox, thanked them for their attention and time and hurried down the steps into Savile Row turning left to go to Piccadilly to find a cab.

Harry returned from the front door to find Drew downloading the photos onto his computer.

'Well, he's gone with the goodies,' Harry said unnecessarily.

'I think he'll be back. I hope he'll be back.'

'Really, you don't see any problems?'

'That they've been recently dug up?' Drew asked cheerfully.

'You noticed too, eh? I suppose we can get them professionally cleaned and thereby remove the traces of earth in the chip engraving. The coins we can leave?'

'Oh yes, one of the raven types has iridescent toning, just as a silver coin would tone if open to the air. I can't see that we've got a problem if we stick to the great-grandfather story and try to leave out any mention of Ireland.'

'And what do you make of our Mr Armstrong?'

'Pleasant enough chap,' Drew offered, 'but he's obviously the courier or go-between for the finder. I suspect his appointment is with somebody else in the trade and they'll go with whoever provides the highest estimate. Who knows what they're worth? We could just have easily quoted two million for the lot.'

The estimating of lots like the find was a perennial bore to Harry as it became a lottery, usually the highest bidder amongst the auctioneers getting the spoils and the skill was to pitch them at as high a figure as possible without over-cooking it and finding oneself saddled with perfectly good lots but unobtainable reserves.

'I'd also like a spectrometry test on the metal content of each item but we would have to compare it with something already dated, and that something is sitting in Dublin. Anyway, let's get the things in for sale first,' Harry said, knowing full well that it was not up to them any more.

5

It was only whilst he was sitting on the train back to Shrewsbury that Jonathan realised that he had not taken in a single detail from his meeting in the city. He had taken some notes and had provided enough doodles on his agenda for an analyst to mull over for days in an effort to find out what was on his mind. If the answer was a million pounds sitting in the briefcase by his right ankle then the analyst should go to the top of the class, and if quantified by further detecting his mix of delight and worry about a million pounds, then a distinction was in order.

His house wasn't worth a million pounds for goodness sakes.

He had tried to phone Octavia with the news but as it was a Thursday, he remembered that she took Livia for riding lessons after school. He sat in the train with his briefcase on his lap the entire way watching the countryside shoot past. He rarely took the train and always drove if they went away, so the chance to see a verdant England from his elevated position was a novelty. In normal circumstances his thoughts would have been with badgers and copses, hedgerows and Black Redstarts, a pair of which he identified during his brief stint as an amateur ornithologist, aged 10, but the prospect of a half a million windfall rendered the landscape an irrelevance. The enormity of his smuggling from Ireland didn't seem too bad when he didn't know what they were worth but had now assumed new, worrying proportions.

If, his energetic imagination threw up, they offered the pieces to the museum in Ireland, then they would have to take them to Dublin for their consideration. Could they then say that now that the hoard was back in the country, that is where it will stay and they would be back to square one? On the other hand, they could invite the authorities over to England and they could inspect them there. Where? In a solicitor's office, he decided, in Birmingham, no, much better, in a smaller town, keep it as unbusinesslike as one could and get them to think that they could buy them for a song. Once they had inspected the items and convinced themselves that they had to own them, they would be given the bill for an even one million pounds.

How could he justify such a price? Upon advice received from several dealers and auctioneers who were all eagerly awaiting the consignment for their latest sales or exhibitions. The money could be paid in instalments and would be interest free up to ninety days and normal bank interest, British, not Irish, would be levied thereafter, and title of the goods would not pass until the entire amount was paid. That was the businessman in him and this antiquities market was just like any other except the commodities were esoteric and there was, as Gatacre and Knox had pointed out, no price index to consult.

Was a million enough? If nobody knew what the things were worth, was it not a good policy to ask for more and come down, for one could hardly go the other way, unless, of course, they didn't offer the find as a private deal but put the lot up at auction where, as he had been told that morning, there was no upper limit. Or was he being greedy?

What would Seton think? Would the amount kindle a Nationalist fervour compelling him to surrender the find with the possibility of it reaping no reward at all other than a remote chance that it would be known as the Nisbet Hoard henceforth? How was he going to explain half a million pounds in his bank account? Cork farmers didn't spring five hundred thousand pounds from share portfolios or the sale of something that had been hidden for generations. That was Jonathan's reasoning before Death Duties and Capital Gains Tax floated through his mind and then Swiss Banks and Cayman Islands came into the equation but would the Irish Government issue a cheque to a numbered account in Zurich without questioning the title of the goods?

Shrewsbury station was a contrast to George Town, Grand Cayman, and landed Jonathan with a jolt of reality as he struggled past a group of backpackers blocking the carriage doors. He walked to his car feeling light headed; the magnitude of the news he was soon to pour out to Octavia creating a euphoria. He had never been able to give such joyous information before, perhaps the birth of their three children put him in the same frame of mind but this was so unexpected, it was a lot more thrilling than finding the hoard in the first place, although if they knew then what he knew now then their elation would have been all the greater.

Octavia's car was in the driveway, the front passenger door still open as Livia had rushed inside forgetting to close it whilst her mother had not noticed. Jonathan parked the Range Rover behind it, closed the door of the car as he passed and walked round the house to enter by the kitchen door.

'Hello?' he shouted, putting the briefcase on the kitchen table. There was no answer. He walked into the hallway and down to the morning room where the television was on but nobody was watching. He had news to tell and there was nobody to tell it to. He was about to go up the stairs when he heard a clattering in the kitchen.

'Where are you?' he called.

'In the kitchen, how did you get on?' Octavia replied, her voice betraying the fact that she was in motion.

'Don't use Lonergan's, you can tell your tennis chum that,' he started.

'Why,' she asked, 'what did they do to you?'

'Just bloody rude and obviously customers interfere with their day. I walked out on them.'

'Oh,' Octavia replied disappointedly, 'so we still don't know then?'

'I then went round to Trotman's which is where quite a few people recommended. Much nicer, less flash, couldn't be more help if they tried.'

'And?'

'Do you want to know what they're worth or what they are?'

'Just get on with it,' she urged.

'The coins were struck in York whilst it was under Viking occupation, one is English, the artefacts are, as I had correctly identified, Celtic, 7th-8th century.'

'And?'

'Patience woman. They are collectively worth around a million pounds.'

Octavia sat heavily into her Windsor chair against the Aga and was, for the first time Jonathan could recall, quite speechless.

'Good news isn't it?' he asked nonchalantly.

'It's .... it's stunning news. What are we going to do now?'

'I've got to phone Seton and we need to discuss strategy. I think we've got to auction them here, or rather, in London.'

He discussed the thought processes that had occupied his train journey and the best part of his day since finding out. Fifteen minutes after arriving home he realised that he could not remember the car journey from the station, the details of which had, along with the contents of his meeting, been completely overridden by a seven figure sum sitting at his fingertips.

Octavia agreed with his calculations and was forming a mental shopping list that started with Ballingaddy itself, after a decent interval of course, a car and some luxuries that a mortgage and then school fees had denied them. Jonathan was still talking whilst she ran through her catalogue of material desires. Who said money couldn't bring happiness?

'I don't think the children should know,' she heard Jonathan say.

'No? Why not?'

'We've got to do this very well. I've lied to the people at Trotman's, it's the first lie I have ever told of this seriousness, we are obtaining money by deceit. If there is the slightest chance that the story could be broken down by an ill-timed or injudicious remark by anybody then the whole thing will be in jeopardy. I think it is therefore best not to put the children in a position whereby they could say something to the wrong person. If we eliminate that possibility then it is one less thing to worry about.'

'What about Livia's cross?'

'Well, just tell them all, if they ask, that the things are under negotiation but it is secret, it involves governments and that they must not tell anybody about it otherwise we can all get into dreadful trouble.'

'Are they going to believe that?'

'They're going to have to, what else can we say?'

'Tell them the truth, right from the Irish law to your and, more importantly, Seton's attitude to such a law. London to a brick they'll think the same.'

Jonathan considered it.

'No, we can't, there's too much at stake now; if it were tens of thousands then perhaps it wouldn't be so important but it's hundreds of thousands, Tavie, and they aren't all ours either, we have a responsibility to Seton as well.'

Octavia demurred to her husband's logic, a rare enough occasion, but bemoaned the fact that she couldn't share the news with anybody else, presumably not even after the sale in case title was ever disputed. They would then spend their money in as unobtrusive manner as possible and the children would be told that the items had to go to the State and that whilst Seton got something, they did not. It was dawning upon them both that the hoard was not only a blessing but was becoming something of a burden on their consciences.

Jonathan had waited until after nine o'clock to call Seton so that Livia would be in bed and Seton would have finished his supper. Janie had answered the phone and as Jonathan was not sure quite how much she knew he didn't mention the hoard but they swapped weather reports and discussed the later stages of her pregnancy and the fruitless discussions she and Seton had been having about names. Jonathan sympathised with them as he and Octavia had managed to fall out over the same thing;

whilst the boys had been easy, girl's names had been particularly hard and when Livia did arrive she was faced with being labelled Fulvia at Octavia's insistence. A classical scholar friend suggested Livia and Jonathan won her a reprieve, although many friends had been heard to say that it wasn't much of one.

Seton eventually wrestled the telephone from his wife so that he could have his say about names which all had Irish origins and couldn't have been further apart in spirit and meaning from those Janie had earmarked. They had a long way to go Jonathan warned and only a couple of weeks before the issue would be forced upon them.

'Have you been to London?' Seton asked eventually.

'I have, I went today, to a company called Trotman's. Are you sitting down?'

'Fake eh?' he replied.

'No, they're absolutely genuine. Viking coins struck in York, don't ask me to explain that, and Irish Celtic artefacts of the 7th and 8th centuries.'

'Are they worth anything?'

'That's why I want you to sit down,' Jonathan urged.

'Alright, I'm sitting down.'

'A million the lot,' Jonathan said, relishing the drama.

'Are you serious?' Seton asked weakly.

'Of course I am.'

'Oh, hell.'

'You sound disappointed.'

'Shocked. We haven't even found the fourth corner yet!'

'I've shown the things to them now, I don't think that I can conjure up the last bit, it's St. John just in case you were wondering about it.'

'Who's Saint John?' Seton asked.

'The missing corner should depict St. John.'

Seton didn't reply.

'What do you think we should do?' Jonathan asked.

'I haven't a clue. A million quid, eh? Well, the first thing is that we have an agreement that the money is split evenly between the two families. None of this I get so many thousand first lark, that just gets confusing.'

'Agreed, but you are being too generous. Now what do we do, offer them to Dublin or auction them? I'll tell you what I have learned during the day.'

He then went on to describe the thoughts of Trotman's, his and Octavia's and invited Seton to throw in his own, but he was happy to go along with anything Jonathan suggested, saying that it was so much money that arguing over the pennies would be 'unseemly'. He reiterated that he had no special feeling about the 'Nation' as he mockingly referred to his country and that in light of the theory propounded as to how the hoard got there in the first place, he considered that the original export would have taken place over a thousand years ago but just failed to arrive at its destination.

'I'll have to find a way to pay you without throwing your income into a ridiculous tax bracket. Do you have a tame accountant with whom I can be frank? I mean I will have to tell him everything,' Jonathan explained.

'I've just sacked the family accountant in Cork. There's apparently a good chap in Clonakilty but I don't know him and I wouldn't want to chance it, we might end up finding a rarity; an honest accountant - present company excepted,' he hastened to add. Seton's suspicion of accountants rose from nothing either he or anybody else could source but, Jonathan believed, was possibly due to his insistence that he do everything himself, from fencing to tractor maintenance, projected income to three year plan land usage. His inability to do the accounts satisfactorily each year, despite completing accountancy courses, was, to his mind, nothing to do with his mental capacity but had been made impossible by accountants over the years who were working to ensure their own continuance in that profession. Doctors and lawyers were tarred with the same brush and as far as dentists went, his last visit had been when he was seventeen and having survived twenty-five years without a filling he decided that his teeth were the sort that didn't need a half yearly check-up provided he maintained them as he maintained the tractor. Farmers were the only professionals he knew that he could totally rely upon.

'I might just have to read up on Irish tax law myself,' Jonathan concluded, 'after all, we may end up living there yet.'

'Buy Ballingaddy?'

'I don't know if the McNamara's would sell although they are going to have to spend some money on it soon, it's getting a little shabby.'

'I know that Brendan has been talking to them about it, trying to get them down to inspect the place. They haven't had it let since you left and I think there were some lean weeks in June and July as well.'

'Might be just the time to move on it,' Jonathan thought out loud, 'anyway, are we happy to sell the things at Trotman's at the reserves they have suggested?'

'Yes, go ahead, the sooner the better. Talking of shabby houses it would be nice to get one of the bedrooms sorted out upstairs for you-know-what in eight weeks time.'

'I don't know how long it all takes, I'll have to talk to Trotman's tomorrow and work out some sort of timetable. I'll be in touch. Tavie sends her love.'

'Bye, Jonathan, send mine, thanks for the call,' Seton said and put the telephone down. Turning round, he found Janie sitting in the armchair near the door to the hallway having thought that she had gone to the kitchen to watch the television which he could hear in the background.

'What's worth a million, darling?' she asked.

'Something of Jonathan's,' he parried.

'Why does he need your permission or even advice to sell it?'

Seton had no alternative but to tell her the whole story using the current denouement of establishing values as the point at which he was going to tell her; it was no use getting her hopes up if the things turned out to be copies or worthless. Janie accepted his excuses to a point but made it perfectly clear that in a marriage, most things are done with the agreement of the other half and that she would have liked to have been included in the decision to smuggle the hoard out of the country, an act she found reprehensible and likened to the second coming of the Vikings themselves. They argued for hours, neither of them from any position of knowledge of the law, history of the period in which the hoard was deposited, moral rights, patriotic duty, for which Janie showed a hitherto undeclared enthusiasm, and, finally, the astonishing premise that they might have violated a grave.

Seton was accused of thoughtlessness whereas he had considered that he had thought very hard about it and was happy that he had come to the right conclusion. They exhausted themselves trying to score points off each other and in the end Seton merely asked if she wanted half a million pounds or not, to which she replied 'Yes', and before she could qualify it he grabbed her hand and led her upstairs.

6

The Professor flicked through the series of photographs as though each image was of little importance to the corpus of Celtic art. His hand movements were at a variance to his thoughts, it was the way he had flicked through thousands of pages of students' work trying to find any innovation that decades of students had failed to come up with during his time in the department of pre-conquest British and Irish history. The coins were already known to them and merely added to the numbers rather than the knowledge but the cross and mounts were of particular academic significance.

He visited Trotman's every Friday to primarily see if anything had turned up that would be of interest and also to be served coffee and chocolate cream biscuits by the red haired and very shapely Julia Ellis, all three of which, at his advanced stage of life's progression, were on the banned list. Every Friday he listened to the week's haul from Harry Knox and Drew Gatacre, whilst observing their secretary busying herself at her desk, quite aware that she was being watched but what harm could a seventy-nine year old, frail and unsteady Professor do her whilst she could provide him with some purely visual pleasure? God only knows he needed some cheering up.

Professor Thornton Bethune was desperately dishevelled, a failing that was exacerbated upon the death of his wife. The entire British and Irish department at Trotman's attended Mrs Bethune's funeral, although not one of them had ever met her. Some distant relatives also attended as did some former colleagues in academia but it was a sparten gathering at their local church in Holland Park. He was a rock at the service, the vicar gave praise to somebody's life, about which he knew nothing, and it showed, and two weeks later, everybody received a card from the Professor thanking them for their kind thoughts on the day. He recommenced his visits to Trotman's soon afterwards, some days unshaven, other days with odd socks or shoes on and his clothes either unclean or washed but unironed. His hair, a cascade of white strands swept backwards, grew longer and curlier, his collars frayed and his hands were turning yellow as the previously banned cigarettes came back into his life.

He was, fortunately, rarely odious to the nose, had impeccable manners and a mind honed like a sharpened spear with which he could pick out minor details on an object to place and date it with unerring accuracy. Harry often made the comment that he was wasted as an academic, although the library behind his office desk boasted three, well-used books written by the Professor, but did not go as far as to include his name amongst the list of consultants that Trotman's regularly used and whose only payment was a free subscription to all their catalogues. This he repaid many times over with his perspicacious catalogue entries on the occasions that Trotman's had something to animate him. This could frustrate Harry because the Professor was very choosy about the items he would describe and the final entry, invariably prolix, was such that editing was out of the question.

'The paten is definitely that which originally accompanied the Ardagh Chalice. It has the same bands of filigree around the rim and the rope twist appliqués are identical to the foot of the chalice. The enamelled studs match but I am surprised that there is no chip-carved boss to the middle of the plate or a medallion matching that of the chalice. It is possible that instead of the paten going on top of the chalice as we see in medieval illustrations, it served as a base, the foot of the chalice sitting so,' he said placing the tips of his fingers and thumb upon the plain central section of the photograph of the paten, 'like a Renaissance rose water ewer and basin.

'It is a competent piece of work and, no doubt, you have the appropriate institution lined up in your sights, eh?' he asked mischievously, he was no fan of commerce invading his chosen subject.

'The mounts I like, I would have liked them more if St. John was with them but I can't have everything. You think Celtic don't you?'

Harry doubtfully nodded his head, this was when he was going to receive a lecture.

'They're Anglo-Saxon, no doubt about it and they are late ninth century. If they were Celtic then I would date them as being earlier but there is nothing with which to compare them in Irish workmanship. I concede that they could have been engraved in Ireland by an English workman but their origins lie in Northumbrian manuscript painting. They are every bit as fine as, say, the Fuller Brooch in the British Museum, and I would contend, of the same vintage. Being gold, they mounted the front cover of the Gospels belonging to somebody very important, not a cleric but, for instance, royalty. These are extremely significant.'

'I see, and the cross?' Harry asked.

'Marvellous. It has certain Byzantine qualities but has been made with so much attention to detail, from what I can see in the photographs, that it is by an individual with transcendent talent and it was, again, made for somebody of great standing. The lack of enamel could indicate that it pre-dates the introduction of that process although it was considered that Byzantine influence on northern objects and enamelling came hand in hand, as you know. What date did you have on it?'

'Eighth century or earlier,' Harry said, ready for the correction to come back at him.

'You're too timid, Harry, sometimes, other times you go too far, but this time I believe we are looking at one of the earliest extant Christian symbols made in these islands. Don't ask me which island because we have so little to compare it with.'

'Hazard a guess,' chanced Harry.

'I've given you my guess, 6th or 7th century, British Isles.'

Harry felt a smugness coming upon him, he had, at last, defeated his Professor and mentor by producing something he couldn't immediately identify.

'Do you want to do the entry if, and when, we get them?'

'I'd be delighted, I'll do all three if you want. Drew can do the coins, wax lyrical on the rarity and condition and no doubt find an investor to deny them to the true numismatists,' he said, with his characteristic venom for investors in art.

'If it wasn't for them, most of this stuff wouldn't come out,' Harry reasoned.

' "Come out"? Is it going for a dance, Harry? Where did it "come out" from anyway?'

Harry relayed the story of the hoard being found in Ireland at the turn of the century but did not add his own thoughts that it had only recently been dug up. He did, however, say that the vendor preached caution as it was only a family rumour and that three generations had passed since the event.

'Well, of course,' started the Professor, 'they could have been found anywhere, here, Ireland, Scandinavia, mainland Europe, even Mediterranean countries, you can't rule any of them out, but one would lean towards northern Europe for obvious reasons. Do we know where in Ireland exactly?'

'No, I'm inclined to leave Ireland out of it, as it might be misleading.

If your theory about the mounts is correct, then England might be a more likely deposit spot, especially as the coins are not circulated.'

'What's this "if" business?' the Professor asked crossly.

'That was your initial thought on the evidence of a photograph. You may change your mind once you have seen the actual pieces.'

'I'm willing to take a bet that I'm right but then who are you going to get to argue the point with me that I would respect? The buffoon Griffiths?'

"The buffoon Griffiths" was a former colleague of Bethune's who had joined the ranks of Paris dealer, Ducat, where his academic excellence was apparently tainted by economic rationale, according to the Professor, and he tended to catalogue items as being much rarer and finer than they actually were. The professional jealously between the two came to a head in a Paris courtroom in a case about the origins of a gold torque that Bethune maintained had originated in Syria whereas Griffiths said it was French and at least two centuries earlier. Griffiths won the day because the French judge wanted the thing to be French but most people in the know who had actually handled it said it was, without doubt, either from Syria or Constantinople. Hence Ducat could sell it for three times more than the going rate for an Eastern Mediterranean torque and Bethune's hitherto unquestioned record was thereafter under some scrutiny. It was for this very reason that he did not like his name to be on the inside front cover of Trotman's catalogues as a consultant.

'Is there any more coffee, dear?' he asked Julia, who leapt up and refilled his cup, his eyes never leaving her cleavage once as she bent over the desk to pour his coffee.

They chatted about a few other things that were on offer and then got on to the Professor's other pet subject, socialism, a contrast of minds between a left wing scholar and a right wing capitalist, as Bethune called Harry. They whiled away half an hour calling each other mildly insulting names, at the end of which the Professor left, recharged with his weekly dose of pre-medieval art and post-Thatcher politics, to return to his books in his lonely flat in Holland Park.

Harry had the photographs strewn across his desk and was trying to work out the movements of Jonathan Armstrong after he had visited them the day before. He would have gone on to get another opinion, perhaps two, then he would have to report to whoever he was acting for and then he would wait a few days so that everybody would stew. That seemed, to Harry at least, the way they did things, and then he would bring them in to him for sale. He couldn't imagine anybody quoting more than a million, if they quoted a price off the cuff at all, particularly not Peter Grier at Lonergans who was notorious for estimating items, printing the estimates in the catalogues and issuing corrections during the viewing with his latest thoughts, whether they be up or down. He would then ring the vendor either the day before, or morning of, the sale, to lower reserves accordingly.

'Harry, it's a Mr Armstrong on the phone,' Julia announced, interrupting his reverie, and switched the call over to his phone.

'Good morning, Mr Armstrong, how are you?'

'I'm fine, thank you, a little shattered after yesterday's news but all the same, on a day like today, who could feel any better?' Jonathan said, looking out at the pall of smog hanging over a windless and humid Birmingham.

'Quite so. How can I help you?' Harry asked, his heart beginning to thump a little harder.

'I've discussed the possible sale with my co-benefactors and we think that we would like to proceed.'

He'd won.

'Yes? Good.' Harry said, as though somebody consigned a million pounds worth of stock to one of his sales every day.

'How do we go about it?' Jonathan enquired.

'Whereabouts are you?'

'In the West Midlands, I work in Birmingham,' Jonathan said, although it wasn't something he liked to admit.

'Either I can come up there or you can come down to me. I'm free at the beginning of next week, Monday or Tuesday?'

'I'm away next week, I suppose it will have to wait until the week after, I'm coming to London on Wednesday the 21st, how about then?'

Harry hated waiting, in twelve days anything could happen and the Armstrongs could get cold feet but if Harry had the items locked up in the safe behind him then a change of mind meant a lot of inconvenience and couldn't be done without difficulty.

'We have a deadline of a week today to get the catalogue to bed, as it were, otherwise you will have to wait until March for the next appropriate sale. Is time an issue?'

'March?' Jonathan questioned incredulously, 'when is the sale you are about to have?'

'November the 26th, we have actually closed off the catalogue but because of the importance of your lots, we would do a separate section at the end of the sale so it won't slow down the printing if we get the information in late. Is there somebody else who can come down with them?'

'No, not really. I wouldn't want to give them the responsibility, it's a lot of money.'

'Yes, yes it is,' said Harry, 'I tell you what, could I arrange to meet you tomorrow either in your office in Birmingham or at your house?'

'I'll be at home tomorrow, isn't it a long way to come? I'm afraid I don't live in Birmingham but in Shropshire, half way between Telford and Bridgnorth.'

'That's fairly easy to get to, isn't it?'

'On a Saturday it's fine, but don't talk to me about the M54 and M6 when I'm in a cheerful mood.'

They agreed to meet at midday at Jonathan's house and they would give him lunch into the bargain. Jonathan gave him the directions which were not complicated, until the last few miles, but Harry assured him that he was armed with his mobile and would call if he got lost.

The smile stuck on his face told everybody in his office that the hoard was on its way to them. News spread through the building that Trotman's had secured firstly, a publicity coup, and secondly, a highly important consignment against the bigger auction houses, particularly those with tentacles out in every region of the country, who were apt to get stock by their local presence rather than by the expertise within the company. Trotman's were well known in the field of antiquities in which they specialised, and were becoming well known for offering Renaissance and Reformation works but they were not a household name and could rarely compete in the publicity stakes with those auction houses that spent huge sums to ensure that their name was on everybody's lips. The rarefied type of material they usually handled also required a certain amount of intelligence to grasp and was therefore above the attention of all but the better newspapers and even then they had to grab them on a slow news day.

Harry hadn't been totally honest about the catalogue deadline, it was another week away from the date he had told Jonathan but he was too anxious to get the material in and it seemed as good an excuse as any other without appearing too hasty and avaricious. Two weeks, however, hardly seemed enough time for them to catalogue the three artefact lots with relevant references. He lined up their photographer to spend all Monday getting the right shots, put the printer on standby that there would be at least another twenty-four pages, possibly thirty-two, for the November catalogue and then decided that they would do a separate catalogue for the hoard, hype it as no other Trotman sale had been presented; a one-off treatment for a one-off sale.

He phoned the Professor to give him the good news and to promise him an office and the close attention of Julia Ellis for two weeks, at which Bethune's voice trembled slightly.

Harry had a quick meeting with the managing director about the offer he was to make Armstrong on commission rates and costs. He telephoned Dublin to secure an image of the Ardagh Chalice and inquire about the cost of reproduction without revealing why it was needed. Harry promised that several copies of the catalogue would be sent to the Museum.

Satisfied that all was in place for kick-off on Monday, he collected Drew Gatacre whose head was stuck in Viking coinage books and various Sylloges to catalogue the coins as accurately as possible. He hadn't seen the coin expert so animated in years and was going to leave him alone when Drew suggested that they go to lunch.

'Lunch?' Harry questioned, 'I'm off to get pissed but you can eat something as well if you want.'

7

It was quarter past twelve when Harry drove up the drive of the Armstrong's house. Either side of him were copses of horse chestnut which opened out onto an open field, a haha and then the lawns of the house before the stark Georgian facade, unadorned by any foliage, blocked his view any further. Behind, he could see the tops of more trees which seemed to come right up to the back of the house but once he was inside he could see that there was a fifty foot wide garden before the woods started. He had spent the past twenty-four hours musing over the sort of house that Mr Armstrong would live in and out of all his mental pictures not one matched this.

He drove up to the front door and got out of the car noticing that it was one of those English country house front doors that nobody used; no clutter outside like a boot scraper or walking stick indicating its use. He was about to follow the road round to the side of the house when a lady appeared inside the door moving something out of the way before she could open it properly. She was clothed in a long, flowing Indian cotton dress, was shoeless and her hair was tied back in a dark red band. She wore a dozen or more silver bangles, some of which were lodged half way up her arm but was otherwise without any jewellery and her well tanned face was devoid of any trace of make-up. Harry didn't think he was expected by her appearance but her greeting proved otherwise.

'Hello, Octavia Armstrong,' she said holding out her bangled arm, 'found us without any problems?'

'Harry Knox, no problems, they were excellent directions.'

'Jonathan's usually so hopeless,' she said uncharitably, 'always misses a turning or stretch of road when giving directions although he has been driving along the same route for twelve years now, five days a week. Do come in.'

Harry went into the hallway, sparsely furnished but a set of the Cries of London hung with military precision along the walls. Octavia showed him into the drawing room and excused herself to get Jonathan who, she explained, was doing some last minute work before his trip to New York on Monday.

He sat in the room looking about, trying to assess the sort of family who either dug up antiquities in this generation, acted for those that did, or whose antecedents were the archaeologists, with successive generations ignoring the results until now. He didn't know exactly what it was that would give the game away, perhaps a David Roberts lithograph of Thebes or a regimental photograph of great-grandfather in front of the officer's mess in an Irish barracks, taken c.1900. There wasn't anything so simply illustrative, just a few Victorian landscapes, some miniatures and silhouettes that could best be described as 'provincial' and some portrait photographs of three strikingly similar children and their mother, each taken when the children were less than a year old and both sitters in each photograph stark naked. He recoiled from looking at these too closely and switched his attention to the furniture which was very much in the Victorian taste but thankfully not veneered walnut nor toffee apple polished. Perhaps that told of a British Army officer stuck in Ireland with time on his hands to go round digging up the countryside? The period furniture was mingled with modern conveniences like large cushions on the floor and art pottery lamps to take it away from being a conventional country house drawing room although the Staffordshire figures on the mantelpiece and silver ashtrays and figures of pheasants dotted on every flat surface gave it that air.

'Mr Knox, good morning, so kind of you to make the journey at such short notice. My wife tells me that you didn't get waylaid,' Jonathan said, knowing Octavia's propensity to tell people that he couldn't find his way out of a paper bag.

'Excellent directions, I can see how people could get lost though,' Harry replied, standing up.

'Can I get you a drink, gin and tonic, beer?'

'I'd love a beer, if that's possible,' he replied. The idea of a gin and tonic after yesterday's over-indulgence made him feel quite ill.

Jonathan returned with the beers and left again to get 'the things'. Harry poured half the glass down his throat which tingled with approval, he was a great believer in the restorative qualities of a cleansing ale. He was about to exclaim 'aaah!' as they do in the beer advertisements when Octavia joined him and seeing a full beer glass on the table, picked it up and did the same thing.

'Thirsty work, mothering,' she said in way of explanation.

'It's another warm day, we're in for another Indian summer I think.'

'Whereabouts in India do they have a summer like this do you think?'

she asked before sitting on the cushions on the floor.

'I think it's something to do with North American Indians and a period of calm weather between summer and winter storms.'

'Is it?' she asked, 'goodness, I've learnt something. Are you sure?'

'Yes, it's quite a well known error that people make, they equate it with the Raj and verandas, languid days and servants cooling the air with fans. Wasn't your husband's grandfather in the army?'

'They all were, the fighting Armstrongs, wasn't a day between Malplaquet and Korea that there wasn't an Armstrong in the King's Own somethings. That ended when Jonathan's father resigned when he was born, Jonathan I mean, both being only children there were no brothers or uncles to continue the tradition and Jonathan's hardly the army type.'

'It's sad when traditions end like that. I mean, there aren't any Trotmans left in our company, they all decided that there was something better to do than follow the family line into antiquities. The family still exists, in fact I think a few of them hold onto some shares, but none of their names appear on the letterhead, more's the pity.'

Jonathan poked his head round the corner.

'Ah, you're here, drinking my beer,' he said to Octavia, and deposited his briefcase on the floor before disappearing again, this time only for a few seconds to get another can of beer and a glass.

'Cheers everyone,' he said, raising his glass and Harry and Octavia acknowledged the salute.

'Now we'd better get the business side out of the way first, don't you think?' Jonathan continued.

They set themselves up around a glass and chrome coffee table, Harry being seated on a Gothic sofa, Octavia to his side and Jonathan sitting opposite them on the floor. The paten, cross, mounts and coins were placed on a well thumbed copy of the March Tatler and Harry got out his receipt book.

'Firstly,' he said, finding the next available page of his book, 'we have to agree on the reserves and commission rate. Now, I think the figures I gave you on Thursday are pretty spot on but the cross could be worth more than I indicated if our preliminary research is anything to go by.'

'What did you put on the cross?' Jonathan asked.

'Two hundred and fifty thousand pounds. I'm prepared to put three hundred thousand pounds on it and estimate it at three fifty to four fifty. It could prove to be worth a lot more but we won't let it go below the three hundred mark, okay?'

Jonathan and Octavia sagely nodded without understanding quite what they had agreed to.

'The paten,' Harry continued, 'we'll keep at half a million and estimate at six to eight hundred thou.. Yep?'

Again they nodded.

'Then the mounts are also worth a little more than I said, but we'll keep them at a hundred flat. The coins were a thousand for the Edmund, five thousand each for the raven types, and seven and a half for the triqueta type of Sihtric which Drew Gatacre has fallen in love with,' he said, adding the flippancy to disguise his relief and excitement in getting the hoard in his hands once more.

'Now, our normal commission rates for property of this value are ten per cent and an insurance cover of one per cent of the final selling price or the reserve price in the case that a lot is unsold. There is no commission charged if the lot is unsold but a fee may be levied for the cost of photography and any expense we go through to catalogue the items.'

The Armstrongs were aware that they were listening to a recording. Harry could be selling them double-glazing.

'You also charge a buyers' commission, don't you?' asked Jonathan.

'Yes, I was just coming to that, we charge a fifteen per cent buyers' premium up to and including thirty thousand pounds, ten per cent thereafter. However, we have an alternative plan. We could put these in a separate catalogue, 'The Armstrong Hoard' or some such ...'

'I don't want my name anywhere near the catalogue,' Jonathan hastily interrupted.

'No?'

'Absolutely not, for personal, or rather, family reasons.'

'That's a stumbling block then. We have to call it something for promotional purposes. Usually a hoard is named after the place in which it was found but we don't know that so we go to the next best which is the name of the finder. Am I right in assuming that your great-grandfather was an Armstrong?'

'Yes, but you cannot use the name,' said Jonathan firmly.

'Okay, we'll come up with something else, it's not too much trouble. Anyway, as I was saying, what we would do is charge you only five per cent commission and you pay for the catalogue, photography and printing.'

'How on earth am I to know how much a catalogue costs? Which one offers me the best value?'

'The catalogue will be about twenty-five thousand pounds, which, if you sell the lot for a million represents two and a half per-cent.'

'I'll be saving another twenty-five thousand?'

'Yes.'

"And the reason for this altruistic approach by yourself?' Jonathan asked.

'Okay, putting it bluntly, and you're obviously a numbers man, if we fail to sell any of these, we will have covered our major expense, the catalogue production, in the light of not receiving any commission. It's an option we can only give in the case of a single owner catalogue.'

'Are you that worried that you might not be able to sell them?' Octavia asked, picking up the cross and dangling it from an imaginary necklace, the cross resting between her prominent collar bones. It seemed to acquire a lustrous quality missing whilst lying on a table or magazine.

'It suits you,' Harry commented, 'I am very confident that we will get them all away.'

'Why the offer then?' Jonathan pressed.

'It's something we are told to offer by management. Quite honestly, I think it's quite a good deal.'

'I'll tell you what,' Jonathan said, getting a propelling pencil and note pad from his briefcase. He scribbled away, all the mathematics being done in his head. Harry couldn't see what he was writing as it was upside down but after a minute he drew a line under a figure and turned the page round for Harry to see.

'Five per cent commission and we'll contribute fifteen thousand to the cost of the catalogue, payable from the proceeds. I agree to the one per cent insurance fee but there will be no other expenses paid, no cataloguing fee, no photography, those you can take out of your buyers' commission.'

Harry looked at his figures in an attempt to find some time to think of a retort. Tricky vendors were part and parcel of the system nowadays but this was not a sale that they could turn their backs on; it was worth a lot in publicity as well as a six figure commission, it was a lot of black Eturian ware beakers, Byzantine coins or bronze arrow heads and he wouldn't be forgiven for turning up on Monday without the hoard.

'That's very tough of you,' he said eventually.

'I've only got one go at it, Mr Knox,' Jonathan replied.

'Okay, we've got a deal. I'll fill these little boxes out here and get you to sign at the bottom of the page. On the reverse is our conditions of sale for vendors, no man traps other than we've agreed and, once signed, this represents our authority to sell and that you guarantee them to be your property.'

'That's fine,' Jonathan said, and waited for Harry to fill in the receipt, explaining as he did that a more formal typed receipt would be on it's way as soon as his secretary could get round to it.

'Will you come to the sale, Mrs Armstrong?' Harry asked.

'Rather not, I'm sure it's all very exciting but I'm not very good in London. Bridgnorth is about all I can stomach.'

'Marvellous place, London, although I live near Aylesbury now. Right, here's where you sign,' Harry said, indicating the spot on the page and noticing that Jonathan read the entries that he had made before signing at the place Harry had indicated. Once done he handed the book back and Harry flamboyantly tore the top copy out of the book and gave it back to Jonathan. In the meantime, Octavia had packed the hoard back into its protective bags that she had made in Ireland and handed them over to Harry who put them in his briefcase.

She then announced that it was a kitchen lunch and led the two men through to the large refurbished room where the paraphernalia of every day life cluttered up the surfaces and indicated that it was where they spent most of their time. Above the fridge hung an enlarged photograph of a beach and tucked into the bottom was another of a rundown farmhouse.

'Where's that?' Harry asked, pointing at the beach.

'In Wales,' Jonathan replied, without missing a beat, outwardly at least.

'Pretty.'

'Do you mind cold, Mr Knox? I haven't had time to cook,' asked Octavia.

'No, it's more than kind of you to feed me at all.'

'It's the least we could do after cutting into your weekend, I must say its a relief not having them around any more now we know what they're worth.' Octavia said.

'It was only the catalogue deadline that made it necessary to come up and bother you otherwise it would have waited.'

'Take a seat Mr Knox, I'll fill your glass,' Jonathan said, happy that the photograph had been forgotten.

8

Socialising had become a necessary part of Harry Knox's job as he wooed buyers and sellers alike in an attempt to demythologise the auction business and introduce people that could become collectors to the world of antiquities. These people were usually either students of history who had money or who were highly educated and thus had the mental capacity to become interested in a complex and broad field such as collecting "dead people's pots and cash" as Professor Bethune liked to call them. Generally speaking, very rich people did not collect antiquities, although quite a few would make a foray into the market and buy something spectacular for the reception area of their holding company's offices, especially something flashy like a red figure vase or an Egyptian granite sculpture.

One couldn't cater for these fly-by-nights, although their money was very welcome, because their decision to invest in the antiquities market was usually unheralded and short-lived. However, it didn't stop Trotman's, and every other firm, from dangling their wares in front of tycoons by sending a barrage of invitations to their homes in the hope that vanity might get the better of them and the chance of a photograph in the gossip columns lure them to a viewing.

Harry had spent many a fruitless hour and an unhealthy amount of Trotman's money in clubs and restaurants in many of the western world's capital cities trying to persuade chief executive officers and their fellow board members that the ultimate status symbol was not a Rolls Royce, Lear Jet or Sikorsky helicopter but a collection of aureii of the Roman Emperors or a Greco-Roman marble bust of one of the deities. His success rate wouldn't put him up amongst the champions but he had managed to get one or two of these elusive men through the doors, mainly Americans and Europeans, the British seemed to stick to their own and were much feted by the British furniture, silver and painting departments for their custom.

When he and his wife, Patricia, first moved to Aylesbury they were looked after by their neighbours and introduced to many like souls, and some unlike souls, whom they could follow up if they so wished. During this introductory period they repeatedly heard the names of David and Tracy Reeves but for a long time never actually met them. Opinion on David Reeves varied from being considered uproariously amusing to a loud-mouthed bore and that Tracy was the tolerant but silent partner. Everybody talked about them but they never seemed to materialise and Harry was beginning to wonder whether he was the victim of an elaborate hoax until he read all about David Reeves in a listing of Britain's one thousand richest people. He had apparently invented a gadget that the automotive industry could barely do without and was an extremely wealthy young man, having been born east of the Bow Bells and left school aged 15 without a single qualification, but with a male youth's enthusiasm for tinkering with car engines.

The riches that he now enjoyed were self generating and he spent much of his time running a motor racing team on the circuits of Europe, hence his scarcity that first summer that the Knox's spent in Buckinghamshire. However, in September, they finally met at a drinks party held by a mutual friend. Harry had imagined somebody older and fatter than the slim thirty year old man who was introduced to him, but his mental picture of Tracy as a statuesque bottle blond awkwardly wearing expensive clothes and far too much makeup was close to the mark.

David Reeves turned out to be closer to the bore than funny on Harry's scale, his lack of education hidden behind endless put downs of anything great and noble and far from casual name dropping of Hollywood's darlings and Europe's courtiers. Harry tried to avoid him after the first few occasions but it appeared that David Reeves had found a long lost friend in him and stuck by his side at every opportunity whilst Tracy assumed great interest in their two daughters, she being, as yet, childless, that bordered on the embarrassing, especially when she showered them with gifts that the Knox's couldn't afford.

Harry often surmised that David's friendship was purely so that he could mock him and his education, referring to him as "the Prof." and passing on any inquiry: 'ask the Prof., he'll know.' But the bravado that produced this boorish behaviour was only evident when there were other people around which became apparent when they invited the Reeves to a barbecue about a year after they first met and the other couple rang to cancel at the last moment which left just the four of them. That night, David became introspective revealing a quiet intelligence and thoughtfulness, for whom education was designed, and Harry's perception of him was turned on its head. Thenceforth, the mocking of Harry's accent, the constant references to "the Prof." and mention that education doesn't necessarily bring riches were finished as David admitted to rueing the day he turned his back on scholastic achievement.

He started to drop round to their house on a wet Sunday afternoon with some cans of beer and ask Harry to tell him about the fine art world; what made something worth more than something else and why anybody would part with their money for a pile of bricks or a canvas painted bright blue and called "No. 2". Harry lowered him into the deep waters of the fine and decorative art ocean slowly, unconscious that he was doing as much on those Sunday afternoons as he would achieve over a Chateaubriand and Beaujolais at the Savoy Grill with captains of industry, nay, admirals even. David didn't rush into things though, he absorbed almost everything Harry told him but he didn't buy anything although in the two years that they had known each other, David's wealth, he revealed one day, had more than doubled without him spending a single day at the office.

In the evening of the day that Harry had collected the hoard from the Armstrong's house, the Knox's were to attend a dinner party at the Reeves'. Harry didn't face the thought of being entertained with any alacrity after the excesses of the previous day and the hours spent driving to and from the Armstrongs. When he got back home he took the hoard to his office and played with the items on his desk. He had spent most of his life looking at such marvellous objects through glass in museum cases but now he could feel them, turn them over, trace his fingertips over the beaded decoration of the cross, bring the paten to his eyeglass and study every square millimetre of the cast decoration and enamelled studs. His mind kept returning to how he envisaged the catalogue and to what extent they would illustrate the items without overdoing it.

He had resolved to photograph the cross on a black velvet background but that was too obvious and the overriding image that he now saw was the gold against the tanned and freckled skin that stretched over Octavia's clavicle, the suspension ring clasped between her long, sun-bronzed fingers with their perfectly symmetrical, unpainted, fingernails. Was he in love with the cross, or Octavia, he wondered? He had been thinking about it from the moment he sat down to lunch with the Armstrongs and thereafter, everything she did made her more perfect to him and so confused was he that he made towards her to kiss her goodbye and she cleverly extended that bangled arm to shake his hand before he made a fool of himself. But then he had made a fool of himself because she knew exactly what he was going to do and only she was quick-witted enough to prevent it.

Which Octavia was she? Was she Atia or Archoria's daughter, or Nero's neglected wife? She was the noble Octavia, Anthony's wife, mother of five and step-mother of Fulvia and Cleopatra's children by Anthony, the revered Octavia, the one that had died in 11 B.C. and had come back bearing a gold cross whose lustre was enhanced by the touch of her skin.

Auctioneers didn't fall in love with the wives of vendors, he told himself and then rubbed the smooth metal of the back of the cross, the side that had touched her throat. No, he was in love with the cross but he could only have it for two months before it became locked up in an investor's bank box, or a glazed cabinet in a museum, where it would lie admired, but not loved as he loved it, not as loved as Octavia was by him, his bare-footed classical sculpture.

'Darling, it's time to go, are you ready?' Patricia called from the hallway.

'Five minutes,' he replied, packing up the hoard and putting it in the central drawer of his desk.

They were half an hour late by the time they got to the Reeves' house. They had to drop their daughters off at Patricia's mother's as she was still lame after a fall and couldn't be expected to babysit at their house. They promised that they would be back by eleven but knew that they would be lucky to escape from a Reeves' dinner party before twelve o'clock. It hadn't mattered that they were late as David was only just pouring everybody's second drink when they arrived.

'Thought we'd lost you,' he commented, when they walked into the large room. They were introduced to the other guests, eight people all of whom were unknown to them, apparently friends from the racing circuit and whose names Harry forgot within seconds of being told. None of the ladies had a name like Octavia, he noted.

The dinner dragged on, the food was, as usual, exceptional, as Tracy didn't pretend like others and openly talked about the caterers and that she had problems making a cup of tea. Harry was sitting next door to her so he concentrated his conversation in her direction and rudely talked about things only they knew anything about, thus excluding the mechanic sitting on her other side. Patricia had been put next door to David and more than once Harry heard his name mentioned, no doubt pilloried for his sagacity.

The rather nasty Vienna regulator in the hallway which Harry could see from his place at the dining table told him that it was quarter past eleven and the pudding was only just on its way. It wasn't so much concern for his mother-in-law, although that was the excuse he used, as wanting to be back in company with Octavia, that made him stand up and offer his apologies to his hostess. Patricia thought it odd and rude of him but could not show a callousness once he had mentioned her unwell mother, and made the same noises. Tracy remained with her guests as David let them out.

'You're not yourself, Harry, have you sold a fake to somebody important?' David asked.

"No, I'm quite tired, been to Telford and back today. I've got something I want you to see, are you coming round tomorrow?'

'Yeh, course I am, a few beers and a chat, eh?'

'Yes. You'll like what I have, I think it's very you.'

'Can't wait, night 'Tricia.'

David kissed her goodnight and they walked to the car.

'What on earth do you think you are doing, darling?' she said, once they got into the car.

'I'm sorry, but I've got one hell of a headache and I don't think your mother is up to staying up until midnight.'

'We've just left in the middle of a dinner party!' she continued, 'I've never known such rudeness. David was right, you aren't yourself. I know that your performance at lunchtime yesterday, from all accounts, was partly to blame, but there's something else.'

'Women's intuition?'

'No, your behaviour tonight. I noticed that you didn't talk to anybody but Tracy other than a few grunts and groans during drinks.'

'They weren't my sort of people, darling. They thought that torque was something in an engine, not a Celtic piece of jewellery. Yes, I've had a hangover, but it's gone and now I'm merely tired. They didn't mind at all, I think they knew that they had invited us with the wrong lot.'

Patricia didn't reply, but Harry could hear her indignation even over the noise of the car. They arrived at her mother's house to find that she had gone to bed so they quietly retrieved the girls and carried them to the car, bundled them up in their duvets and set off for Aylesbury, a ten minute drive. Harry caught himself going to sleep along one darkened stretch of road but once they got to lit streets he was alert and awake to the omnipresence of the police waiting to pounce on the few motorists out this late. They got home without bothering anybody and Harry parked the car by the front door as it was easier to carry the children that way rather than having to negotiate the corridor between the garage and the stairs.

Patricia carried their bedding as Harry took their eldest daughter to her room and then went back to fetch the sleeping younger daughter. When he re-entered the house Patricia was standing at the bottom of the stairs looking bewildered.

'We've been burgled,' she said simply.

'Oh Christ!' he replied, and handed their daughter over to her before running into his office. He knew the second he saw the centre drawer of his desk open that the hoard had gone, they had taken the whole bag, his laptop, the silver inkstand presented to him by his father upon gaining his first from Oxford, his camera, even his mobile telephone and charger were gone.

He heard footsteps above him and realised that he had left Patricia holding their daughter and that she must have taken her upstairs to bed. He went back into the hallway and then into the drawing room where, again, every electrical appliance other than the lamps had been taken and anything silver, or coloured silver had also gone.

He walked into the dining room to find the drawers and cupboards of the sideboard opened and anything looking vaguely valuable had gone. Glass, porcelain, furniture and pictures were all left untouched. Patricia joined him by the sideboard and put her arms around his waist.

'Everything?' she asked.

'Everything that looked valuable.'

'What about the things you picked up today?'

'Gone.'

'I'll call the police,' she said.

'What about upstairs?'

'My jewellery, your cufflinks, the silver photo frames. They don't appear to have gone through the clothes or, if they have, then they've been neat about it.'

Harry's headache had gone now.

Patricia telephoned the police who said they'd respond as soon as they could, but still took more than an hour to arrive. In that time the Knox's had established that the burglars had broken into the house through the kitchen door which wasn't that difficult to do unseen as it was around the back of the house.

Harry sat in the kitchen writing a full description of the items in the hoard because it was those that were most recognisable although the merciless nausea that swept over him told him that the gold items would have been melted down within twenty-four hours of being stolen. Octavia's cross had gone forever.

The two policemen that arrived were very sympathetic but Harry heard a distinct tutting when he informed them that the house was not fitted with a burglar alarm. He then gave them a list of the household and personal items that had been stolen which they thanked him for but didn't offer up any hope of recovering.

However, their reaction when he informed them of the theft of the hoard was quite different, galvanising them into action as a million pound hoard was now C.I.D. business and they had better be thorough if C.I.D. were going to be involved.

'You haven't touched anything?' one constable asked.

'Not in the rooms where anything has been taken, no,' Harry replied sullenly.

'Well, we're going to have to do a thorough forensic test. We won't be able to set it up until the morning.'

'I'm sorry if it has inconvenienced you,' Harry said, loading on the sarcasm, 'perhaps you get more Brownie points for those motorists just over the limit, eh?'

'Where we score our Brownie points, sir, is preventing crimes from occurring and advising people how this can be done. Not drinking excessively before driving is one, ensuring that one's premises, especially those containing million pound Celtic treasures, are secure before leaving them empty is another. Now I understand that you must be feeling very upset and the missing artefacts are not going to be easy to explain to your company's insurance assessors; I'm not sure an unlocked desk drawer in a house without any form of alarm is going to impress them.'

The local detectives arrived soon afterwards and Harry had to repeat the whole story to them. They looked in all the rooms that had been burgled and then turned on Harry as though he had something to answer for.

Who were the other guests at the party? Who knew that he had the hoard in the house? How much were the mounts and cross worth if melted? Could the dish be converted to disguise it? Did he regularly bring clients' stock home? Did anybody else within his organisation know his house and that he was going to collect the hoard? Did the Armstrongs know that he was taking them home and wouldn't have them in a secure place until Monday?

They then grilled Patricia who knew so little about the hoard, even the contents, that she could hardly have been the slightest benefit to their enquiries.

Harry spoke to the uniformed constable who seemed to be a lot more attentive and they discussed the probable disposal of the hoard and the household contents.

Harry explained that the numismatic and art trade had a worldwide warning system, whereby he notified the Trade Association who emailed or faxed all its members and other Associations throughout the world. He could also register the items on various websites. The constable agreed that it seemed to be an excellent system and it would be a good idea to get them listed first thing in the morning in case any of the items were offered for sale to a dealer.

'Not only that but I've got the photographs of the hoard in my office. I can get them to you tomorrow too if they'll be useful.'

'Definitely, we're going to have to come back in the morning for the fingerprint dusting, etcetera anyway so you can give them to us then. In the meantime, can you not enter any of the rooms downstairs other than the kitchen and try not to use the kitchen door nor the path through the garden until we've given it a thorough going over.'

'What time will you get here?'

'It won't be me, of course, but the forensic detective sergeant starts when he likes, depends on how many jobs he's got after a Saturday night. Don't expect him before seven.'

Harry looked at his watch, it was twenty past three and he still felt sick.

9

The sharp click as three digits of the alarm clock changed from 6.59 to 7.00 woke Harry with a start. He had a knack of being able to wake up at an appointed hour without an alarm clock and could even tell the time when he woke up without a clock beside him, but old habits dictated that the clock sat on the beside table, the alarm rarely ever set. He hadn't slept well in the past three hours and the children had decided, that particular morning, to wake and play just after six o'clock, so Patricia, too, had a short sleep.

He wasn't, however, drowsy and seemed to have his wits about him as he formed a list of what to do and in what order. He had initially put the Armstrongs uppermost on his list as they were bound to be contacted by the detectives and they should hear the news first from Harry. Then Trotman's managing director took top billing because he was going to have to contact the company's insurers. Drew Gatacre should be told so that he could get the numismatic trade's early warning scheme under way for the coins whilst he could email the antiquities dealers from home himself. His thoughts took him to the underworld and what they would do with the hoard; melt as much as they could and get rid of the paten and coins for whatever they could get. They were probably sitting in some market stall in a Sunday Fair somewhere in Britain as he lay in bed thinking about them.

At half past seven he decided to call his managing director, Sam Reid, it being not too desperately early but, for a Sunday, early enough to show his sufficient concern. He dressed and went downstairs, careful not to disturb anything but he did venture a look into his office just in case it had all been a bad dream. The desk drawer remained open and without the small cloth bag in which he had collected the hoard. Moving on to the kitchen he found Patricia giving a portly, balding, ruddy cheeked man a cup of tea.

'Detective Sergeant Bodden,' Patricia announced, 'this is my husband, Harry.'

'Not at all pleased to see you,' Bodden said cheerfully, 'less I see of you people the happier I am. Your wife kindly offered me a cup of tea, I've been up since four thirty with a decapitated body in the Grand Union Canal.'

'How grisly,' Harry replied.

'Good clean job, no hacking around with kitchen knives, those are the messy ones.'

Patricia coughed in disapproval of the subject matter at breakfast.

'Better be getting on with it. Is the detective constable here?' Bodden said, raising himself to his feet.

'I don't think so,' Patricia replied.

'You know where they got in and where they went through?'

Harry led him from the back kitchen door, into the corridor and along to the drawing room, dining room and his study. Bodden went back to his car, parked in the driveway and changed into white hooded overalls, vivid purple surgical gloves, white elasticated shoe covers and a face mask before he collected his equipment which he set up in the dining room. He emerged from the room after five minutes.

'The bastards have wiped it clean,' he announced, 'we've a professional team on the job here.'

This did not deter him from his job and he thoroughly inspected every likely surface but his foe had been equally exacting in cleaning up after themselves. He continued to chat as he went displaying a deep hatred of those who perpetrated crime but by the time he had got round to the office was beginning to show some begrudging admiration for this particular 'lot of scum'. He agreed that the gold items would have been melted down or the cross possibly given to one of their girlfriends because it came to them cheaper than they would have had to outlay in a high street jeweller. The coins, he added breezily, would be put into soft drink machines in the Mall.

Whilst he studied the route from the driveway to the back door, Harry sat in the kitchen flicking through his address book trying to find the home number of his managing director but he didn't seem to have it. He did, however, have his mobile number and it was this that he rang, but it was out of range or turned off. He called Drew instead, who, at quarter to nine, was obviously still asleep. They chatted for a minute or so about their Saturday whilst Harry waited for him to wake up so that he wouldn't have to repeat himself. He then told him about the robbery. He should have chatted for longer because the news rendered Drew mute for a minute and Harry kept asking him if he was there, knowing that he was.

'Jesus Christ, Harry, yeh, I'm here. What the hell are you going to do?'

'We've got forensics and detectives on the job but I need a huge favour from you. Firstly, do you have Sam's telephone number at home?'

Fortunately he did.

'Secondly, can you go into the office, do your early warning thing amongst the coin people and get the photos we took onto a CD and bring it here? We'll get the police to run off copies and distribute them.'

'Yes, I'll go. I won't be with you before, say, one o'clock. Is that alright? Are you alright? What did they take of yours?'

Harry ran off a list that had been imprinted in his mind but he did have household contents insurance and was inwardly not too disappointed at the prospect of renewing some of the more outdated photographic equipment that had been taken.

'Have you phoned the Armstrongs yet?' Drew asked.

'Not yet,' he answered miserably.

'Rather you than I, old boy,' Drew said sympathetically, 'I'll see you at one.'

Fortified by the positive way in which his colleague eventually took the news he called his managing director; the master himself answering the phone. Harry was no friend of Sam Reid, there was an unexplained friction between the two, which, because of their indifference to each other was never resolved or even discussed, it just remained as it was.

Harry had to tell him the story twice, during which the only reaction or interruption from Sam was to swear vociferously before concluding that he would be over to his house within the hour to discuss the case with the police. Upon Harry's enquiry, he thought it highly unlikely that their insurance cover was adequate for such a cock-up and that it looked to him as though Harry had managed to lose a million pounds for Trotman's, some sort of record, he added.

Harry felt even more depressed than before but immediately called the Armstrongs after Sam had slammed his received down.

'Jonathan Armstrong,'

'Ah, Mr Armstrong, it's Harry Knox here.'

'I've been trying to call you on the mobile number you gave me.'

'Did anybody answer as a matter of interest?'

'No. We've got the police here now, what's going on?'

'I've been burgled, the hoard has been stolen from my desk. I am really very sorry, you are covered for insurance, of course, but that's not the point.'

'Did they ransack you? They did it to us about twelve years ago, whilst we were actually in the house. You'll get over it, it's the only consolation I can give you. It does seem the most extraordinary coincidence that you only collected the things from us that afternoon. Do the police have any leads?'

'Not yet, but we are putting everything we can in place to track the hoard down, it's not as though they can sell the things on the open market. I can't tell you how wretched I feel about it, I was so looking forward to compiling the catalogue and organising the photographs, it was probably the most exciting lot to come to us in a decade or more.'

Jonathan was proving to be a good tonic as he placated Harry by suggesting that the thieves had proven themselves to be electrical goods and jewellery experts and, with exception to the cross, would look at the hoard with disappointment as it would not be immediately saleable. He talked as though he had little concern, perhaps buoyed by the fact that Harry had assured him that they were covered by the insurance clause they had agreed to the previous day even though Harry wasn't at all sure that would be the case. They parted, promising to keep in touch, and Jonathan wished him good luck and told him to keep a positive frame of mind.

Detective Sergeant Bodden was in conversation with a suited man in the back garden when Harry rejoined him. He was introduced to him as Detective Inspector Longfield but Harry thought that he must have misheard as the man was younger than he was.

'Detective Inspector?' he asked.

'Longfield, yes. Scotland Yard, Art and Antiques Squad. Sad business, Mr Knox. Detective Sergeant Bodden tells me that they've done a good job.'

'Unfortunately, yes,' Harry replied.

The Detective Inspector saw Bodden to his car before returning and taking a look inside at the downstairs rooms. He looked over the dusted areas with what seemed, to Harry, to be a cursory glance but he had presumably been fully briefed by Bodden.

'The hoard was in here?' he asked, pointing to the drawer of the desk and Harry nodded. He pulled the chair back and indicated that Harry should sit in it whilst he sat on the edge of the desk.

'Mr Knox, what would you think if you were a policeman faced with a crime like this?'

Harry shrugged his shoulders and was about to confirm that he hadn't a clue when Longfield continued.

'You see, this has all the hallmarks of being an inside job, and whilst I doubt it, personally, the possibility has to be ruled out, do you understand?'

'Yes.'

'Please don't think that I am putting you up to this because I can see you are a decent family man and are visibly distressed. I've met people who think that they can pull one over the police, Mr Knox, and you are not one of those.'

'I'm even more distressed to find out that our company insurers will contest any claim, according to my managing director. I somehow suspect that not only have I lost the hoard, most electrical appliances outside the laundry and kitchen and my family's silver, but, by tomorrow morning, my job as well. I think you can rule me out, Detective Inspector,' Harry said, not a little hurt at the suggestion.

'Not insured?'

'I thought we were, under the company policy of goods in transit, but apparently they are not "in transit" if they are sitting in my desk drawer at home. If I had known that, I would have driven straight to the office and put them in the safe there.'

'Things get a bit easier for us if there is no insurance claim and some assessor poking his nose in. Not so good for you though. Now, I believe there are photographs of the items on the way? Yes? Good. There are two ways of doing this, go quietly and see if the pieces bubble to the surface because the thieves don't know what they are, and recover them thus, or, and this is my preferred way, we hit the press, illustrate the items and scare them into getting rid of them. This is a risk because, as I'm sure you are aware, it could panic them into melting the gold or selling it for scrap somewhere or, the latest scam of the underworld, ransoming the pieces once they know what they are worth. This works very well with insurance companies who can see a way of not having to honour their full commitment of paying out the insured sum but only a portion thereof. Of course, your premium remains the same and you lose all credit they may have extended in various bonuses, but that's the way it is.'

'Charming,' Harry commented.

'The world is a charmless place when fighting crime. Anyway, I think that the risk of them melting down the gold for a fraction of their worth as works of art is greater than them trying to ransom the pieces. We can still catch them if they try to do the latter but it's too late as they drop into the melting pot.'

'How do we do it?'

'Once I get the photographs we'll have a press conference, no need to wait, they're outside your gate right now,' he said, nodding towards the window overlooking his front drive. Harry got up from the chair and peered around the curtains. Sure enough, camera crews and photographers were on the pavement taking shots of the house. A few reporters with microphones were standing about but a policeman had closed the gate to prevent their gaining an interview with the victim of the million pound theft.

'Don't worry, we can keep them off your backs, for a while anyway. The best approach with them is to issue a short statement, say how marvellous the police have been, of course, and tell them that it is all they are going to get. We'll follow that up with an official bit that they can print and then a warning that due to the nature of the goods stolen it could be part of an on-going crime and therefore everything they print has to either go through us or risk the consequences if they mention something prejudicial to a possible conviction. Usually does the trick. They love bad news, the press, thrive on it, but then we buy the newspapers and watch the news, don't we? They also love an art story, especially a forger or anything to do with fake paintings, it's all part of the mystery and romance, isn't it?'

'Seems to be. Comes down to earth a bit when it's stolen though,' Harry commented.

'I'm afraid that just adds to the story. The local police have got a headless body in the Grand Union Canal this morning. It's none of my business but it was a murder to be followed up on, never nice when something major is missing like a head. Anyway, Gerry Bodden says it was a clean blow, one swipe with an axe and off came the head. So then they had an axe murder on their hands which isn't common but one of the constables finds a fitting from a Japanese sword lying nearby and it looks as though we have a murder using a Katana and the press vultures are there baying for blood, and they write paragraphs about Japanese swords and the sort of things they can cut through. It's actually stomach churning but they write it up all the same.

'That you've been deprived of a million pounds worth of your company's property...'

'Correctly,' interrupted Harry, 'the property of clients of my company, in transit between client and company premises.'

'Quite. Yes, well, the loss to you is of no interest to them but they'll play on the artefacts side and the most expensive single item stolen from a house in the district, which I'm sure it is when we discuss the plate. They want superlatives and statistics, the get-a-story-and-bugger-the-victim style of journalism in which the thieves are invariably called "daring" and their methods are "meticulous".

'Aren't they, in this case?' Harry asked.

'They haven't finished yet. The successful burglar is one who steals, sells and is never a suspect. We generally get them in the end but we don't get them for the number of crimes they have committed, sometimes only a fraction and a small one at that. A theft of this magnitude and of items so unusual will attract the vultures and may place the normal house breaker or fence in a position that he takes the wrong turn and into the welcome arms of the C.I.D.'

'We'll have to wait for my managing director, who should be here in half an hour, to give permission for the publicity. He has the company name to think of.'

'He's not really going to sack you is he? I mean you are a victim of circumstance amongst anything else. They could have been stolen from the owner's house for goodness sakes. It could have been prevented, granted, but that's fine in hindsight. Have you ever been burgled before?'

'No, not even when I lived in London where it was almost expected. People swapped burglary stories at dinner parties but I could never contribute and then they'd all turn round and say "your day'll come." Here it is and it's every bit as frightful as they said.'

Sam Reid had some trouble getting through the gate as Harry and the Detective Inspector had forgotten to give his name to the constable controlling the flow of traffic. It didn't improve his mood. He had a conversation with Longfield out of Harry's earshot before he went into the office to look at the hoardless desk drawer, perhaps, Harry thought, just to check that there was a desk at all, he couldn't think of any other cogent reason for having a look.

'What would your thoughts be about making the whole thing public?' he asked Harry without the preface of a greeting.

'I think that it is best to leave it to the police but I have to say that I speak from inexperience. I'm sorry that you have been dragged out on a Sunday.'

'Why didn't you take them straight to the office?' Sam pleaded.

'I quite often bring things home that I want to research, it's so much easier than taking my library into town. You can't spend your life thinking that you are going to have your house burgled that evening.'

'You can if you've got a million pounds of somebody else's property in it,' Sam replied indignantly before leaving the room and rejoining Longfield. Harry stared out of his office window at the gathering outside the gates of his house. One of the camera crews were packing up, no doubt off to film the stretch of the Grand Union Canal for that night's head story, whilst there seemed to be more people just standing, gaping at the beech hedge that separated the road and his house. He had never been a victim before and he was starting to feel like a curiosity rather than a subject for sympathy.

This, in turn, just as Longfield had told him would happen, transmuted itself into anger that the thieves had won over him whilst he wasn't there and only had the physical barriers offered by bricks and mortar to conquer. It must have taken them more than an hour to clear everything out and clean up afterwards. Had they been watching for days or even weeks and realised that when they took the children out in the evening it meant that they would be out for more than the requisite hour or hour and a half?

He was also now convinced that they had chanced on the hoard and were now looking upon it with some trepidation. Whilst they had all the right people and channels to blend the household goods into the stream of second hand goods offered all over the country, the hoard items, if not taken as mere jewellery, presented a problem. Problems brought investigation and why risk a very successful business cleaning out houses on the chance that they could earn a little more pocket money? Don't think like a policeman, he decided, think like a criminal, and he sought the officer in charge to offer his new considered opinion.

Everybody disagreed with him and said that they should go for the publicity to flush the hoard out of the criminal element. It did not matter how vehement Harry was, everybody was against his judgment that the hoard would pop up at some dealer's premises, unrecognised as anything other than a silver dish and a gold cross and be a lot cheaper to recover than having to pay a ransom set by the thieves in light of its worth.

The argument was settled on the publicity option until Drew Gatacre arrived with the compact disc containing the photographs and who, after hearing the choices, sided with his fellow director, Harry, and wanted to wait forty-eight hours. The police took the CD off to their labs with an impressive, to Harry anyway, order of two hundred prints of each which meant four thousand eight hundred photographs in total and his mind was sufficiently relaxed to try to conjure what that many photographic prints looked like.

Detective Inspector Longfield left the choice to Sam Reid as to whether they told everything to the press or just let them know the basics. It was already reported on the local radio that a massive theft of jewellery and antiques had taken place in Aylesbury and that it was rumoured to be worth over a million pounds. In light of that, how could they explain the value against the number of items that were taken without elaborating in more detail on the hoard, Longfield argued.

'I'll talk to the owners,' Harry suggested, 'shouldn't they have a say in this?'

Longfield thought not, as the aggrieved party seemed to be Trotman's and not the Armstrongs. But Sam Reid thought it to be a good idea to show the Armstrongs, who, he explained to Longfield, would not be getting as much as they might if the items were put up for sale, that they were doing their best in the circumstances.

'Mrs Armstrong?' said Harry unnecessarily, 'it's Harry Knox.'

'You'll be wanting Jonathan. He's taken the dogs for a walk and will be back at two thirty. I'm sorry to hear about your robbery, we had one years ago and I still can't get over the audacity of the people. They never found a thing, you know, but I don't suppose that is of the slightest comfort to you. We're a bit confused this end; which of the values is taken as the insured value?'

'The reserve,' Harry admitted.

'But if the items are valued at three hundred and fifty thousand to four hundred thousand with a reserve of three hundred thousand, presumably we should get four hundred thousand less your commission?'

'No, three hundred thousand, the reserve, less the commission.'

'So, when it sells for four hundred and fifty thousand, do we pay one per cent of three hundred thousand or one per cent of four hundred and fifty thousand?'

'The latter. However, you could have insured them for as much as we mutually agree but they are, or were, insured at the reserve as per the sales agreement I left with you.'

'The small print, I assume,' she said tersely.

'Not in the slightest, I specifically said the insurance cover was on the reserve price until it was sold, or, if in the case of remaining unsold, until it is delivered to you. I'm sorry if you have got the wrong impression.'

His ballooning love for her was immediately deflated.

'It seems to be a real winner for your insurance company.'

'They're like that. I'd prefer, of course, not to have to do all this at all.'

He went on to describe the two options and she agreed with Harry but left the final decision to Jonathan.

He rejoined the gathering in the kitchen to find that David Reeves had bypassed the police cordon and had calmly walked into the house with eight cans of beer in his hands. He introduced everybody and was told by a uniformed constable that "the D.I.' was onto something and was discussing it on his mobile in the back garden. Harry told the story to David, who, out of range from flapping police ears, duly informed him that they hadn't a prayer of finding the gear and that, in all likelihood, it would be in the Middle East paying for one liberation army or other.

'I should know,' he said, in a sotto voice, 'I was brought up with all the villains, they do all their business offshore now.'

He offered everybody a beer and they all refused at first but Harry joined him when he proceeded to pour himself one, the presence of company dictating that he should use a glass. The situation they found themselves in had all but silenced them as they waited for Jonathan's call. David tried to enliven the group by telling his latest crop of jokes, gleaned from the pits of his racing colleagues, without exception at the expense of a racial minority and forced a smile from even the grim-faced Sam Reid.

Jonathan called at a quarter past two and listened to both sides of the argument. His input to the debate provided nothing new but in the end he sided with Harry and Drew.

Longfield graciously bowed to their advice and compiled a statement to the effect that a substantial amount of jewellery, silver, artefacts and household goods had been stolen during a random burglary at a residence in Aylesbury. The word 'amount' was intentionally ambiguous, it did not differentiate between worth and quantity. The artefacts were of a nature that immediately identified them and the relevant antiques dealers had been informed at the earliest opportunity. In the interim some of the household items were marked and could also be identified to those that knew the markings. This was a practise widely recommended by the police and greatly assisted them in their ongoing battle to identify second hand goods of uncertain ownership.

The press were not at all satisfied by the bland statement and asked for more. What period were the artefacts, were they easily transportable, were they national treasures, was there a black market in such goods, was the jewellery antique or modern, was not the owner an antique dealer, was the house completely cleaned out, where were the owners, why didn't the alarm go off and did they have any leads?

Harry was still inside the house but could hear every word Longfield said. He admired his sang froid and he left nobody in any doubt that not only was he on top of the case but a suspect could be expected in for questioning at any moment. His constables listening in the same room rolled their eyes and allowed themselves a chuckle every now and then at one of his more pithy replies to the inane questions fired at him. He finished his interview asking that the household be respected their privacy in light of their experience and a majority dispersed when he promised them any further news via the media liaison unit at his station.

The police, too, melted away when Longfield left after Harry had supplied him with a list of antiques dealers throughout Europe that he intended to email that afternoon and evening. The message merely described the items but did not place a monetary value on them that might have been leaked to the press.

Drew promised to help him as he had brought his laptop in which he had the Trotman's mailing list and Sam Reid, satisfied that everything that could be done either had or was going to be achieved before nightfall, also departed.

David Reeves drank more beer and was more of a hindrance than help as far as the toil of their tasks was concerned but nobody minded his cheerful prattle provided he knew when to stop.

Patricia was adept on the telephone fending off members of the press who chose to ignore Longfield's request for their privacy. She had assumed the tired voice of an overworked receptionist that had even fooled her father-in-law who had seen the film footage of the exterior of the house on the early news, and who asked her to give a message to his son or daughter-in-law to call as soon as was convenient and to pass on his condolences at the dreadful news.

When he finally settled himself between the sheets that night, Harry felt he had a lot more friends than had seemed evident in the morning and that whilst most people thought that they had seen the last of the hoard, there were others that were prepared to work towards its recovery in an acknowledgment that all was not lost.

They had been deluged with telephone calls after the evening news by friends, relatives and neighbours who were curious to know what they could have had in the house that was so valuable. They palmed them off by saying that it was a bit of an exaggeration which worked until a thoroughly unpleasant man who lived in the parallel street said that the average house burglary was not reported on the national news and that the Knoxs had brought the whole neighbourhood to the attention of the "lower orders".

If that was all that was to bother Harry in the near future then his mind would be at ease.

10

The door bell of Bill Coates' shop rang once, briefly, as though the ringer was tentative about entering. Coates emerged from his office behind the shop counter and pressed the catch-release button. A respectably dressed young man entered and said good morning to the shopkeeper who enquired if he may be of assistance.

'I'm just looking,' he replied and, to his word, started to look at the displays.

'I have more specialist stock in trays,' the shopkeeper explained.

'Yeh? Well, I'll start here and if I can't find anything of interest, I'll ask for help. Another lovely day out.'

Bill Coates agreed that it was another lovely day out but was beginning to be suspicious about his customer. Usually, a person came into his stamp and coin shop in Stevenage either requesting items from a particular area or country or modern or colonial issues, ancients or modern proofs, first day covers or cancellations or were totally clueless and were buying for a relative as a present and needed help. This man was neither, his "looking" involved the study of cheap packaged stamps for the young philatelist, a small selection of war medals that Coates had taken on consignment, a display board of low denomination British West African banknotes and some bullion gold coins. Such eclecticism usually indicated that he was a fellow dealer looking for a bargain, and the mobile telephone strapped to his belt, expensive trainers and collarless cotton shirt that was all the rage amongst the successful computer-wise young, was very much the uniform of the new breed of coin dealer.

However, he could equally be an undercover policeman looking for stolen material as Coates had been investigated before, and charged with possession of stolen goods, a charge to which he had to plead guilty although even the judge admitted that he was an unfortunate pawn in a much larger game and said that it would be more gratifying to have a back line player in the dock instead of Coates, before giving him a suspended sentence.

The third possibility was that he was being cased for a robbery, another experience that he had endured when he was held up with what the police later identified as a sub-machine gun. The two perpetrators entered the shop as bold as brass, leapt over the counter, went into his office and removed the tape from the security video camera, took only gold and the small amount of cash he had in the till and told him to lie on the floor for the next five minutes before they cheerily said goodbye and left. He had lain on the floor for a minute, or perhaps two, before gingerly getting up and reaching for the telephone. They had ripped the socket from the wall so he walked up to the glass front door and seeing nobody like them in the shopping precinct sought to run to the coffee lounge next door to ring the police. The robbers were thorough though and had locked him in from the outside so he had no alternative but to use the hold-up button which had a direct line to the local police station and hastened a patrol car to his premises.

He could see the red rectangular button now, beneath the lip of the counter, and on the floor was the foot button that operated the video camera which he casually pressed whilst he cleaned the glass of his counter. The customer then started to look at the coins in the trays displayed in the counter, first bending over, then getting down on his haunches and finally his knees as he studied the lowest tier of trays, the ancients, a few Greek tetradrachms and some Roman denarii and sesterii, nothing too expensive because they were there more as an advertisement that he bought such coins than as a stock display for purchasers.

'Is that really a coin of Julius Caesar?' the customer asked.

'Yes,' Coates replied, quite used to the question.

'What, for two hundred quid?'

'Yes.'

'I mean, a genuine two thousand year old coin for two hundred quid?'

'Yes.'

'Come on! Pull th' other one. It's not a copy or a fake or nuffing?'

'No, it's absolutely genuine. I'll give you a certificate of authenticity with it if you wish but I only sell genuine coins.'

'But that's ridiculous,' the customer continued, ''ow can you buy a two thousand year old Roman coin for two hundred quid?'

'Get your money out and I'll show you,' Coates said, not for the first time in his life.

'Do you take credit cards?'

'Yes.'

''old on, I've got some dosh 'ere, discount f' cash?'

'Not for that amount, perhaps with a larger purchase.'

'Cor, an 'ard man. Still, if you says it's genuine ...'

'I'll give you an invoice and if you ever have trouble you bring it back and I'll refund the full amount, no questions asked.'

The customer peeled twenty ten pound notes from the thick roll he had produced and placed them on the counter whilst Coates took the Julius Caesar denarius from the tray, put the coin in a plastic envelope and wrote up an invoice fully describing the coin. He wrote out a receipt as well which he stapled to the invoice, folded it all up and placed everything in an envelope which he gave to his dealer / undercover policeman / armed robber who left still smiling in wonderment at what he had been able to buy with only a slight lightening of the wad in his pocket.

Coates had wanted to ask him if he was in computers because he wanted to put his stock on computer like the bigger dealers. He was progressive as smaller dealers went in that he had a computer, he surfed the 'net, he found material for his better clients with taste beyond his budget from dealers across the world and was beginning to question the wisdom of having a shop with all its inherent security implications and tying him down whilst he would like to attend the coin and stamp sales in London to restock and to catch up with colleagues with whom he dealt on the telephone or e-mail.

Monday morning was always a day for the accounts and stock-taking, a laborious business for a coin dealer who could sell literally hundreds of coins for less than a thousand pounds but who had to work out his unit cost price for V.A.T. purposes and his accountant. How much easier, he had often thought, to never sell anything for less than a hundred pounds and to concentrate on stock worth more than a thousand pounds per coin. Stamps he would happily discard altogether but it was the encouragement he gave to young stamp and coin collectors who might have a pound a week to spend that paid dividends in the future as they kept to their hobby when they had a hundred pounds a week to spend. Behind every serious philatelist and numismatist was a childhood mentor, be it a geography or history teacher, a relation, or quite commonly, a coin or stamp dealer.

Bill Coates fiddled with coin tickets and trawled through a collection he had bought in the dying hours of Saturday trading from somebody obviously in need of some money for their Saturday night entertainment. They had been happy to accept his one hundred and fifty pound offer, in cash, and he had already found six hundred pounds worth of coins at ticket price, perhaps two hundred and fifty if he were to knock it out to another dealer to save him the trouble of ticketing each item. Nobody knew what every coin was worth and therefore there were books to consult with price guides accompanying each date and denomination of all the nations of the world. Every coin dealer's wish was to find the elusive date rarity in a pile of "junk" and there were often tales of, for instance, United States 1792 silver centre cents cropping up amongst piles of Victorian pennies.

Lunchtime approached and Coates thought that it was nearly time to check the e-mail for messages although Monday was usually a lean day unless he was expecting something from the Far East. He spread out a selection of George V and VI colonial silver coins, mainly African and Asian but there was nothing of a rare date or sufficient condition to warrant ticketing and adding to his trays. British colonial coins of those two continents rode the crest of a wave for a long time but were beginning to pall as the Asian economy slackened. He could say, however, that one particular collector of his who had served in the foreign office in Kuala Lumpur, Singapore and Hong Kong, had done very well by his collection over the past fifteen years and was looking at a handsome profit.

Just as he was ready to nip next door for a cup of coffee and a sandwich, the customer of the early morning was at his door again and, before he could ring the bell, Coates pressed the catch-release button once more. He has come to return the coin, he thought; there went his forty pound profit for the day.

'Hello again', the young man said.

'Hello, back so soon?'

'Yeah, well, I've been finking, I want to buy some more of them Roman coins, they jus' seem so cheap an' that, so I was wondering if there is a book or somefing I can read about 'em?'

Coates did stock a selection of coin books for beginners and had access to a specialist bookseller in the capital to obtain the more obscure titles for clients of a more advanced stage of collecting. He produced a few titles that he thought might serve the purpose of getting his new customer interested in the subject and then he flicked through and read the blurb on the back cover, putting two to one side.

'Whilst we're at it,' said the customer, digging into his pocket, 'my uncle was a merchant seaman and 'e left us all this stuff.'

He produced a small plastic bag full of base metal coins from all over the globe, exactly the sort of loose change a merchant sailor or post war soldier would collect and throw in a drawer.

Coates emptied the bag onto a tray and spread the coins out with the tip of his forefinger.

'Nothing here, I'm afraid, all base metal and of average circulated condition.'

'Never mind, I jus' wondered, they didn't look much. What about this then?' he said and produced a small thin silver coin which he tossed on top of the others. Coates picked it up and pushing his short-sighted glasses onto his forehead, brought the coin closer to his right eye in which he placed a black plastic eye glass.

'It's Anglo Saxon or Norman,' he announced, 'I'm not sure which, I'd have to look it up.'

A frisson of excitement went through him as he reached for his catalogue of British coins, this was the sort of find that justified the expense of having a shop. He ran through the pages of early Anglo Saxon coins but couldn't find this particular example but the average price for a very fine example on the page he studied was between one hundred and fifty and four hundred pounds, so he settled on a figure of two hundred and twenty pounds, an exact amount that looked as though he had worked it out with precision. He knew, however, that it was a coin worth considerably more than that as it was a type that he had not previously encountered.

'Is that all?' the young man said.

'You have to understand that coins are not uncommon and especially coins minted or in circulation during troubled times as they tended to be buried in hoards and are actually quite plentiful. During the late Anglo-Saxon period, for instance, the Danes demanded tens of thousands of pounds from the English, each pound having two hundred and forty of these coins,' and he held up the penny for effect.

'I fink I see,' said the young man and he added a third book to the pile.

'Now,' he said, 'that lot comes to thirty-eight quid, right?'

Coates added them up and they came to thirty-five, eighty-five but he didn't say anything.

'Wot I fink is, I give you the Anglo-whatsit, and you give me my two hundred notes back and I take the books. Is 'at alright?'

Coates thought for a second or two.

'Alright, but I have to do the paperwork correctly.'

He produced a carbonless copy book into which he wrote the details of the coin, as sparsely as he could, at a price of two hundred and twenty pounds and turned the book around asking the customer to fill in his name and address and to sign at the place he indicated.

The young man didn't hesitate in filling out his name and address and even offered to show some identification but Coates assured him that he had done all that was necessary, tore out the top copy of the form, counted out the two hundred pounds and gave him the money and document. He put the three books in a carrier bag with a receipted invoice and put them on the counter, the customer, a Gary Lewis, he noted from his purchases book, taking them from there.

'There might be more of those pennies, I'm not sure, would you be interested?' he asked whilst walking to the door.

'Most certainly, I can't always pay cash though, it depends on how much I have in the till.'

'I'm quite happy to swap 'em wif more Roman stuff, I like the Roman ones. See ya.'

Bill Coates raced next door for a very basic lunch whilst he dug around his mental storehouse to try and identify the coin he had bought. The small cross in the centre of one side convinced him that it was issued by a Christian king or leader but the stylised bird on the other didn't indicate an Anglo-Saxon king. He nearly scalded his mouth on his coffee so eager was he to discover quite what he had bought and within twenty minutes he was back in the shop and in amongst his books.

He had tried to read the legend on both sides of the coin but it was never easy reading them in the first place if one didn't have a start by knowing what to expect. He was beginning to doubt that it was an English issue at all and that he had bought a European coin for which his library was totally inadequate and for which he had absolutely no market. In the end he became frustrated and he put the coin to one side whilst he did something else to clear his head, a methodology he employed whilst tackling the crossword in his newspaper during his morning break.

He had one message on his e-mail but it was only one of the interminable Numismatic Dealers' Association's early warning notices which usually referred to obscure and extremely expensive Ptolemy decadrachms that had been stolen in the post between Dortmund and Miami, Florida. He scanned the details and was satisfied that it was unlikely to refer to anything he was going to handle when his eyes caught the words Hiberno-Norse Vikings.

He returned to the neglected section of his British coins catalogue and looked up the issues of various Viking rulers whilst based in York and there was his penny, illustrated on the page with a valuation of five thousand pounds. He looked back at the computer screen and confirmed his worst fears, he had bought one of the four stolen coins and was mindful of "Gary Lewis'" parting comment that there were more of them to come; presumably three more.

He looked up the entries for Lewis in the telephone book and, although he could have been ex-directory, there was nobody by that name at that address. The shopping centre in which he had his shop was also host to a first floor of offices, one of which housed the operation room for one of the local taxi companies. The day time receptionist was an acquaintance of his, they often queued for their lunch together and she always waved when she passed the door of his shop. He locked his door and raced up the stairs to her office, knocked gently on the door and peered round as it wasn't shut. She was sitting at her desk typing something into her computer keyboard, the earphones of a dictaphone slung around her neck.

'Hello,' she said, continuing to type.

'Hello. Look, I don't want to be a bore but I was wondering if you could confirm if an address exists, you know, if you've got street maps, that sort of thing.'

'For here?'

'No, for Hitchin, in fact.'

'You've come to the right place. The boss 'as bin driving mini cabs in 'itchin for donkeys. I'll get 'im.'

'I don't want you to go to any trouble,' he said weakly as she disappeared behind a partition.

The boss emerged, an enormous man whose shirt front did all it could to contain his stomach, his trouser waist obviously having long given up the battle and was snuggly imbedded in the fold twixt tummy and waist.

'Where d'you wanna know guv?'

'No. 4 Lake Drive.'

'Nah, not in 'itchin. Lake Drive's in Welwyn.'

Coates checked his purchase book to confirm the address, 'Gary Lewis, 4 Lake Drive, Hitchin, Herts.,' and for good measure showed it to the boss.

'Nah mate, it just doesn't exist, 'less the bloke's confused. 'old on, 4 Lake Drive's the Lakeview 'otel, y'know, the one on the adverts, "Welwyn's Premier Accommodation". That's No. 4 Lake Drive, Welwyn, not 'itchin.'

'Odd isn't it?' Coates said, although it was exactly as he suspected; a fake address. He thanked the big mini-cab man but before he could go he was asked, as everybody did when they had a coin dealer to one side, what a 1934 crown was selling for and seemed satisfied with the answer.

Once back in his shop he looked at the coin, the e-mail message, checked his catalogue again, and realised it was no mistake; he had bought one of the stolen coins and it was of such rarity that there was no chance of slipping it onto the market without it being noticed. He had no choice than to be a good corporate citizen and report the purchase hoping that in so doing he would, by owning up to handling something he had later found to be stolen, somehow exonerate himself or even expunge his record from the police files.

When he rang the police contact number on the e-mail, a London number, he was put through to Detective Inspector Longfield with great haste when he said he had some information. The Detective Inspector told him that he was on his way and that he must lock his shop up so that the man couldn't try to sell him the other three before he got there. Coates could hear that Longfield was flicking pieces of paper on his desk as they spoke.

'Did he offer you anything else other than coins?'

'No, why would he? I'm a coin dealer,' Coates explained.

'No scrap gold?'

'No.'

'Do you buy scrap gold?'

'Not very often, I buy bullion coins which I send down to a dealer in Hatton Gardens but I don't, as a rule, buy old rings and gold bracelets, there isn't the money in them unless you cheat on the weight.'

'So you have no sign saying "Scrap gold bought?" '

'No. I have a sign saying "Bullion Coins Bought, Spot Prices".'

'Okay,' Longfield said, struggling into his jacket, 'where can we meet, not in your shop?'

'How long will you be?'

'A good hour, say hour and a half.'

'There is a coffee shop next door to mine. I'll be in there from three o'clock onwards.'

Longfield checked the address of the shopping centre, told a detective constable to accompany him and another to telephone the coin expert at Trotman's, he'd forgotten the name, and somehow get him to the shopping centre in Stevenage by three o'clock, three thirty at the latest.

11

Bill Coates waited nervously in the coffee shop as though it was he who had done wrong. He had caught a thief once before shoplifting a packet of stamps worth one pound fifty but he had observed the stocks of similar packets dwindle mysteriously over a number of months and he had little doubt that he had caught the thief of them all. He had thought twice about calling the police over something so trivial and in the end made the child telephone his parents to come and fetch him so that Coates could embarrass him into ceasing his pilfering.

The father duly turned up, apologised for his son's behaviour and gave the shop keeper one pound fifty. He didn't as much give it to him but threw it at him and stormed out of the shop dragging the boy behind him. That night he received a call from the security company who patrolled the shopping centre to say that petrol had been poured through the letter box in his shop door and set alight. Fortunately it burnt itself out before any major damage had occurred but it took the best part of a week to rid the shop of the smell of smoke and petrol, replace the carpet and clean the soot from every surface. All for one pound fifty.

Now he faced a serious crime, a coin worth five thousand pounds that he had purchased, with cash, for two hundred and twenty. It was the sort of transaction that gave the trade a bad name and his only defence was that he honestly did not know what he was buying and therefore erred on the side of caution. He had thought up all sorts of tall tales to cover himself such as the Caesar denarius and Viking penny was a straight swap, that "Gary Lewis" asked him to pay two hundred and twenty pounds for it although such a figure was unlikely and that it was a down payment until he researched it further which begged the question, then why did the seller give a false address if more money was due? He had been caught buying something cheaply and whilst nothing in the statute books could bring him to court, his reputation, already sullied through no fault of his own, was about to spread through the trade like blood in water.

He knew the three jacketed men that entered the coffee shop at twenty past three were policemen. Policemen, in his experience, did everything as though they owned the place, no doubt the result of assertiveness training or whatever they had. He stood to greet them although he was the only other man in the place. They introduced themselves, two from the Art and Antiques Squad in London and one from the local police. The Detective Inspector from London asked Coates if he was alright for a drink and when he replied that he was, his offsider went to the counter to order for them.

'This could be the breakthrough we're looking for. It's very good of you to let us know. We'll try and make sure that you're not out of pocket on this, there might be reward money from the insurance company but I can't promise anything,' Longfield said, settling himself in the booth that modern coffee shops think is de rigeur for their sort of establishment.

'I did it because I was handling stolen goods, unwittingly of course, but I can see how people can get trapped. I'd like this guy caught and prosecuted for putting me and my business under threat of another charge. Technically, I suppose, I am guilty of the same thing but what can one do?'

'I fully sympathise with you, Mr Coates, our job would be made all the easier if we left the minnows alone but the jails are full of them whilst the big fish are still at large. This time, however, we have a rare chance at hooking a sizeable catch and you've laid the bait, keeping to a piscatorial theme. What we need first are the details, any details you can give me about the man.'

Coates told him the story including the subsequent investigations that he had carried out regarding the address. Longfield took everything down in a note pad and then asked for a description of the man which the dealer attempted to recall but could only give the basics. Even though he had been suspicious of him at first and it was less than three hours since he had last seen him his mind was a blank when it came to describing his facial features. It was whilst he was struggling that he remembered that he had activated the video camera during his first visit.

'Do you have the cassette with you?' Longfield asked.

'It's still in the machine,' Coates replied.

'Well go and get it! We can run prints of the bloke and then make some discreet inquiries, the Lakeview Hotel being our starting place, don't you think Falls?'

His assistant nodded.

'Go and get it now?' Coates asked.

'Yes, and we'll get it off to be processed immediately.'

Coates returned to his shop to retrieve the video cassette. The machine was in his office at the back of the shop and as it would only take a minute he left the front door open although the sign on the door stated that he was closed and the lights were not on. When he came out of the office, however, there was a man standing patiently at the counter.

'Hello,' he said, 'are you open?'

'Er, yes, I suppose. I'm actually in a meeting. How can I help?'

'I'm told you buy coins,' he said.

'Yes, what have you got?'

The man reached into his pocket and produced a folded piece of tissue which he laid on the counter and carefully unwrapped revealing a small silver coin.

Coates immediately saw that it was another Viking penny, identical to the one he bought off the young man at lunchtime.

'Goodness, these seem to be growing on trees,' he commented.

The customer pretended not to know what he meant.

'I bought one of these a few hours ago. Has a hoard been found?'

'I've had this for years,' the man claimed, 'it came from my grandfather.'

'Ah, just a coincidence then,' Coates said, 'it's a very fine specimen. Did you have a price in mind?'

'Haven't a clue, I'm led to believe it's worth a few hundred, two fifty perhaps, would that be right?'

'Yes, fairly spot on. I'll just check it in my records, make sure it's not a rare variety. Hold on one second,' he said before returning to his office where he re-read the e-mail warning the trade about the stolen coins. It confirmed that there were two raven type coins of Olaf Guthfrithsson, the one on the counter was obviously the second.

A six inch thick brick wall separated him from the police force and he had one of Longfield's "big fish" in his shop. He couldn't telephone because the customer would hear the conversation, he couldn't activate the video because his one and only cassette was at the counter ready to hand over to the police. However, he considered it to be good work to recover the coin and if he spent two hundred pounds there was the possibility, as Longfield had said, of receiving a reward which was usually ten per cent of its worth, nominally five thousand pounds, so there was a tidy profit to be made.

'I can give you two hundred and twenty pounds for the coin,' he said emerging from the office.

The man picked the coin up and turned it over in his hand.

'Two fifty,' he said.

'Well, I bought an identical coin this morning for two twenty and they're not the easiest of things to sell. Two of them is a drag on the market. Two twenty is the most I can offer.'

'I'll take it elsewhere,' he said and began to wrap it up in the piece of tissue.

'Two thirty in cash,' Coates offered, he couldn't let it go for the sake of thirty pounds but he couldn't capitulate too easily.

'Two forty in cash,' the man countered.

'Oh alright, there goes half my profit. Now there aren't any more of these hanging around?' he asked jovially.

'Not that I know of, not from me anyway.'

Coates made great play at looking through the cash in his till which he knew only contained a hundred pounds flat.

'I'll have to nip next door to cash a cheque. I'll be back in a jiffy. If you sell anything, there's ten per cent of the profit in it for you,' he said making a dash for the door, cheque book in hand.

'Have you got two hundred pounds in notes?' he asked the two policemen who both nodded at his strange request. 'I've got a different man selling another of the coins in the shop at his very moment. What the hell do I do?'

Longfield leapt up, approached the girl on the till of the coffee shop and producing his warrant card, asked her if there was two hundred in the till.

'No, but Ricci has the banking.'

Ricci produced two hundred and forty pounds from the bank book on the assurance of Bill Coates that he would get it back that day.

Coates dashed back to the shop, he hadn't been gone for more than a minute and the man was still waiting patiently at the counter looking at the coins on display.

'Here we go,' Coates announced waving the money in his hand, 'now all we have to do is fill in the purchase note and you can be on your way.'

He opened the book at the next available form and filled out the details of the purchase before handing it over to the man and explaining that he needed name, address and signature at the place he indicated.

The man hesitated by reading what had been written on the page and then wrote down a name and address and signed it with an extravagant flourish. Coates turned the book round and nearly chuckled at the lack of imagination, "John Smith" of "6 Railway Street, Royston, Herts." He counted out the money, slowly and purposefully, wondering when

Longfield and Falls were going to make their appearance.

The man took the money, folded it in two and put it in his pocket. He accepted the paperwork which he folded with less care into quarters and put in his other pocket. Coates picked the coin up and put it on the shelf behind the counter. The man lingered a little by the counter peering at the coins before saying thanks and goodbye and leaving the still unlit shop. The dealer stayed behind his counter whilst he watched John Smith turn to his left and walk briskly away. He expected to see the three policemen hot on his trail but after a minute the two from London entered the shop with broad grins on their faces.

'Did you get the coin?'

'Yes, did you get your man?'

'We don't need to, my chum in the local police knows who he is. Did he give you his name?'

'He gave me a name, John Smith, not very original is it?'

'Oh, there Mr Coates, you are wrong,' Falls said, 'it is, in fact, his real name, conveniently for him.'

'He's apparently a very bad boy, John Smith,' continued Longfield, 'you remember our little chat about minnows and bigger fish, well John Smith is in the middle but he talks to the big boys all the time and he plays with the minnows as a sort of recreational pursuit, you know, keeping his hand in just in case the big boys give him the shove, as they are apt to do. The Hertfordshire Constabulary are waiting for him at home so that he won't put his arrest down to you.'

'That's thoughtful, thank you.'

'Now, I'd better have the two coins, Falls will give you a receipt, and the video cassette, if I may?'

Just before they left for the local police station, Drew Gatacre, accompanied by another of Longfield's men, entered the shop. He identified the two coins as being those stolen and showed Coates the identifying features of the other two. Much to Drew's regret, the local police wanted to retain the coins as evidence but Longfield assured him that they would be returned as soon as possible, he had no wish to be a guardian over expensive items such as those.

Longfield and Falls were informed over their car radio that John Smith had been arrested and was awaiting their arrival at his house which was ten minutes' drive away from the shopping centre. They got directions from the Cad-room dispatcher and drove through the outskirts of Stevenage to an estate which overlooked the busy A1. After several attempts they found the right house, or, rather, the presence of a police car in the street indicated that they could be close and it turned out to be a correct hunch.

John Smith maintained that the coin was his grandfather's. Even when shown the photograph taken by Trotman's on the previous Thursday, he did not stir from his story. The uniformed police searched the modest house but found nothing obviously connected to the robbery in Aylesbury. Longfield was beginning to lose his patience.

'Let me show you something, John,' he said, extracting the remainder of the photographs from his jacket pocket.

'You see this gold cross?'

'Yes.'

'Did you melt it down?'

'I ain't never seen the cross.'

'I see. The weight of the cross is about two ounces and what's an ounce of gold worth at the moment?'

'Why ask me?'

'I thought you might be up on this sort of thing. If you melt it you may get four or five hundred quid, right?'

'S'pose,' Smith replied.

'Do you know what the cross is worth?'

'You just told me, four hundred quid.'

'To melt it, yes, but do you know what it's worth as a work of art, Mr Smith? No? How about one thousand times that. Yes! Unbelievable isn't it? This little gold cross is worth four hundred thousand pounds or thereabouts. Where is it Mr Smith?'

''ow would I know?'

'Because the coin you sold today, the coin you have admitted selling today and this gold cross were close companions for many hundreds of years. Now, your colleague, young, er, you know, whatisname ...'

'I don't 'ave a young colleague or an old colleague or any sort of colleague.'

'But you do, Mr Smith. He sold the companion coin at lunchtime today, to the same poor dealer. The cross and some other things and these two coins and two others were stolen from a house on Saturday and you and your colleague, we've got him on video, by the way, are selling them two days later, thirty miles away from the crime scene. It's not clever is it? And if it is the measure of your intelligence then I thought you ought to know what the cross is worth, just in case you sell it for scrap. Do you understand me, Mr Smith?'

'I don't know what you're on about.'

'I think you're lying to me, Mr Smith. Now what I have to work out is where you fit into all this. I don't think you're the thief because that

117

means lifting heavy objects like televisions and trays of silver cutlery and you're a lazy bastard. Then you could be the fence for the whole lot but that's a bit beneath you as well, can't see you flogging a video player in the King's Head somehow.

'What I think,' continued Longfield, 'and I stand to be corrected if necessary, is that you've branched out, expanded your horrible activities, just to keep us on our toes.'

'You talk in riddles,' Smith muttered.

'I think I'm getting closer, aren't I? You are the overseer of a house breaking operation ...'

'That's just rubbish!'

Longfield turned his back on Smith and placed his hand on his chin in an overacted gesture of pondering.

'Are you goin' to charge me or what?' Smith asked.

'All in good time Mr Smith, let us not be too hasty now. I have a problem in that I can only charge you with handling stolen goods and any judge is going to smack you on your wrists and tell you to be on your bike. I, however, am a great believer in not wasting the court's time so when you come before the beak on a charge brought against you by me, it will be for a long stretch so that you can't interfere with my day for many, many years. House breaking is a much more satisfactory charge and a man with your burgeoning record, Mr Smith, can expect little leniency.

'Entertain me for a while: If you are masterminding, I use the term loosely, of course, a house-breaking enterprise then you are going to need to store the gear before you pass it on down the line. Your distribution network thus far has not been very efficient. You do a place over on Saturday night, divide the spoils on the Sunday whilst you should be at Matins, and twenty-four hours later are caught selling some of your gains. Pretty rotten luck, eh?'

'I don't know why you are persisting with all this, it's all crap,' Smith said, shifting himself in his armchair.

'It's called theory, Mr Smith.'

'Well, it's still crap, theory or not.'

'That's up to me to decide. I'll continue. So you do a job in a prosperous looking house in High Wycombe ...'

'Aylesbury,' Smith corrected.

Longfield paused and then turned to Falls.

'Aylesbury, Detective Constable Falls? Have we mentioned Aylesbury?'

'I don't believe we have sir,' Falls said with a grin.

'Oh Mr Smith! Fallen for the oldest trick in the book. It really isn't your day is it? Now, all we need is the address of your lock-up, the keys would be a bonus to prevent wear to our sledgehammers, ever thoughtful of conserving the public purse, and it'll be a good day's work.'

'I don't have a lock-up.'

'No! Well where is the gear?'

Smith was poised to say something and then reverted to his sullen demeanour.

'You did the job and then you found a treasure trove in the drawer of the desk but it's not the sort of thing you usually handle and you're out of your depth.'

'I never did no job. The gear came to me yesterday, you know, some electrical stuff, I was told it come from Aylesbury.'

'So you have the video and telly and stereo system, mobile phone?' Longfield tested.

'Yeah.'

'We're getting somewhere now. And whoever supplied these goods threw in a coin or two for good measure?'

'No.'

'Well, did they come through the letter box mysteriously or fall from the sky, pennies from heaven, eh? Look, I don't really care about the video and mobile phone, that's for the local police, what I want are these,' Longfield said spreading the photographs of the pieces in the hoard on the coffee table, 'have you seen these?'

'What do I get for co-operating?'

'At the moment you get four to six years. Keep talking.'

Smith hesitated and then picked up the photographs of the coins and the paten.

'I can get me 'ands on the plate and the other two coins.'

'What about the cross and those triangular things?'

'Do you know Duncan Ewart?'

'No. Local boy?'

'He's a mean heap of shit. Comes from the wrong side of Hadrian's Wall and should be shipped back there. He done the robbery and he's not a learner, know what I mean? He's moved into this area and I thought if you can't beat 'em then you've got to join 'em. He's got the gold and he give us the silver.'

'Us?'

'Gary Bell, the guy on your video.'

Falls wrote the information down.

'Where do we find Messrs. Bell and Ewart?' Longfield pressed.

'Gary works at the Lakeview Hotel in Welwyn, he's a trainee receptionist. He's alright Gary, he knows a lot of people and can shift some gear. He and Ewart are best mates, that's where Gary went wrong because Ewart is a right regular bastard.'

'Do the local police know Ewart?' Falls asked, pre-empting Longfield.

'He's too clever by 'alf, teflon coated he is. He gets everybody else to do the grafting whilst he just pulls in the dosh. But he's upsetting the wrong people and the system.'

'Where do we find him?'

'You didn't hear nothing from me.'

'Of course we didn't.'

Smith then gave a description of Ewart and the places he frequented during the day and night. Nobody knew his home address nor his domestic arrangements, he had, as Falls observed, the perfect personality for a crook; a loner, they were always the hard ones to track down.

They took Smith to the local police station to be charged with the fairly minor offence of handling stolen goods for which he could plead the time honoured defence of not knowingly handling stolen goods but that he was told of their status after he had handled them. Another detective went to the Lakeview Hotel to pick up Gary Bell who apparently had the other two coins and the paten.

Longfield spoke to D.I. Prasad, his equivalent in that district's force, but he had never heard of Ewart, nor was he in their records, but he granted a clearance to pick Ewart up and the services of a C.I.D. sergeant to make the task easier. However, Ewart was not to be had in any of his regular haunts, if indeed, and which looked increasingly unlikely, Smith had given the correct locations. Most people denied ever having heard of Duncan Ewart, some knew of him but were ignorant of his whereabouts and, after visiting six establishments, Falls made the observation that Ewart would be well alerted by now and that they should perhaps be trying the travel agents on the off chance that he might be in there booking his flight to Cyprus or Brazil. They tried one more cafe where the waitress admitted that he had been in that morning and that he had left at about twelve o'clock which was a four and a half hour lead on them.

On their return to the station they found Gary Bell with the two coins and the paten and a statement to the effect that he had bought them from a man in a pub at lunchtime on Sunday for one hundred and fifty pounds the lot, and that it was John Smith who lent him the cash at the time and who was given one of the coins in repayment. Smith had separately corroborated this story except that there was a lot more money involved and that the man in the pub was Duncan Ewart, although he had never seen Ewart with the goods.

When asked about a gold cross and shown the photographs of the book mounts, Gary Bell, too, denied ever having seen them or knowing anything about them. He did, however, freely admit to being acquainted with Duncan Ewart as a friend rather than involving any business, and no he didn't know where he lived but they normally met at The Green Man. Longfield handed Bell his mobile telephone and told him to arrange a meeting that evening but, obviously frightened, he refused to have anything to do with police efforts to bring Ewart in, regardless of incentive.

Longfield took Falls out of the interview room.

'What are we going to do now, sir?' Falls asked his superior.

'I've stuffed this one up, good and proper,' Longfield admitted, 'how come nobody's got a photograph of this man? I can get the entire bloody Hertfordshire police out looking for him but we don't know what he looks like.'

'The only thing we can do is let Bell know what the cross is worth. At least it might prevent Ewart from melting it down.'

'And alert him to the chance of ransoming it? We are taking on the huge assumption that he does actually have it in the first place. If that is so, then it's worth the risk because we'll know where the threat is from. On the other hand, it has struck me how extraordinarily clumsy Smith and Bell have been and how very convenient it was of Smith to be dissatisfied enough with Duncan Ewart to drop him in it. There's more to this than we think, Falls.'

'Yes sir,' Falls replied, wondering when they would finally get their cup of tea.

12

There were four people waiting for attention in the reception area of Simon & Simon, bullion dealers for six generations who were scrupulous in their dealings and had managed to feed several families on the meagre percentage that they took on each deal by undertaking a lot of business. There were two schools within the business; old and new, Imperial weights and decimal, slide rules and calculators but fathers and sons, uncles, nephews and even nieces, rubbed shoulders in a harmony that could not shake the ubiquitous use of the adjective "traditional" when describing the company's activities. They were still family owned, and although various crashes in the bullion price and wild fluctuations in exchange rates had placed them at risk every now and then, they continued to serve the jewellery trade and bullion investors alike with the knowledge that they had to satisfy no shareholders other than themselves.

Every deal was handled in the same manner, whether it be for a hundred pounds or a million pounds, which made every hundred pound customer feel as though he or she were buying or selling a million pounds and every million pound customer feel as though they should be spending or selling more. Nobody was accorded special treatment although regular clients were dealt with by the same dealer within the company and were therefore thought to be favoured but their two per cent per deal was gathered in exactly the same manner as a casual client's.

Duncan Ewart felt out of place in the pillared reception area with its marble floors and hushed atmosphere. A guard stood by the door and CCTV cameras played on every area within Ewart's view. He was eventually motioned to one of the partitioned seats for clients by a suited man in the public area who directed the movements of everybody that side of the counter to ensure that everybody was attended to as soon as possible. He waited for a minute before a girl leant over the counter and asked him how she could help through the glass louvre window. He pulled the gold cross from his pocket and told her that he wanted to sell it.

The young lady took the cross and examined it under a jewellers' loop.

'I'll have to test it,' she said, 'to determine its purity.'

Ewart nodded, said 'fine' at which she turned around and carried out her testing. Satisfied that she had established the carat she then weighed it on electronic scales writing down the results of two readings, calculating the figures and returning to Ewart.

'It is a touch over 18 carat, at today's prices we can pay a total of three hundred and eighty-seven pounds.'

'I've got these as well,' Ewart said, handing over the three book mounts.

The lady repeated the process, they were of less pure gold and weighed slightly less than the cross, she was prepared to pay three hundred and twenty-eight pounds which made a total of seven hundred and fifteen pounds.

'Can I have it in cash?' Ewart asked, his brogue making the last word sound like a threat.

'Of course, I'll just take your details.'

Ewart gave his correct name and an address in Stevenage that happened to be a nightclub that he currently favoured. He tendered his drivers' licence as proof of identity which was politely waved away as unnecessary. He was given the top copy of the receipt and the money was counted out in front of him. Business thus concluded he thanked the young lady for her time and efficiency and vacated the seat for the next customer.

He walked to the door which the security guard opened for him and thanked him for his business. It had taken less than three minutes from the time he had sat down at the counter to being returned to the outside world and he was seven hundred and fifteen pounds richer.

He hadn't been in London for several months and with his money burning a hole in his pocket he went to the West End to buy some clothes and some shoes, he was in particular need of shoes that reflected his growing importance within his own circle. People noticed shoes, especially when he eye-balled them and they were forced to look down.

He had always been a neat dresser, insisted upon a clean shirt every day with two vertical ironed stripes back and front and never the slightest sign of frayed collar or cuff. Those were consigned to the clothing bin in the supermarket car park although he was prepared to admit that it upset him to think that they would probably no longer be laundered correctly.

He bought a pair of plain black shoes in Bond Street, exactly the same type as the man wore in the bullion dealers, the man that directed everybody to their right places, obviously a man of military training. His shoes were spotless or perhaps there was the slightest scuff mark on the right inside heel, a blemish unnoticed by the wearer who would think ill of it when he discovered it later in the day.

Ewart toyed with the idea of buying a pair of brown patterned brogues but decided that they were too old fashioned for the remainder of his wardrobe. He remembered his father's employer wearing that type of shoe and corduroy trousers and a woollen jersey with holes at the elbow when he came to their house to announce that his father was no longer required to turn up for work at the farm.

That took them off the land and into East Kilbride and his training for the way he chose to make a living commenced. Most people in his profession were either scruffy and in need of a bath or gaudily vulgar and still in need of a bath. He had decided that the less money went on flash and more that went into dash was money well spent. Even his car was a model of conservatism and it was for this reason that he went around largely unnoticed whilst being feared by those with whom he had come into contact.

His leisurely amble, window shopping in the West End, took him away from the people with whom he normally consorted. This was his sort of world; Piccadilly and Regent Street, elegance and wealth on display just as he wished people would see him in a few years time when he had turned his back on Stevenage and people who refused to wash regularly.

He caught the tube to Hendon where he had parked his car, as his navigation in London was not good and there was the chance that he would damage the silvered blue livery of his latest purchase.

The evening rush hour was just beginning and the A1, especially around the junction with the M25, was at a snail's pace. He was patient though, he had never seen the use of barging from queue to queue in the remote chance that you would be three cars ahead in ten minutes time.

Once they had got through the South Mimms junction the traffic started to go faster and he was on the outskirts of Stevenage fairly quickly. He left the motorway at the junction signposted Hitchin and Luton although he wasn't going as far as that; he only needed to go to St. Ippollitts where he had bought a small cottage with the proceeds of the sale of his parents' house in East Kilbride.

He would change and head back into town for a few drinks and possibly a Chinese meal with some of the lads if they were allowed out on a Monday night. As more of them married or lived with their girlfriends, his choice of dining companion dwindled to a smelly few for Mondays.

The thought of getting home and having a bath to wash off the London grime was most appealing. He could almost see his small cottage dwarfed by two horse chestnuts and a blue spruce that had reminded him of his childhood in Inverness.

A flash of red came through the high hedgerow and his attention was diverted for a split second, time which would have been better spent slowing down. The last thing he saw was the driver of the tractor throwing his arms up against his eyes to shield himself from the inevitable crash. Then silence.

When the splintered debris settled, Ewart's body slumped onto the steering wheel and the drone of the car horn alerted the neighbours less than a hundred yards away.

'Longfield', the Detective Inspector said briskly as he answered the phone.

'Guess what?' asked D.I. Prasad.

'You've found him?'

'Yes, in a manner of speaking.'

'Is he co-operating? Has he shown any signs of knowing about the cross?'

'He's beyond all that. He's dead. Died in a head-on collision on a country road.'

'Damn it!'

'Quite. I've established his address and I'm getting a warrant to search it. The body is being taken to the morgue now although it's fairly obvious what he died of. His eyes were apparently hanging from their sockets, he must have been travelling.'

'Is the cross on him?'

'Negative, but there are his wallet, various bits of paper, and four hundred pounds in cash. They are bringing that in here now. Do you want to come back?'

Longfield was at home, more than an hour's drive back to Stevenage.

'He can't do anything with it now, can he?'

'I doubt it, that's if he had it in the first place.'

'Oh, he's got it, or had it, it's just a matter of what he has done with it and the other bits. I'll come over tomorrow and you can take me to his house, we'll see if there is anything there to link him to the Aylesbury robbery other than the gold. Keep me informed if you find anything. Thanks for the call.'

Half an hour later, the contents of Ewart's car and pockets were placed in a plastic bag on Detective Inspector Prasad's desk. The four hundred pounds was in used notes but he had obviously had more when they inspected the contents of a plastic bag containing a pair of shoes, men's, black, and a receipt for two hundred and fifty pounds. There was a freshly laundered white handkerchief, some loose change and a folded piece of paper which Prasad opened.

On Simon & Simon's letterhead was a receipt for an 18 carat gold cross, value £387, and three 15 carat gold carvings, value £328, paid in cash to one Duncan Ewart. The initials of the company representative that undertook the transaction were R.F.S.

Without ringing Longfield first, Prasad telephoned Simon & Simon, and despite it being after the advertised hours on their form, the telephone was answered. The person to whom he wished to speak was, according to the operator, Rebecca Simon, a buyer, and he was put through to her telephone. It rang twelve times before somebody, obviously harassed, answered. Rebecca had gone home. Yes, he could see that transaction in her book but he did not know what had happened to the pieces. Usually, if a purchase was considered to be worth more as a piece of jewellery than its intrinsic value then it would be retained but there was no indication that this was so and there was nothing awaiting inspection in the safe. Normal procedure would be to consign it to be melted that day. No, he didn't have Rebecca's home telephone number, this was not the sort of business where that information was given out freely due to the possibility of staff being kidnapped and forced to open office doors and safes.

'But I'm a police officer!' Prasad protested.

'How do I know that?' the harassed man replied.

'Alright, this is what I can do. I can give you my telephone number here at the station. You ask for me, Detective Inspector Prasad, you will be put through and thereby prove that I am sitting in a Police Station trying to prevent a priceless work of art from being melted down.'

The man relented and went off to get Rebecca Simon's number which he passed on to Prasad.

'How priceless are they?' the man inquired.

'Half a million pounds or so.'

'And she's paid seven hundred and fifteen?' he asked, looking at her purchase book.

'It would seem so. However, they are the proceeds of a robbery and must be returned to the owner. Can you guarantee that no more is due to go out for refining today?'

'Yes. The afternoon shipment goes at four o'clock. If they've gone for melt then they're history, there's nothing we can do about them now.'

'That's why somebody will be on your doorstep tomorrow morning to carry out a search of your premises,' Prasad said, without any such authority in his powers.

'I'm not sure you can do that,' the man protested.

'Don't worry, you'll be sure when it happens,' he replied.

Prasad tried the number for Rebecca Simon but there was no answer nor was there an answering machine. He then tried Longfield.

'Seven hundred and fifteen pounds!' he cried incredulously down his telephone.

'Yes, seems like a bargain, doesn't it?'

'And now Simon & Simon don't know where the goods are?'

'Yes. It would appear that they have been melted but we can't confirm it one way or other.'

'What about Ewart's house?'

'First reports are that it's clean. Nothing of any suspicion found but they're still at it.'

'Keep me posted and find Rebecca Simon. Do you need any help with contacts in the Met.?'

'No, I've got some of my own. Do we search Simon & Simon in the meantime?'

'You'll never get a warrant now. The key to the whole thing is this Rebecca Simon woman.'

Prasad wanted to go home himself but had to wait for the uniform police searching Ewart's house. In the meantime he repeatedly telephoned the number he was given for Rebecca Simon. He was going to leave it for the night when he thought that he'd check the number in the London telephone book and when he ran his finger over the R. Simon's he found that the second last digit was incorrect, either the harassed man had given him the wrong number by mistake, or intentionally, he wondered, or he had copied it down wrongly. He blamed himself, it was quite possible that he had written it down incorrectly. He dialled the revised number.

'Is that Rebecca Simon?' he asked the girl who answered.

'Yes.'

'I'm Detective Inspector Prasad of the Hertfordshire Police. Can I have five minutes of your time?'

'What about?' she asked suspiciously.

'Do you recall a transaction you did today with a Duncan Ewart? You bought a gold cross and some gold book mounts.'

'Yes.'

'Can I ask what you did with them?'

'They were consigned to the scrap pile. Why do you ask?'

There was a momentary pause.

'They were definitely put in the consignment to be melted?'

'As far as I know, yes.'

'Oh.'

'You haven't told me why you are asking about them.'

Prasad told her the whole story up to and including Ewart's fatal meeting with a tractor at high speed. She listened impassively to the tale whilst playing with a pendant on her necklace, a gold cross with minute beaded decoration, something she had bought that day and was beguiled by the execution and design. She had reimbursed her company with the seven hundred and fifteen pounds it and three enigmatic gold mounts had cost, and taken them home.

It was now apparent to her that she was in possession of stolen goods and that she had lied to a policeman.

13

Each time that evening, and the following morning, that she looked at the cross she grew more desirous of owning it but it was forbidden fruit. She knew that she would have to return it to the scrap pile in the office and telephone Detective Inspector Prasad to say that it had not been sent for melting the previous day after all. There may even be some sort of reward for saving it and the mounts from their fate at the refinery.

The Inspector had said that the cross was Celtic and eighth century or earlier but she considered it to be too fine, not that she would necessarily know, and thought that it was probably a Victorian or Edwardian machine-made copy.

She only retained the mounts so that the deal was opened and closed neatly and she was going to make them into something; she hadn't yet established what but she was friendly with many of the jewellers that came into her office and they could have not only suggested a use but have done the work as well. She hadn't been able to work out what they were all about but had liked them, nowhere near as smitten with them as she was with the cross but they had presence and she was sure that they would come to some good use sometime.

Now that she had been told that they were book mounts, it was obvious to her and she arranged them on the corners of an interior design book she had on the coffee table. She then decided that they looked better on a black background so she folded a piece of black cloth over the book and replaced the three mounts, the bottom right hand corner sadly missing.

She had wondered what her conscience would say if she kept them, not for monetary gain but because she liked them. They had already been stolen and it was only her intervention that had prevented them from being destroyed for good. Was there not something that entitled her to keep them for a while and then return them or donate them to somebody whilst the insurance company paid out?

It was only a momentary flash of whimsy as her heart knew what she had to do. Her father had told her that if he were dishonest then he would have been a much richer man than he found himself but his compensation was that he could hold his head high and truthfully say that he had never levied a commission not due to him nor denied monies to his creditors. That maxim had been Rebecca's too although the opportunities to break either were very few and far between and now she was considering turning her back on his words once a sore temptation came her way.

It was a very relieved Detective Inspector Prasad who took the call from her at nine o'clock the next morning. She didn't even relate the story she had concocted whilst lying in bed but simply told the truth and apologised for having misled him the night before.

Prasad telephoned Longfield whose morning agitation had been exacerbated by his previous night's choice of curry for supper which was having a furious argument with his ulcer. He cheered up immediately he got the news of the recovery of the gold, it had meant that the hoard was now reunited without loss although the other household items were still missing.

There couldn't, of course, be any prosecution of the thief, as he lay, mangled, in the Hertfordshire Constabulary morgue, but they could possibly charge John Smith and Gary Bell with more than receiving but his heart wasn't in it. Hopefully Bell would be suitably chastened to re-route his life and to avoid the companionship of the Duncan Ewarts of the world but he was one to watch.

'I'd better accompany the extraordinarily lucky Mr Knox to Simon & Simon to recover the gold. He can come to you to get the plate and coins, is that alright?' Longfield asked.

Prasad phoned an equally relieved Harry who was under threat of "possible action" being taken against him regarding the loss of the hoard. Trotman's insurance company had immediately said that it was not covered under the "in transit" clause in their policy whilst Trotman's lawyers had come to the conclusion that the items were "in transit" under their definition and that a challenge could be mounted against the insurers.

Harry's relief at the recovery was such that he omitted to ask if his household goods had been found at the same time. His nausea that had bubbled away within was quickly suppressed and the alleviating dullness that overcomes anxiety set in before he thought of informing his managing director and colleagues of the good news.

Longfield telephoned him and asked if he could arrange the exchange straight away as he was awaiting a forensic report from another case upon which he would have to act immediately it was to hand and which would tie him up for a few days at least.

Longfield was in his office within half an hour imparting his own thoughts as to Harry's luck.

'I'd like to say that it happens all the time like that, but it doesn't. In my experience fine art and antiques that have been stolen disappear into the ether and we blithely say that they've been swallowed up into a vast underground black market where the very rich bid for stolen property for their secret collections. I don't, and I'm speaking strictly personally, believe it for a minute but I'm blowed if I know where it does go. We've been monitoring stolen artworks for decades now thinking that it must reappear but it rarely does.'

'All very depressing, Detective Inspector,' Harry admitted.

'They haven't found anything else,' he said, 'I've put out a notice on the silver canteen and inkstand.'

'I suppose they'll melt those down?'

'Usually, but sometimes silver gets sent to Italy and is sold for more than scrap. Was it a nice service?'

'Pretty ordinary, fiddle pattern but it was same date and maker; that might make it better if these people know anything about these things.'

'I can't guarantee anything but it might just turn up. Was the inkwell inscribed?'

Harry couldn't follow the train of thought.

'Inkwell?'

'Silver presentation inkwell,' he explained.

'No.'

'Well, how is it a "presentation" inkwell?'

'I probably told them. It was a present from my father but it wasn't inscribed.'

'So it was modern then?' Longfield continued.

'No, it was an antique. 1830 something.'

'No date, no maker?'

'I couldn't recall what it was when I gave them the list. It was three in the morning.'

'You are an auctioneer of antiques and you didn't have a proper list of your own house contents?'

Harry was ashamed to admit that he had nothing more than a rudimentary listing.

'I'm not going to lecture you,' Longfield said, as a preface to a lecture, 'but how do you think we are expected to find your gear if we don't know what we're looking for?'

Before Harry could think of a reply, Longfield launched into a catalogue of woe that was the policeman's lot with retributions brought against them for poor recovery rates and accusations that they could hardly have tried to find stolen goods when everybody knew that you only have to check out the contents of so and so's car boot at the Sunday markets to find half the stolen goods in such and such an area. When, however, they do investigate so and so's car boot they are harangued and accused of harassment and have to answer to the "Super" who is attacking them from both sides; better results and no complaints from the public.

The journey from Savile Row to the City was occupied by Harry listening to this tirade against all and sundry, wondering where his misdemeanour came into it: Somewhere near the top, he concluded, as they neared Chancery Lane.

They were shown into an office off the reception area of Simon & Simon where Rebecca received them with unnecessary contrition. She introduced her father to Harry and Longfield and they all agreed that the items in the photographs and those laid on the table were one and the same.

After the D.I. made the comment that they didn't look much like half a million pounds it was up to Harry to explain them. His confidence returned as his hands touched the objects once again and he didn't fail to notice Rebecca's eyes as her gaze flitted between the cross and him. They were dark and deep set with the hint of make-up but her face was devoid of artificial colour apart from some lipstick and she had a complexion of light brown silk which reminded him of something, a piece of fine grained wood perhaps, he couldn't place it and he knew that to look at her cheeks for too long betrayed his illicit interest.

Despite a few good questions from her father and the occasional comment from Longfield, Harry held the stage as he enlightened his audience with a display of knowledge that couldn't help but captivate them. He wanted to hold the cross against Rebecca's angular face but sensibly didn't, he compared Octavia's skin to Rebecca's, a plum mahogany to her flame figuring and couldn't help wondering if the cross would gain the lustre it displayed when held against Octavia's chest. He had never looked at skin before, his was pallid and covered in impurities, so too was his wife Patricia's but he had met two women in the space of a few days who had opened a door for him and the handle of that door was the cross.

He handed her a cheque for seven hundred and fifteen pounds

explaining that the question of reward money was being addressed, a lie he was told to repeat by Sam Reid. She waved her hand as though to dismiss the idea of a reward; her father had said that the goodwill would still be paying dividends long after any money had gone.

He had come equipped with tissue paper in which he wrapped the mounts and the cross, placed the pieces in an envelope and put them in his jacket pocket, tapping the outside once done to show that they were now safe.

'When are they to be sold?' Rebecca asked.

'At the end of November,' Harry said, 'would you like a catalogue?'

'Oh please!' she enthused, 'here's a card, send it to the office. Can I come to the auction?'

'Of course.'

'As long as you have no designs on owning any of the lots on offer,' her father instructed.

'No Daddy, of course I don't. I just feel a little attached to them, that's all. I owned them for nearly a day. You can't help but wonder who else owned them.'

'I must admit that I think more of the person who made them, where he found his inspiration, what restrictions were placed on them by the person who commissioned them, size, cost, amount of time he was given to make them, that sort of thing,' Harry said.

Ownership was transitory but the design and execution were the work of one or perhaps two people and their work was the important ingredient as far as he was concerned.

Harry returned to his office alone as Longfield had received the call he was waiting for and was headed towards the next case. The foyer of Trotman's was as quiet as ever. He asked the receptionist if there were any messages for him and she replied that Julia had one but that she was out at lunch.

On the staircase he met Drew and calmly informed him that he had 'got the stuff back.'

'Your stereo and things?'

'No, the cross and mounts.'

It was then that Harry realised that he had told only Sam Reid about the recovery of the hoard and that it had not been passed on. The news was a tonic to the entire company and he wondered why Reid hadn't told anyone. The cross and mounts were laid out on Harry's desk so that everybody in the building could see the cause of such mixed emotions over the last five days.

Harry then phoned the Armstrong's house and it was answered by a young girl.

'Is Mr or Mrs Armstrong there?'

'No, Mummy's mending a fence in the five acre field and Daddy's in America.'

'Ah, yes, I recall he said would be away. Could you take a message for your mother? Do you have a pencil and piece of paper?'

The girl told him to 'wait a sec.' whilst she collected both items.

'Now,' Harry continued, 'could you say that Harry Knox called?'

He spelt out his name.

'I've got some very good news for her. We have found the gold cross and mounts and I will be collecting the paten and coins tonight. Have you got that?'

'My cross?'

'I'm sorry?'

'You've found my cross, the one that Seton's got?' she asked.

'Seton? I'm afraid I don't follow you.'

'I found the cross and the plate thingy. Seton's got them.'

'And where is Seton?' Harry ventured.

'At home,' she replied.

'Where's his home?'

'At Castle Nisbet.'

'Ah ha, we're getting there. And where is Castle Nisbet?'

'In Ireland, of course,' she replied.

'What part? I've never heard of Castle Nisbet.'

'In Cork, west Cork. It's where we stay when we go to Ireland, Nisbet's Cove.'

'Oh yes, now I know. You found the cross eh? In Seton's house?'

'No silly, in the ground, after the cliff fell down. I found the plate and then one of those funny triangle things and later I found the cross on its own and Daddy said that it was my cross. Is that it, it's got bobbles on it?'

Harry looked down at the cross with bobbles on it. He was not hearing what he wanted to hear, however much he and Drew had suspected it.

'Where does Seton come into it?' Harry asked.

'He owns the farm we found the things in.'

'In or on?'

'Both, we had to dig to find the coins and the last triangle brooch.'

'Okay. Look, I'll give you the number to ring, can you ask Mummy to call me as soon as she comes in?'

He gave her the number and asked her to repeat it. She thought that she wouldn't be too long as it was nearly lunchtime.

'And what's your name?'

'Livia,' she replied.

'Olivia?' Harry asked.

'My Dad calls me that when we are in Ireland. He thinks it's hilariously funny. No, it's Livia, '

'Ah, Livia,' recalled Harry, 'Augustus's wife?'

'So I am always reminded,' Livia sighed.

'And Claudius' grand-mother.'

'You're very clever,' Livia said genuinely.

'And you're very kind. Get Mummy to ring?'

'Okay, goodbye Harry Knox.'

Harry Knox had once again lost his appetite.

14

'Harry, for God's sake, we knew that they were dug up. All we need to do is get them cleaned,' Drew pleaded with his wavering colleague.

'We didn't know, we suspected. Now we know when and where and it is our responsibility to report the fact.'

'It's our responsibility to earn some money and kudos for Trotman's and a little of the latter for us as well. You can't acquire a conscience now, or if you do, it'll be a bloody expensive virtue and not all at your cost either. I mean, you were on the brink of being sacked, Julia got it from his secretary, what's her name?'

'Jenny?'

'Yes, Jenny. They have organised a meeting with the top lot.'

'But I'm on the board!'

'They can hardly have you in on the meeting! Anyway, that's not the point, it's all over, but you won't be doing yourself any harm by putting the hoard up and hyping it to Hell and back. If you now go to Reid and tell him that you don't feel easy about putting it up in light of information to hand, I'll give you six months.'

'That's plain stupid! They can't sack me for being honest,' Harry said, looking at the cross under his magnifying glass for the fiftieth time.

'Not sack, dear boy, just fail to promote. You know, make it clear you're not wanted.'

'If that's what it takes ...'

Drew leant over his desk.

'I don't know about you, but I have no qualms at all about selling the coins. That they've turned up in Ireland is of some note but there are other Viking coins found there so we know that they were there, that's all the evidence needed and they've got it. The other kit, well, that's your subject, but quite frankly, they could have been taken out of Ireland a thousand years ago and nobody would be any the wiser.'

Harry put the cross back onto his desk, leant back in his chair, put his feet onto his desk and his clasped hands on top of his head. His obligation, he had thought, between putting the telephone down to Livia and telling Drew the news, was to the historians and archaeologists, the ranks of which he considered he belonged. Drew was arguing that his obligations were to his company, the ranks of which he also belonged although they were mostly at odds with each other. Had he, as Professor Bethune maintained, switched camps or was he hedging his bets with a bit each way?

He also had a craving to own the cross, not just until such a time as he had to part with it after it was sold, but forever, until he died. He had seen thousands of objects going through Trotman's sales and in museums over the globe and none had an attraction, a desire to own, like the cross. He couldn't possibly attain to own it, even if he sold his now pillaged house in Aylesbury and his innate honesty prevented him from ever considering purloining it, but he wanted it.

His innate honesty was sorely tested in the knowledge that the only way he could own it, and only for a brief moment, was to ignore the information he had tricked out of Livia and sell the hoard. However, if Livia had told him, who else had she told and how many people would she tell?

'I give up,' Drew said.

'You give up what?' Harry replied, only barely conscious that Drew had been talking to him.

'I give up with you. You've got to "get real" as they say. Go upstairs to Classical Antiquities and ask them where all their stock comes from. Don't for God's sake, mention the tombaroli up there, they all develop a nervous twitch and pretend they can't speak Italian. I, for one, can categorically say that I have handled hundreds of coins taken from hoards that weren't declared in their country of discovery,' Drew said, with some misplaced pride.

'In England or Ireland?' Harry asked.

'England, yes. Don't know about Ireland. Because we were invaded so often and were beating each other over the head with wooden sticks, coin hoards are almost common in Britain. Only a few varieties turn up in the Celtic series every now and then that's of interest to the academics but numismatic collections in British museums are bursting at the seams with coins, duplicated over the country. It is no skin off my nose to deny them a chance of squirreling more away in the rare chance there might be one they haven't got but it's on their list because the next city or county's museum has got one.'

Harry's right foot, resting on his left ankle was wriggling as if his mind were wavering between wrong and right.

'Okay, if we sell them in the knowledge that we know their origins, and that's something we can't deny, what do we do if it is made known that that was the case?'

'Don't get you, old boy,' Drew said obtusely.

'What if we get caught?' he said plainly.

'I've pre-empted you there,' Drew replied smugly, 'we write a memo to Reid, telling him everything we know. He's not going to suggest we spill the beans but rather turn a blind eye to it. I know he's done it before with something that came from Paris that we'd been offered from Athens. All reference to the Athens offer was destroyed and we happily flogged it on behalf of the French client.'

This was news to Harry.

'How do you know all this?' he doubted.

'I'm in coins, everybody outside the coin department tells me what's going on inside theirs. They think that I'm immune to questioning. I know more about what goes on in this business than Reid can ever know. He will get the memo, tell us to get on with selling the hoard with the original story that Armstrong told us. We might have to check some facts up but now we know the true story we can tell the Armstrongs the reasons for investigating their great grandfather rather than having to pussy foot around them.'

'Who writes the memo?'

'We both do.'

They sat at Harry's desk composing their excuse for their impending actions. The wording had to be such that the approval for Trotman's to sell the hoard was entirely in the hands of their managing director or higher. Harry's secretary, Julia, was let in on the plot and it was her contribution that was the most significant to the memo. She even acknowledged the fact that she knew the contents by including her initials in lower case adjacent to those of Harry and Drew in upper case and was about to finish the document when the telephone rang.

'It's Octavia Armstrong for you, she is getting friendly,' she said transferring the call.

'Mrs Armstrong?' Harry asked.

'Mr Knox. I've been sitting by the phone for ten minutes before I found the courage to pick it up. I believe Livia has told you a story?'

'Is it not true?' Harry asked, hoping upon hope that Livia was capable of making it all up.

'Absolutely true, I'm afraid. The hoard was found in the remains of a collapsed cliff in West Cork in August. We smuggled them into England when we came back, for the very reasons you kindly pointed out when you came here on Saturday. I suppose we should now return them to the proper authorities in Ireland? If we did that, is there any reason why they should know we smuggled them over here in the first place?'

'Well, hold on,' Harry started and then put the two points of view to Octavia, surrender them or sell them. If the latter, then he was going to have to say that he had only ever been told the first story of her husband's great grandfather recovering the hoard in Ireland or, to confuse the issue, purportedly in Ireland.

Octavia grasped the options quite clearly; if, for whatever reason, they were caught selling goods unearthed and smuggled out of Ireland, then Trotman's did so without knowledge of their origins, the liars were the Armstrongs. Was she prepared to accept that?

'We always have been,' she said, 'that's why we never told you, it would have been better for you if you didn't know.'

'Much simpler,' Harry agreed.

'But now that you do, it doesn't change anything in our eyes. The owner, as you may have gathered, is the farmer on whose land they were found, we are the couriers and we are to split the proceeds.'

'We can't pay somebody in Ireland for them!' Harry exclaimed.

'No, you pay us, we pay Seton. My husband, you'll recall, is an accountant, he has already worked out a way.'

'There is one other point,' Harry continued, 'if your husband inherited them from his father, how come they have never been valued for probate through the generations?'

'You don't miss a trick, do you Mr Knox?'

'I try not to,' he replied.

'My father-in-law died in New Zealand where he was a resident. There are no death duties in New Zealand and therefore no need for probate when there was only one beneficiary to a will, as was the case in both Jonathan's and his father's case.'

'Clever, very clever.'

'It's true!'

'Is it?' Harry asked surprised, 'well, you couldn't have invented a better sequence of events.'

'That particular sequence wasn't invented. Nor, indeed, is the story of the discovery, it happened as Livia related.'

'The cross is hers?'

'Yes, she found it and was mature enough, as a ten year old, to tell us that she found it. It was actually found below high tide lying on the sand. We wondered about its status as it was not dug up?'

Harry laughed.

'We can't get involved in a legal argument otherwise people might start to ask questions.'

'I see, yes. What do we do from here?'

'I want you to do a bit of research. I'm confused as to what is true and what isn't. Did Mr Armstrong's great grandfather really serve in Ireland?'

'Apparently, yes.'

'Do you know where and when?'

'No.'

'Can you find out?'

'I couldn't tell you. I think that Jonathan tried to find out but if he did he didn't tell me. I'll be speaking to him tonight, I'll ask him. Do we have to be involved at all?'

'Hopefully not,' Harry said, 'but it's better to be prepared if any questions are raised.'

They parted on the understanding that everything was as before. He wolfed down a ham sandwich whilst trying to reorganise his photographer and had a brief chat to Thornton Bethune arranging to get him into the office the next day to start the cataloguing.

The message that Julia had taken earlier was from Detective Inspector Prasad asking him to pick up the paten and coins before five that night or to report to his sergeant if it was to be after that hour. He phoned Patricia to pick him up at the Stevenage police station at five and got Julia to find out the train times. He was feeling pleased with his efforts and satisfied with his progress when he was summoned to Sam Reid's office.

'Why did you send me this?' he asked, holding the memo between his forefinger and thumb as though it emitted a distasteful odour.

'I thought you ought to know. I think you'd be pretty cross if it was discovered after the sale and you weren't in the know.'

'So you're shifting the blame onto me?'

'Not at all, we are all as guilty of being accessory to this particular case.'

'And what are our chances of this being discovered? Could it be, in fact, a plant?'

Harry hadn't entertained such a thought.

'Not when you know the people involved. The family are very straight laced, normal people, he's an accountant, they live in a marvellous house. They have a great story covering their tracks, even down to probate and death duties.'

Reid put the memo on his desk and wandered off to his window to stare at the empty street below him.

'I want you to destroy every copy of that memo because if we are to sell this lot then we deny we know anything about Ireland. We stick to the vendor's original story. You and Drew and Julia will stand in any dock in the country and perjure yourselves, do you understand?'

Harry understood but didn't like it.

'I'll destroy all the memos but I won't perjure myself. If asked if I know the origins of the hoard I will truthfully say no because I don't know the exact location but if I am asked if I knew that they were smuggled out of Ireland I will say 'yes'. I've weighed up the risks and I consider us to be almost beyond reach.'

'How many more people in this building know about Ireland?'

'Just us four.'

'It will remain that way. Loose lips and all that. No doubt the opposition will raise a few salient points about the hoard and try to undo it. I, for one, am looking at getting our name on the front of every paper in the country. I want academics arguing about the workmanship, I want politicians involved about 'saving them for the country' and I want overseas interest to fuel that particular debate.'

'I must admit, I was thinking of a New York, Dublin, Belfast, London viewing, taking the three hoard lots and the better pieces from the general sale.'

'What about the coins?'

'They aren't really worth taking,' Harry said.

'But they are part of the hyping, the Viking dimension bringing the thing to life. For once Trotman's are presenting something that film makers could use; longboats sailing up the Shannon, rape and pillage, treasures stashed away until discovered ...'

'By Major Armstrong in 1900,' Harry interjected quickly.

'Yes, good old Major Armstrong. "The Armstrong Hoard"?'

'Not allowed to use the name. I was thinking the "945 A.D. Hoard" but it's a bit bland.'

'Why not "The Viking Hoard"? Take the pennies on the tour and you'll get on every television screen in America,' promised Reid, 'and we'll bring them to their knees in desperation to own the things.'

15

Rosie Spillane carried the ponderous title of National Arts Funding Co-ordinating Director. If asked to summarise her job in circumstances which required brevity she described it as signing cheques and scrambling around the depths of the government's handbag looking for loose change. It hadn't taken her very long in the job to realise that funding for the Arts was not exactly a priority with governments although none would ever admit it. Hospitals, education, roads and social services had the run of the money, even tourism was better supplied, although the arts overlapped into that portfolio.

"The Arts" was such a broad term and was split into "performing arts", "heritage", "fine arts" and "Gaeltacht" with several subtitles again under each of those. Writing books, for instance, was considered a "heritage art" rather than a "performing art". It look a small army housed in Merrion Street, Dublin, to sort out the monolith that was "the arts" and the person to whom they all turned in the end was Rosie Spillane.

If a curator wanted to buy an important Irish document then he usually went to Rosie to top up the coffers so that they had some chance at competing on the open market, most usually at auction. Some curators were particularly good at finding funding by corporate sponsorship but Rosie had to help those that were shyer and less bold in courting the rich and famous to help maintain Ireland's heritage. Their success rate was not on the right side of 50 per cent but they could get marvellous publicity when they did manage to pull off a coup. A lot of the funding came from the other side of the Atlantic where Irish antecedents weighed on the consciences of successful businessmen and who showed their largesse in purchasing an item or donating a collection for one of the many institutions set up around the country to accept these items.

Rosie was the one who gathered these funds in and distributed them, ensuring that the benefactor's name gained some sort of immortality in return. It was sometimes a thankless task as many curators perceived bias after certain allocations and almost all grumbled at Rosie's innovation in retaining funding if the particular item or items were not eventually purchased.

The spending of funds had been the preserve of individual curators and directors within their particular institution but this was heavily orientated to Dublin and as they came under the tourism minister's preview, it was decided that provincial institutions should be on an even footing. This brought grumbles from Dublin but, when analysed, they still received the vast bulk of the money by virtue of their standing in their particular fields. One didn't get the prefix "National" without it being recognised as such.

Rosie's problem was getting acknowledgment that the arts were worth spending public monies to retain. Patronage of the arts had slipped out of the private domain and into public spending. Whereas the rich and cultured would have commissioned art for their homes just as they had commissioned an architect to build the house to hold it, this was no longer the case and there were hundreds of artists, sculptors, actors, craftsmen, potters, writers, film makers and theatre directors and producers holding out their hands for government patronage. This came in many different ways, through tax breaks, support for some particular aspect of a project such as advertising or assistance from a governmental department, the use of government owned assets to sponsor projects or finally a plain cash donation. In some cases, entire contemporary art forms depended on governmental support.

The hardest part of the job was disappointing people and she had to do that all the time. She also shared the disappointment but it was rarely seen like that and she was often mistaken as the villain. In her heart she would give everybody everything they wanted but she didn't have the resources. She did, however, make sure everybody got a fair hearing from her despite the fact that the funding often didn't follow. She was able to steer people in the right direction or help them with their applications and not one was just flicked over on the desk of a junior clerk before being consigned to the bin.

This meant a lot of work for her department and demanded patience, tolerance and dedication which, over the three years she had been in the job, seemed to be the qualities of the few who stayed with her. It was something of a joke within the Arts and Heritage Department that longevity under her was akin to a snowflake approaching Old Clootie's lair.

The requests received by her department varied from those that were professionally compiled, to scraps of paper with some additions and a figure underlined at the bottom of the page. Some of the latter were made the more deserving cases as some of the former had already cost the applier a considerable sum and therefore showed a lack of money sense. The claims in some applications were often extraordinary and some downright fraudulent but her team sorted them out although she knew that one or two had slipped through the net. Those she most feared were the applications made by museum or art gallery directors as they knew more about the subject than she did and they usually involved large sums of money. Was it better to buy one object of "national importance" or fund twenty small theatre groups who were bringing tourists to less visited areas? Sometimes, but less frequently, she thought herself to be beyond making such decisions.

Rosie attended a seminar on Cultural Ireland, a project mooted by the tourism board which would whisk tourists through Joyce's Dublin to Paul Henry's Connemara and a thousand places between in a celebration of Ireland's contribution to the arts.

On her way out she was confronted by Seamus Dullea of the Irish Heritage Department in the newly formed Museums' Confederation. He was her most persistent adversary and she had reason to believe that he was the author of several anonymous, libellous letters that had circulated throughout the civil service with headlines such as *The Dyke Strikes Back* and *Lesbian Theatre supersedes William Orpen in Irish Importance* whenever one of his requests for funding were overlooked. She wasn't a dyke, nor had she, to her knowledge anyway, funded a Lesbian Theatre group and the nation owned all the Orpens it needed at the time.

'I've got something rather special,' Dullea said outside the conference room.

'It's the first I've heard about it,' she replied mischieviously.

'This is extremely important. I haven't time to do a report that will do justice to the items but we have been tipped off that at the end of November some Celtic artefacts are being offered in London.'

'Oh?'

'One of them is the paten to the Ardagh Chalice.'

'And doubtlessly you have to buy it?' she said with an emphasis on the "have", just as he always stressed.

'It would be nice to re-unite them,' he replied sarcastically.

'But you have the Derrynaflan chalice and paten in the National Museum. Isn't that enough?'

Her knowledge of the national holdings was legendary and had caught out many an applicant who had tried to obsfucate the true position.

'I'll have to arrange a meeting with you, at least we've got two months to work on it,' Seamus continued.

'Makes a change for once,' she commented quite used to having twenty-four hours to find funds when somebody dropped out at the last minute. 'How much is involved?'

Seamus hesitated, he loathed the cap in hand requests he had to make to the unappreciative Ms Spillane.

'A million.'

'Euros?'

'Sterling.'

'Forget it. There is nowhere near that sort of money for decorative arts, Ardagh Chalice or no Ardagh Chalice. How were the two separated anyway?'

'In the eighth century. It's the most extraordinary piece of luck to get the two back together again.'

'You haven't done it yet and you won't if you rely on money from my department. I think you are going to have to ask for a "special" on this.'

'More form filling,' he said dejectedly.

'I'll give you a hand once you've made a formal application. Don't you have any money of your own?'

'A bit, but there is a marvellous rococo soup toureen by Charles Townsend coming up in October. We have allocated funds for that.'

Rosie sat down on a leather cushioned sofa, her briefcase resting on her lap. Seamus sat next to her. She wasn't that unattractive he thought, it was just her mean attitude to his requests that made her lips snarl and her less endearing features all the more prominent. That she was still unmarried had led to speculation about her sexual orientation but she wasn't harmed by the barbs. She looked sporty: hockey, tennis, white water rafting sporty, perhaps judo. If so, how did she keep her hands so perfectly manicured, he mused? Crosswords, that would be it, crosswords with her cat, she had to be a cat lover, sitting on her lap and dreadfully disappointed not to do the big cryptic one on the weekend within an hour. Yes, he decided, a mental rather than a physical toughness, although she was hardly slight in stature.

'What are you doing tomorrow morning?' she asked him after half a minute's silent reflection.

'Nothing that I know of. Can I get back to you? I didn't bring my organiser.'

Her head flicked back by a perceptible fraction of an inch in disapproval.

'Hopefully I'll see you tomorrow morning at 10,' she said before walking away.

Seamus returned to his office and gathered all the relevant experts together. He surmised that he had eighteen hours to get together a submission to start the search for one million pounds worth of funding, whether they could fly over the first hurdle, the formidable Ms Spillane, or not, was his initial worry.

They had heard of the pieces from a dealer in Dublin who had received information about a robbery in Buckinghamshire. The photographs were not brilliant but good enough to tell them that the pieces were of very fine workmanship although some experts rather doubted their authenticity; they were a bit too good and how much easier was it for a forger to base his work on something that already existed, the Ardagh Chalice, for instance.

If they were genuine, and the majority thought that they were, they were items that they would very much like to acquire for the National Museum and perhaps some other projects would have to be put to one side in the meantime.

The chance to acquire something new was a rare treat for curators. Organising exhibitions, demands from other departments, constant consultations with conservators and a good deal of goodwill took up the time of museum and art gallery staff.

Adding to the collection was a laborious task but one of excitement and action, all too infrequent in their world. The most onerous of duties was preparing a report saying what they thought the item to be worth and then justifying it. Not a few curators were tempted to say 'because I think so', under the justification question as the items they sought to buy were invariably of such a rare nature (hence the museum or art gallery did not have anything like it) that evoking a recent market price for something similar was impossible.

If they had sufficient funds in their own institutional accounts then the summary would be placed before the Board of Trustees who said yea or nay to the purchase. If the money was needed from elsewhere then, after being sanctioned by Rosie, a group of suited ladies and gentlemen in the employ of the Departments of Finance and Arts would decree if the nation's coffers were to be opened and possibly lightened.

This was all very well if the items sought had firm price tags but when items came up for auction they had to give an "up to" figure which would include the auctioneer's buyers' premium and any government levied sale taxes which was all too difficult for many people in charge of allocated funds to comprehend.

Therefore, the best submissions, as Rosie had often told her team, were the simplest and whilst Seamus tried to pare down the length of their case, it was still twelve pages long and ended with the precautionary statement that the request was subject to the objects being genuine.

They had approached Trotman's on a casual basis to see if they could be of any help in cataloguing after it had been made known to them that a request had come for a photograph of the Ardagh Chalice for reproduction in the catalogue. They had seen the reports of the robbery and subsequent recovery of the items. It was only when they had been retrieved did they find out Trotman's estimate of their worth, because, when asked, the curatorial team looking at the purchase had all shrugged their shoulders and said collectively that it was anybody's guess.

Trotman's had promised to send all the information and better photographs but were tied up with the catalogue production and wouldn't get back for a few weeks but they did add that they thought that a certain institution would be most interested in the hoard.

One of the more vexing headings in submissions to get funds to buy objects was that of "Ownership". National institutions had, at all times, a responsibility to establish ownership of the goods before public monies were lavished upon them. Most of the time, this was straightforward as establishing provenances for items from the eighteenth century to the present was not a difficult process, especially when the sellers or donors were descendants of the original commissioners or buyers.

Archaeological items however, posed a different problem and that was why, in 1930, it was declared that everything found under the ground was the property of the State, ownership thus being unchallengeable. Museums worldwide had fingers pointed at them by foreign governments claiming that items on display had, at some stage of their life, been stolen or smuggled from their country of origin.

In times of conflict, works of art were taken from one place to another as a sign of conquest. These were then displayed and after several generations were considered to be the conquering country's by right. Now that was being questioned, most famously with the British Museum's ownership of the Elgin Marbles and the Greek's claim to them. The fact that the Earl of Elgin purchased the marbles from the then government of Greece in 1801, which happened to be the Turkish Ottoman Empire, further confused the issue.

Seamus had been given a verbal provenance for the hoard that was entirely hearsay and unprovable. The name of the vendor was not going to be released, even after the sale, but they were English and had apparently been in possession of the items for several decades, but, according to the family, they were possibly either found or purchased in Ireland at the turn of the century. It was a perfectly believable story but was regrettably short on detail.

The curators involved in early Irish works of art were at variance with each other about the workmanship of the items. Frustrated by the relatively poor quality of the photographs they were divided over the country of origin of the three corner mounts which they would all like to be by a goldsmith working in Ireland but were inclined to think that they were made in Northern England.

The paten was definitely of Irish origin but the gold cross was puzzling them all. There was a strong leaning towards it being Byzantine in which case it was of interest in as much that it proved that trade existed that far east but was not really something that would fit into the current collection. However, the overwhelming opinion was that the hoard should be bought intact otherwise it was meaningless. Together the objects told a potted history of early Christian to early Medieval times in Ireland and that a lot of its value, not necessarily in monetary terms, was in its diversity.

By the time Rosie occupied the chair on the other side of Seamus' desk, his team had put together an impressive document which effectively said that the State could not do without the hoard in its entirety and that they were going to face tough opposition, quite possibly from British institutions who felt the same way.

'Can we do a deal?' she asked.

'Who with, the auctioneers?' Seamus replied.

'No, with these British institutions.'

'I don't understand.'

'Well, we either nobble them or combine forces and buy them together. They can have them for a year or so and then we can have them.'

'It's novel,' Seamus said, trying not to smirk at her naivety.

'That's the point, Seamus. Everybody wants to own these things but even your lot is not totally convinced about the origin of the cross and the mounts. If it is fifty-fifty between British and Irish, could we not buy the hoard "in its entirety" as you seem to require, in co-operation with the British?'

'And then spend the next fifty years arguing whose turn it was to display them, who indemnifies them, who pockets the income from photography and reproduction rights? The list is endless.'

'No, it isn't endless. Somewhere the list of difficulties ends and then we go back to the beginning and answer those questions. This ownership bug your museums have is slowly draining the coffers and government patience. If they were undoubtedly Irish then you'd have a case, with the paten for instance. However, Byzantine gold, Viking coinage from York, a penny from Norwich and three mounts from Northumbria throws the whole lot into jeopardy.

'I would suggest that if you wish to buy the hoard in its entirety then you are going to have to join forces with your admitted opposition and work something out for yourselves,' Rosie said, her eyes scanning over the conclusion on the last page of the summation.

'Are you saying that you won't put the request through to the Department for consideration?'

'I'll put it through, far be it for me to interfere, but I'm pre-empting the reply if it goes through like this. I'm perfectly serious about approaching the British. Would it not ease the threat of them refusing an export license?'

She had done her homework well, Seamus thought.

'It would. It's just that it's never been done before.'

'But does that mean that it can't be done?' she asked.

'No, of course it doesn't.'

'It's all in the domain of the new era, European integration, peace in the North, dialogue between politicians in both countries and now a sensible approach to showing our national assets when their origin is questionable.'

Seamus screwed his mouth in doubt.

'I know,' Rosie continued, 'what you are unsure of. As I've told you, it's this ownership thing; you all like to saunter through your empty galleries and think that you own all this. We all do, every Irish man or woman can enter your hallowed portals and say, truthfully, 'I own everything here, including the building.' We all have how many millionths of a share in everything and that is as close as we will ever get. It isn't important to me, and I suggest it will not be a priority amongst the people in the Department of Finance, that these are owned by the nation or shared with another from which they may have come in the first place.

'Instead of pulling the hoard apart, we ensure that it stays together by collaborating. We can't go against British institutions if all they have to do is let everybody else slug it out on the saleroom floor and then refuse an export licence if it's bought by somebody overseas, nominally us, and take six months to find the money.'

'It doesn't happen that way,' Seamus said sulkily.

'It could though, Seamus. We are all susceptible to the winds of change and I feel that there is going to be a re-think about public ownership of art and artefacts. Nations no longer want to be fettered by expensive holdings in art. It would be much better if we asked a private sponsor to buy this hoard and lend it to us if we promise to look after it. It's happening in America already and it's beginning to spread to other countries.'

'If you spent more time trying to crack the carapace surrounding the Revenue Commissioners about a tax allowance for that sort of thing we'll all be in a better shape. You think a change is going to come, well that is where it had better originate', Seamus said.

'I take the point. I'll set up some meetings but it will take many months and possibly a budget to form a workable system. It's not going to help us in our current situation. How about the idea of approaching the British?'

Seamus again hesitated. He had to admit that Rosie had been right on the button about the craving for ownership amongst museum staff who saw acquisition as a measure of their own importance. Even when he had a relatively unimportant job as an assistant curator in Asian ceramics the thrill of acquiring something to augment their collection was a feeling that made the job all the more worthwhile.

Was it more important to keep the hoard together or split it up in order to buy the paten and forget the rest?

'I'll have to go back to the various departments,' he said.

'If you want my opinion, for what it's worth, I don't know, don't give them the choice. Just say it's all or bust, you have to work out a way to share the hoard. Is there any possibility that the British won't be interested?'

'I would say that it would be extremely remote.'

'Right then,' Rosie said, standing up and collecting her papers together, 'you get on the phone to them and work something out.'

As she left his office Seamus noticed how long her legs were, all the better for kicking people, he thought.

16

'What do you reckon?' Drew asked Harry, handing him the catalogue of "The Viking Hoard".

Harry flicked through it, he was very familiar with the layout having worked on it for a week after the items had been recovered. They had managed to take the number of pages to thirty-two, the longest description being for the cross although the paten took pride of place being the last lot to be offered. They began the seven lot sale with the Edmund penny by Eadgar of Norwich, then the two raven type pennies of Olaf Guthfrithsson and the very rare triquetra type of Sihtric Sihtricsson. The gold mounts were offered together, although Harry had considered offering them separately in a ploy to extract more money, then the cross and finally the paten.

Thornton Bethune had written a scholarly treatise on the origins of the cross which he ascribed to a goldsmith knowledgeable in the ways of his Byzantine contemporaries but working in either Ireland or Britain, keeping to his initial thoughts when Harry had first shown him the photographs. He firmly attributed the mounts to a Northumbrian goldsmith, drawing as evidence several manuscript paintings from that region with similar iconography. He had spent an inordinately long time sitting next to Julia correcting her typing off the computer screen and commenting how hot the office was in the hope that she would remove her jumper.

The less she wore, Harry noted, the more effusive his descriptions and the late summer burst of sunshine added pages to the catalogue as he discussed every possibility. He provided everything Sam Reid had demanded; contentious attributions with food for thought, priming an undoubted academic debate initiated by a lecture given by the Professor to the Society of Antiquarians at which the presence of the actual hoard guaranteed a full house. Question time after the lecture was a verbal free-for-all as specialists in the period added their thoughts, nearly all at odds with Bethune.

Nobody agreed that the cross was of a Northern origin but when asked to name a Byzantine equivalent they were stumped to come up with anything on the spot. Bethune loved every minute of the debate; he had the upper hand in that he had not used his time between cataloguing and presenting his ideas idly. As theories built on theories he was in a position to sink most with well aimed replies and by the end of an hour he was in the ascendancy although those that disagreed with his attribution's were well aware that further research on their part was necessary before battle could be rejoined.

The publicity department of Trotman's had never had so easy a task to attract the attention of television, radio and print media. They enlarged on the theory of how the hoard came to be that Harry had proposed as a preface to the catalogue, but there was always the question of why it had taken the best part of a century for the hoard to come to light, the oft repeated tale of treasures lying unrecognised in the attic.

Two days before Harry was to take the hoard and ninety lots from the general sale to be exhibited in New York, he received a telephone call from a journalist who wanted to know why the paten, cross and mounts had been cleaned. Harry, at first, dismissed the call but the journalist was most persistent about it, forcing Harry to spin out the story about having been stored in an attic that was home to several pigeons.

'But Mr Knox, it is quite obvious that they had been cleaned between the time they were photographed for the catalogue and made available to the press.'

'They were cleaned initially for photography, that is quite correct, but it was only a light wash due to the time available to get the catalogue out. After the photography we returned them to the conservators to clean them properly.'

'Clean what exactly?'

'Accumulated grime in the filigree. One never knows what is in that dirt, it could react with the metal.'

'Dirt? Does that include earth?'

'There was bound to be some earth stuck in the finer crevices but we've managed to practise good conservation and have, I believe, seen that nothing untoward can happen to the pieces,' Harry explained.

'Nothing to do with possible tests being carried out on the earth attached to the items that might show the presence of modern phosphates?'

'Modern phosphates?'

'To see if they had been recently excavated,' the journalist explained.

'They were excavated no later than about 1900 according to

information provided,' Harry explained.

'So you say.'

'I wasn't there, that I must admit, but then I suggest that you weren't either.'

The journalist was not to be fobbed off.

'Are you aware of the penalties for smuggling archaeological finds out of Ireland?'

'They weren't in place in 1900,' Harry said.

'That's if they were found in 1900,' the journalist started.

'Look, I'm a busy man, we have given the provenance of the items as we have been told. We can not prove it, we can not disregard it. I was the one responsible for having the items cleaned and they showed all the signs of being in a dusty place for a long time. That is all I can help you with. Goodbye.'

He put the telephone down and immediately set about wondering who had put the journalist up to that particular line of questioning. He had been quite right in spotting that they had cleaned the items after the photography and he was also correct in thinking that they were cleaned for the purposes of removing any trace of modern chemicals with which Seton Nisbet covered his pastures. The conservators were above reproach as they cleaned antiquities for every company and it was self defeating to let on that there was a little more earth on a particular object than should be the case if it were excavated many decades ago.

The line of questioning by the journalist was such that he had been informed by an expert of the points to raise. That expert, Harry considered, was most probably in a rival auction company and the master of it was Peter Grier of Lonergans. He had a propensity to spread ridiculous rumours about the authenticity of major lots in his opponents' sales and question the function of items whose use was uncertain in an effort to make them very much more run of the mill than was the case. He had to expect something of the spoiling tactics as they were stealing a march on their opposition with the publicity afforded the hoard. Try as he might, Harry couldn't get the media to mention the first part of his sale which included some notable items not least of which was a particularly important Caeretan painted vase of the late sixth century B.C.

The lots from the main sale that were to be shown in New York were sent by airfreight to the venue whilst Harry took the hoard with him on the plane. The cabinets and cases were set up in a function room in The Hotel Westbury by Jeff Cane, Trotman's American representative, who had a modest office in 5th Avenue from which he relayed bids from

American clients and gathered goods for sale in the London rooms. He had cleared the air consignment through customs, organised the press and had sent out over a thousand invitations to cocktails on the Thursday night in an attempt to get American interest in the sale.

The Americans were hard work and Harry had long wondered at their folly in lavishing such money on champagne and canapes. All the American collectors he knew were quiet, studious men and women, not party goers at all, who were inclined to attend a viewing during quieter moments when Harry could talk to them seriously. The cocktail set, however, were without a doubt, extremely wealthy but they did not spend their money on antiquities. They, like their European counterparts, were looking for status symbols and their search was aided each month by the various lifestyle magazines they slavishly followed. These magazines were disinclined to explore the depths of classical antiquities other than to illustrate reproduction urns made of concrete "sandstone".

The serious buyers in America usually found the time to attend Trotman's better sales in London and it was also notable that just under half of this American clientele were women whereas in Europe, women would make up less than a fifth of his clients and were often in tow with their husbands. Harry had long attributed the three thousand mile divide of ocean between his American collectors and the classical world for their interest. The absence made their hearts all the more yearning and a method of satiating that was to buy artefacts from those regions at his sales. Theirs was old money and Trotman's was an old firm, not as old as some but also not a slave to every invention of the computer industry. The very fact that the company did not sell anything later than the sixteenth century gave them an air of antiquity which was appreciated the most by their trans-Atlantic clients.

Harry supervised the unpacking of the air consignment whilst Jeff arranged them in the cabinets. Due to the weight they only showed smaller objects, leaving larger statues and architectural items in London. The centre display cabinet was reserved for the nine pieces of the hoard for which Harry had arranged perspex mounts to be made so any budding owner could see how to display them in their own homes.

A press conference was arranged for the print media which was extraordinarily well attended and the ensuing publicity was, in Jeff's experience, akin to that given to a major impressionist painting. "The Viking Hoard" was all the rage and soon Harry found himself a minor television star, appearing on morning television, afternoon television and evening chat shows. The most difficult interviews were those for radio but after three days of saturation appearances, Harry thought that most people would have seen the images of the items anyway. Most interviewers were well read on the hoard but some got it hopelessly wrong, one even spoke of the presence of the Romans in Ireland which Harry was pleased to correct. He did, however, tell New Yorkers that Solinus had noted in about 200 A.D. that Ireland did not have any snakes thus denying St. Patrick his great feat and surprising thousands of Irish New Yorkers with the news. His line about Solinus soon became more of an issue than the Viking Hoard, the first question at each interview being, "is it true that ..." and Harry started to apologise for the fact and steer conversation round to the point that he was selling a collection of antiquities in London and that they could be seen in the Hotel Westbury until Sunday.

The cocktail party went very well according to the number of bottles of champagne and samosas consumed. Harry was asked once about the hoard and twenty-three times about Solinus, the Roman scribe would be pleased his observation had received its long overdue recognition.

The next day a fair number of people came through the viewing, especially at lunch time when they could combine an artistic education with the fine food at one of the down-town restaurants. The crowd were appreciative of the items on display but were apt to equate size with price, hence the paten and cross seemed extremely expensive against a more modestly priced Krater or Apullian vase.

In the mid afternoon, Harry was approached by a timid man in expensive clothes and an accent trying hard to be British. He wanted to know if he would be permitted to examine the paten more closely. Harry took him to the cabinet, unlocked the sliding door and handed the paten to the stranger. He took an eyeglass from his pocket and fitted it into his right eye before examining the bands of filigree.

'And does the National Museum of Ireland agree that this is definitely the paten for the Ardagh Chalice?' he asked whilst still examining the piece.

'They have been remarkably quiet about it, truth be known. I personally have no doubt nor does anybody else I have spoken to. Whilst all the decoration is not the same, the similarities and the workmanship point to the same craftsman,' Harry replied.

'This is, of course, one opinion,' the previously hesitant man said aggressively.

'Modesty aside sir, an educated opinion.'

'Quite so. I'm Arnold McMicking,' he said, holding out his free hand. Harry introduced himself.

'You're the man that told everybody about Solinus!' he exclaimed.

'I rather wish I hadn't,' Harry replied.

'Yes, an Englishman putting down Ireland's patron saint in New York. It wasn't very wise.'

'Oh well,' Harry said, 'now I'm infamous, doesn't happen to many auctioneers. Do you like the paten?'

'Like it? Who can help but like it. But how much will it cost me to own it and is it right to own it?'

'I don't understand "is it right to own it"?'

'Must it not accompany the Chalice now that it has been discovered?'

'Well once you've bought this, we can negotiate on your behalf for the chalice from the museum,' Harry said dryly.

Mr McMicking handed the paten back to Harry without commenting on his suggestion.

'Do you wish to see anything else?' Harry asked.

'No, I wanted to see the paten. When is the sale?'

'November the 26th.'

He looked thoughtful for a while and then extracted a leather bound pocket diary from his jacket. He flicked through the pages, virtually every date having some sort of entry.

'The 26th?'

Harry confirmed the date.

'What time?'

'For the hoard? One o'clock.'

'I'm in a meeting here that afternoon. I can't be in London on the 26th.'

'That's alright, we can do a phone bid if you like,' Harry said. 'Do you have a catalogue?'

'No. Do I want one?' he asked.

Harry gave him catalogues for the general sale and the hoard which followed immediately, or at the earliest, one o'clock. The hoard would only take ten minutes to sell and he had allowed two and a half hours for the general sale.

Had he found the opposition to the museum for the paten? What sort of name was McMicking? Had he landed the catch that the New York viewing was cast for, a rich Irish-American? Jeff Cane had never heard of him nor had anybody else in his network of social contacts. How had an obviously knowledgeable man escaped their attention?

The advent of a new collector was a rare enough occasion but to get an old collector newly into one's own business was an even greater triumph. Presumably McMicking had bought from other auctioneers or privately through the trade but now they had snared him.

The Saturday brought more people and a lot of Harry's established American clients, most of whom were interested in Mediterranean antiquities. They politely looked at the central cabinet but nobody was sufficiently interested to ask to see anything of the hoard more closely.

His entire afternoon and early evening was spent with clients in a small room off the exhibition area, drinking cup after cup of tea ordered from room service. He secured commission bids from five clients for thirty-three of the lots in the general sale and several requests for telephone bids on a dozen or more other lots. Harry couldn't help thinking that they probably would not have bid if they hadn't seen the items themselves and that perhaps the New York visit was something that they would have to do for every larger sale in the future after all. It certainly was not a cheap exercise with air freight charges and hotel bills but Sam Reid was in control of that, Harry just did the work.

The Sunday was a repeat of Saturday, cups of tea and coffee in the small room, commission bids, mostly, annoyingly, on the same lots as those he had received the previous day and none on the hoard. A coin collector looked at all the pennies for what seemed like hours before declaring that it wasn't his particular interest but was "nice to have a look" at the rarities.

The last few hours dragged by with a trickle coming through and at six o'clock, the closing time, a team of shippers arrived to pack the whole lot up again to get the Aer Lingus flight the next day, the same flight that Harry was to get from JFK at six fifty in the evening. The exhibition was demounted and packed within four hours, the paperwork signed, customs satisfied that everything that came into the country was going out again and Harry had the hoard locked up in the hotel's jewellery safe.

Harry spent the next day at the Metropolitan Museum of Art, bought Patricia a present from Bloomingdales and answered several faxed questions from London whilst having a late lunch in Jeff Cane's office just round the corner from the Hotel Westbury.

Drew had sent through a request from Seamus Dullea to view the hoard pieces at his office rather than at the hotel in which Trotman's were holding the Dublin viewing, the Gresham in O'Connell Street, in order to have some privacy.

Harry immediately smelt a rat, he wanted them to himself to see if he could find enough earth to test its chemical composition. Citing security implications and time restrictions, Harry wrote back regretting that his request was impossible but that they may, of course, view the items at the hotel outside the public opening times.

They had wondered if the Irish authorities would seize the hoard on the suspicion that it had been looted. It had happened before when they successfully obtained an injunction to prevent the sale of an item in London on the suspicion that it was an archaeological find, to get it back to Dublin and discover that it had, in fact, been stolen from a Limerick museum some decades before and that the recovery was entirely due to the injunction that had been falsely, but fortuitously, given to them.

Harry was a stranger to Dublin but was met off the flight from New York by Drew who had been doing Jeff Cane's job at the Gresham, setting up the hired cabinets the previous day and arranging media interviews, without any pretence at trying to sell the other antiquities.

Julia and two porters from London joined them for the "Private View" cocktail party, this time for only about one hundred and fifty people, those from their mailing list and some local celebrities invited by a Dublin publicist who was connected with Trotman's London publicity agents.

It was New York all over again; a few items were shown to people during the drinks party, a few people trickled through on the Friday but the Saturday and Sunday were busy, the obvious attraction being the hoard pieces.

Seamus had organised to see the hoard before the opening on Friday morning and it was manifestly apparent that he was not versed in the subject of Celtic or Anglo Saxon art nor did it seem that he was interested. He repeatedly returned to the subject of provenance and seemed to be annoyed that the items had been cleaned, which, he informed Harry, would have been in breach of the National Monuments (Amendment) Act of 1994 had they been found in Ireland.

'The taking them out of the country and failing to report and surrender them to the proper authorities is also an offence, and quite rightly so,' Harry added, bristling at Seamus' suggestions which were, of course, bulls-eye accurate.

'However,' he continued, 'we are told that these were uncovered prior to the introduction of the original act in 1930 and have been in England since that date. They fall outside Irish jurisdiction, therefore, on two counts.'

'That is if we are to believe it,' Seamus said smugly.

'We cannot prove otherwise,' Harry replied, the use of "we" being a clever ploy to think that they were all on the same side.

'Unfortunately not, due to the insensitive cleaning of the items.'

'Insensitive? I beg to differ. Works of art covered in pigeon shit are not exactly saleable. They were sensibly conserved and as far as I could see there were no earth accretions anyway. They would have been cleaned when they were discovered so it is quite possible that they have been cleaned several times. On the other hand, it is possible that they were never buried but found in a building by the vendor's great-grandfather. We are not fully acquainted with the facts of the find, not even if the pieces were found in Ireland.'

Seamus decided to give up the chase; Trotman's and their vendor had found a way around some of the toughest legislation in Europe regarding finds. If Seamus had found the slightest hint of earth adhering to any of the pieces then they were prepared to place an injunction on the hoard leaving the country for the second time and to carry out tests on the soil but that too had been foiled.

He left soon after the public viewing had started and passed Rosie on the steps of the hotel. He took her to the coffee lounge and told her that they were unable to obtain the hoard without paying for it, an option that they had discussed during their weekly meetings to chart progress.

'Are the British being helpful?' she asked.

'The British are being British; decidedly unhelpful. They haven't made up their minds about the hoard as they have not yet had the opportunity to view it.'

'But the idea of sharing it?' Rosie persisted.

'It received a rather derisory laugh but they didn't discount it. How are things here?'

'The same, "possibly but ..."'

'The sale is two weeks away!' he moaned, 'we're going to be the laughing stock of the academic world if we fail to secure this lot. Look at the publicity they're getting, television, newspapers, they're on the Late Late Show tomorrow night. Everybody in Ireland is going to know about the hoard and they'll all want it retained for the country without giving it much thought about how we are to do it.'

'It's not our concern what "the people" want', Rosie explained. 'In a day's time they will have forgotten about the whole thing. Our concern is that we have brought the hoard to the attention of our elected representatives and they, in turn, are weighing up the kudos it is going to give them to announce to the nation that they have spent a million plus euros of their money to keep it here.'

'Will they?' Seamus asked hopefully.

'I don't know. They'll jump at it if you've got the Brits. on side. Anyway, you've seen the actual things now, what are they like?'

'Uninspiring to the untrained eye. The coins are the size of a five cent piece,' Seamus said.

'What size did you think they were going to be?'

'Don't know. Like an old punt I suppose. There's no doubt that they're important for what they are but they don't grab me in particular.'

'Are you losing interest in them?' Rosie asked.

'It's been a long build up and when you get to see them they're small, that's the first impression but I'm never going to be able to lose interest in them with the pressure I've got from the curators.'

They finished their coffees and Rosie went into the room where the viewing was being held. She bought a catalogue although she already had one in her office and made directly for the cabinet holding the hoard. The cabinet was a six foot high square sectioned glass case with two glass shelves. The uppermost shelf had the three artefact lots, the next the four coins, placed on a large black velvet tray. Rosie could see the point about the size but put it down to the fact that the cabinet was too large and the pieces were a bit lost amongst all that glass.

She couldn't pretend to understand the coins but she had been informed by the museum numismatist that they were extremely important and that Belfast had two of the raven types but not a triquetra type and Dublin had none. The penny of Edmund was also not represented in Dublin and whilst they were not pursuing Middle Anglo-Saxon period coinage, the fact that it was found in conjunction with the other three, and possibly in Ireland, made it desirable to his department.

Rosie could see the allure of the paten and cross but found the gold mounts difficult to place in context when the rest of the book cover was not there. She was twice asked if she would like to have a closer look at the contents of the cabinet by different people and she declined but there was something about the cross that urged her to touch it and she asked another man if she could hold it. He unlocked the cabinet and pulled the perspex mount to the edge of the shelf before taking the cross off it. She cradled it her hands, surprised at its weight.

'Who would have owned this?' she asked the man.

'That's one of the frustrating things about my job,' Harry replied, 'I can talk to them but they can't talk back. My guess, and it's entirely that, is that it was owned by somebody of great importance who had been an early Christian convert.'

'A monk?'

'That I doubt. A king perhaps.'

'Or queen?'

'I hadn't given it much thought, but a queen perhaps. It has a manly look about it. I would have thought that a female cross would be smaller, more petite.'

Rosie wasn't sure about that. She handed the cross back to Harry and watched him hook it back onto the stand, push it back into the case and lock the door.

'I much prefer the cross to the paten but you've got more money on the latter,' she said.

'That's because we have a ready buyer for the paten,' he answered indiscreetly.

'Oh?'

'Well, it should be reunited with its chalice.'

'The Ardagh Chalice in the National Museum?'

'Yes.'

'Holding the nation to ransom?'

Harry laughed.

'No, not at all, but we do have them at a slight disadvantage. This stuff is so rare that it is impossible to price so one guesses and doubles it. It's remarkable how right we are sometimes.'

'And other times?' Rosie asked.

'Either it goes unsold and we have egg on our faces or it sells for ten times the estimate and we should have egg on our faces but we wear a grin instead.'

Rosie was about to leave when she tested to see if Harry could be any more careless.

'Have you got much interest in the hoard?'

'Apart from the obvious, er, a gentleman in New York and the coins have all got bids on them. The cross and mounts don't have any bids on them thus far but it's early days. We just hope that your Government does some sums in time.'

'I'll see what I can do about that, thank you so much for everything,' she said leaving the room.

Harry asked everybody if they knew who she was but they all shrugged their shoulders and she had not left her name. How was she going to see what she could do if she wasn't a part of the government? And if she was a member of the government what on earth had he told her that he shouldn't?

17

The television lights were causing sweat to break out on Harry's forehead as they prepared a live cross to the news. The crew had been setting up for nearly an hour making the viewing crowded and difficult and not a few of the viewers were shielding their faces from the camera although it was not running. Harry supposed that they were probably meant to be elsewhere and didn't want to be seen looking at antiquities.

'This is the paytern?' the cameraman asked.

'Pa-ten,' Harry corrected, 'like the general.'

'Right, paten. And these are the coins, small aren't they? What would one of those have bought you?'

Harry had to admit that he was stumped on that one.

'Which one is worth the most?' the man asked.

Harry picked out the triquetra type penny and explained its rarity which seemed to go over the man's head as he played with the cross pretending it to be a medal and hanging it over his left breast pocket. Harry then explained the thinking behind the origin of the cross at which the man nodded at the right moments.

'You'll be talking to a government official in the studio, you'll be able to see her on the monitor over there and we'll fit you with an earpiece so you can respond to her and Padraig,' the cameraman informed Harry.

'I thought we were just going to talk about the items and the sale. Why do I need to talk to a government official?'

'Because we want to do a story on archaeological finds and the laws in this country and this is the perfect opportunity.'

Harry did not like the idea at all.

'You'd better not intimate that these are subject to that law,' he warned.

'Aren't they?'

'Of course they're not!' Harry exclaimed, 'otherwise I wouldn't have them in Dublin, would I?'

'I don't know. There are moves afoot to compel you to leave them in the country,' the man said.

A girl was fiddling around his back with an earpiece.

'If there is one mention, even a hint of these being illegally taken from the ground or out of Ireland, I will instruct our company's solicitors to sue you, the television company, the government, basically anything that moves and breathes. It is a grossly unfair accusation and you've got me here under false pretences.'

The girl asked him to try the ear piece and he heard, faintly somebody doing a sound check.

'I'm not in charge of the discussion, Padraig calls the shots.'

'Well, you call Padraig and tell him that the merest whiff of possible law breaking concerning this hoard is going to mean trouble.'

The cameraman sat in silence looking at the hoard laid out before him.

'So?' Harry asked.

'I can't contact him, we're going live to air and he's reading the news. Don't worry, try and concentrate on the objects themselves. Now which ones were actually made in Ireland?'

Harry ran through them again and the cameraman said that they would concentrate on the paten and the cross. They then waited for ten minutes before they were put on standby for the studio.

'In London in two week's time, some valuable Irish Celtic artefacts are to be put up for public auction. Amongst the seven lots is a paten, quite possibly that which began its life in the 8th century with the Ardagh Chalice, perhaps one of the best known Irish Celtic artefacts in the National Museum.

'We are joined by Harry Knox, a director of Trotman's who are to sell the items. Mr Knox, may I ask you who is putting these artefacts up for sale?'

'An English gentleman. He prefers to remain anonymous.'

'They were found in Ireland?'

'Apparently. The furthest we can go back to is 1900, their history prior to that is unknown unfortunately.'

'They are all Irish?'

'No, the paten is, without a doubt, Irish; the gold cross is possibly Irish; the other pieces originated in England. The coins have dated the deposit to about 945 A.D. which rather confirms the thinking that the Ardagh Chalice was deposited about then, they were obviously split at that time.'

'I see, now the law states that anything found under the ground is the property of the State. Is that correct?'

'As from 1930, yes,' Harry said.

'But these are not covered by that law?'

'They would be if owned by somebody in Ireland. Failure to report an archaeological find and to trade in unreported finds is quite rightly illegal. However, these have been in England and have therefore not come under that law.'

'If I may turn to you, Rosie Spillane, National Arts Funding Co-ordinating Director, what chances do we, the Nation, have of buying these?'

The camera turned to Rosie and Harry groaned when he saw her face on the monitor in front of him.

'We would like to say that we've got everything in place to buy them but they are going to be very expensive.'

'How expensive?' Padraig asked.

'A million pounds,' she replied simply.

'Or more,' Harry added.

'Yes, Mr Knox, take us through the hoard.'

Harry described the items and at the end of each description he added an estimated price. When he said that the three mounts would be worth one hundred thousand plus Padraig interrupted.

'But there's one missing!'

'Worth a lot more with the fourth,' Harry agreed.

'Who would buy these, surely they belong in a museum?'

'I couldn't agree more,' Harry said cheerfully, 'but not everybody is well off enough to donate such a valuable hoard to a museum and nor would somebody in England benefit from a tax trade-off in Ireland.'

'Ms Spillane, is there anything we can do, obviously they are important to the nation?'

'We're trying our best but there are no funds available at present. There are two weeks to go however and we may find a benefactor by then.'

'Lets hope we do,' Padraig said, 'thank you both for your time. In Brussels today ....'

Harry took the earpiece out of his ear and mopped his forehead with his handkerchief.

'That was alright wasn't it?' the cameraman asked.

'Yes,' Harry agreed.

'No mention of these belonging to the State already, eh?' he continued.

'No, governments can be dreadful bullies you know. They have bus loads of lawyers available at a few grand a day to keep the peasants quiet. Is Ireland the same?'

'There is a certain amount of it, yes, but it seems more prevalent on your side of the water. How do you establish ownership of something? I mean, if somebody raised his hand here in Ireland and said that he had sold these after the Act came into being what could you do?'

'I wouldn't bring them here for a start if I thought that what you have suggested was a possibility. It would then be between my vendor and your man, a court case and probably seizure of the goods. Ownership is extremely hard to prove unless one has supporting documentation. For all we know, these could have been stolen from somebody in 1900, dug up from somebody's land who did not receive any money for them, poached, as it were, from his land. Now if that person found out about it and passed the story down the generations, it is quite possible that somebody will come out of the woodwork and stake a claim to them, but I doubt it. The owner comes from, er, good stock.'

'British "good stock" made a particular habit of plundering Ireland over the centuries', the cameraman commented wryly.

A mystery had been answered for Paddy Hearn. Once warned off the collapsed cliff face he was intrigued as to why, and passing Seton's car on its way to the coast road he parked at Nisbet's Cove and made his way to the cliff with his metal detector. He had barely started when his machine told him of the presence of metal and over a large area. He dug about a foot down and revealed three old fashioned sieves, the sort used in nurseries. Somebody had been sieving the cliff fall.

He then recalled Seton's request for the use of his metal detector. He knew that it was virtually impossible to obtain a licence to operate such a machine and certainly not one for archaeological use unless one was attached to a government authority. Seton had obviously found something there with the aid of the sieves and if he had used those, there was little chance of finding anything else. He covered the area surrounding the sieves but found nothing and then walked down the slope to see if there were any signs of digging along the fence. About five feet above the beach he got another signal.

Just a few inches below the surface he found a gold coloured ring, two to three inches in diameter, set with coloured stones that he thought must be of Celtic origin. He put this in his pocket and continued the search for another half hour. A squall of rain soaked him to the skin as there was no shelter and he hadn't thought it worthwhile to make his way back to his van. He took the ring out of his pocket and let the rain wash away any earth still stuck to it. He could make out some raised decoration like intertwined ribbons set between the coloured stones. At the edges he could see silver under the gold and there was a hole in the base of the hinged section, presumably to fit some sort of pin, thereby making a brooch of sorts. Was this what Seton was trying to find?

The rain stopped and he thought about calling it a day but did another sweep further along the cliff fall for good measure without any success. He kept looking at the cliff and the area in which he found the sieves and the brooch. He calculated that anything buried beneath the grass on top of where the cliff used to be would end up in an area that he hadn't screened.

He moved over to where he thought he would strike and was there for less than a minute when his machine again spoke to him. He dug to about a foot deep but couldn't find anything and it was only when he ran his detector over the soil that he had extracted did he realise that he had missed the object. He sifted through the soil, made wet and cloying by the rain until his fingers felt something hard.

At first he thought it was another stone but when he rubbed the earth gold appeared. He took it to the sea's edge to wash away the dirt and found that he was holding a triangular plaque decorated with the image of a man. There were holes in the plaque, obviously for securing it to something but its use and date of origin was a mystery to Paddy Hearn.

He had searched the cliff face for many hours after that but found nothing more. That he was in possession of archaeological items he was in no doubt and he had a friend in Dublin who would take them off his hands although he was a miserable payer. He didn't, however, ask any questions, and if Paddy was caught with such items he knew that it would be jail, again, because he was no longer licensed to use his metal detector and he had told the local garda that he had sold it to a dealer "in town".

He telephoned his friend in Dublin to arrange a meeting but he was brusque and unfriendly, stating that he was busy and for Paddy not to call again. Half an hour later the friend called him from a phone box to tell him that he was under surveillance and that he was sure that his telephone was bugged, hence the theatrics when Paddy had phoned him at home. He said that he would take the brooch and the other item but not for a few weeks, not until the gardai were off his tail.

Paddy placed the two items in an old tin in the shed, put a piece of cardboard over them, filled the rest of the tin with old nails and put it back on the shelf. They remained there for six weeks, awaiting the call from his friend, when a chance glimpse at his television set during the news told him what the triangular gold item was all about. He bought the newspaper the next day and read the report of a hoard found somewhere in Ireland at the turn of the century, a hoard now worth about a million pounds.

In the hoard were three book mounts and, judging by the photographs, he had the fourth. He was also of the opinion that the hoard was not found in 1900 but a few months ago and that Seton and his English friends were the finders.

He saw the items again on the television on Saturday night and the expert interviewed mentioned that the three mounts would be worth a lot more than one hundred thousand pounds if the fourth one was with them.

Far better, Paddy thought, than selling his fourth mount to his mean friend in Dublin who was under watch anyway, he would sell it to Seton who might be a bit embarrassed to find that he had broken the law by exporting the hoard and not reporting it. He, Paddy, knew the law; he had served a prison sentence when caught and had studied the charges to make sure that he never got caught again.

One hundred thousand euros sounded about the right price for his fourth corner and then he'd get the brooch to London and sell it there, much more sensible than giving it away for a few hundred quid to the scoundrels in Dublin.

He didn't like the Nisbets, he never had: They were too smart for their own good, too important to talk to the likes of him the same way they talked to their own and arrogant by naming a geographical feature after themselves and their house a castle as if they were lords of the manor. If he had been around during the troubles in the twenties then he would have made sure that the castle was burned down and the Nisbets no longer felt secure in the area. But everybody said what good people they were and how they had kept the rural community around their property going and how their importance had brought benefits to the district earlier than other remote areas.

Now he had them but it wasn't going to be blackmail; he was going to sell them the mount and one hundred thousand would buy his silence as well, or at least until he needed some more money. How would young Seton react, he thought? He couldn't go to the gardai otherwise he'd be guilty of betraying his English friend and Paddy could say that he had found the corner lying on the ground near the cliff fall and was only trying to sell it. It couldn't be considered archaeological if he didn't have to dig for it.

The Sunday papers were full of the hoard and how sad it was that Ireland could not afford to buy back its heritage whilst the country gave millions of euros a year to other countries in aid. The coins were described as being less than an inch wide and one of them was worth seven and a half thousand pounds.

Temptation got the better of him and he set off for the cliff for one last search just to make sure he hadn't missed anything. It was a bitter day with winds coming down from the north bringing intermittent showers. There was nobody on the beach and the tide was out. He walked along the edge where people sheltered from the westerlies and got to the cliff face just as another shower descended. He waited for the worst to abate before commencing his final search of the area. He was sure that he wasn't going to find anything and the first hour's work confirmed his hunch. He moved further along the cliff towards the rocks to the west and was working out a plan to tackle the area when he saw movement to his right.

Seton Nisbet was descending the scree that formed the cliff, his gaze fixed upon Paddy.

'I thought I told you not to come here,' Seton said, whilst still some distance away.

'I'm on common land,' Paddy explained.

'But you haven't been, I've been watching you go over the slope, precisely where I asked you not to go.'

'An' why would that be?'

'Because it's dangerous.'

'An' it wouldn't be anything to do wi' this now?' Paddy said, pulling the fourth mount from his pocket.

Seton looked at it and feigned disinterest.

'What's that?'

'Well, would I be after t'inking, Mr Nisbet, tha' your friend had taken the udder t'ree to London for sale?'

'What other three, what friend?'

'Now, now, Mr Nisbet, all I have t' do is take this to th' gards an' tell them where it was I found it and isn't it a grand thing too as the others were coming up for sale in London, smuggled, no doubt, out d' country an' I wonder who'd be doin' da smugglin'?'

'You're speaking double Dutch, Paddy. Smuggling and gards and other three bits. Did you have a few too many last night at O'Driscolls?'

'I t'ink, Mr Nisbet, tha' ye oughta start listenin' now. Ye warned me off dis cliff coz y'know that there was more t' find. Well, I found it an' here t'is', Paddy said holding up the mount.

'I'm completely lost Paddy. I must ask you to leave the cliff alone, it is unsafe and it is technically my land although it's not much use to me now,' Seton said coolly.

'A hundred t'ousand euros an' the fourth bit is yours.'

'A hundred thousand euros? What are you on about Paddy?'

'Ye gi' me one hundred t'ousand euros an' I'll give ye the mount; the last part, an' not tell anybody where they all come from. Is it a deal?'

'You're completely mad Paddy. Take it to the gards and tell them how you found it whilst you're at it.'

'A million pounds, Mr Nisbet. What's your share or do ye get th' lot? Ye won't get nuttin' if I turn ye in.'

Seton was beginning to lose his nerve and to disguise the fact he became more belligerent.

'Look Paddy, I don't know what it is that you're on about but you have been trespassing on my land with that machine. I don't know about the use of it but I will charge you with trespass if you don't get off it and stay off it. Do you understand?'

'Well Mr Nisbet, it seems you're missin' a rare opportunity. I'll have no hesitation to take the piece to the gardai and they'll have two weeks to stop the sale and then they'll start their inquiries 'bout who exactly is selling the pieces. D'ye t'ink it'll come back t'ye?'

'Please get off my land,' Seton said. He was trying to weigh up the situation but needed to talk to Jonathan so thought that bluff would be the best offensive tactic.

'I'm not on your land,' Paddy replied petulantly, puzzled by Seton's seeming indifference about his threat to expose the origin of the hoard.

Seton returned to the beach and strode back to his car parked alongside Paddy's van. He thought of nobbling his vehicle but was not quite sure how and to what purpose other than to antagonise him.

Seton thought that Jonathan took the news stoically. It was only after ten minutes of discussion between the two, large moments of which were in silence as they collected their thoughts, did Jonathan say that they would have to pay him the one hundred thousand but could only do so when the proceeds of the sale had been passed over to them.

'That's admitting to Hearn that I am involved!' Seton complained.

'No it's not but it does admit that you know who is involved. It could be argued that you wanted to reunite the fourth corner for altruistic reasons. It doesn't mean that you are in anyway involved and the payment scheme I have devised will distance you from any financial implications. For goodness sakes, we could tell Hearn that we are going along with his blackmail, sell the stuff and then tell him to go and see the gards with the fourth mount. There's little he can do about it, for all they know the first three could have been found a hundred years ago and through modern technology it was possible to go over the ground and find the fourth.'

'Highly implausible,' Seton said, 'and by answering Hearn's threat we admit some guilt. I'll see what I can do with him, we may be able to chisel him down a bit.'

'Chiselling is a very appropriate word when it comes to Mr Paddy Hearn,' concluded Jonathan.

Seton pondered his next move. He wasn't at all keen on giving in to Hearn because he could never be sure that the man wouldn't hold his hand out for a bit of hush money each time they passed in the street. What he did need, however, was the fourth mount, without that Hearn could do little, but with it he could undo all their dreams. He drove back down to the beach but the van was no longer there. He then travelled west along the coast road where O'Driscoll's bar stood in isolation. There were a number of cars outside but no van. The clouds to the north were blackening as an overture to another drenching.

Seton wasn't sure which house on the north side of the coast road was Paddy's. He rarely had occasion to go to the other side. The phone book only told him the house name and the community area which covered over thirty square miles so he traversed the roads that criss-crossed the plateau between the valley leading to Nisbets Cove and one that ran parallel to the coast in the hope of seeing his van or the house name *Corr Eisc Teachin*.

In the end, he stopped at the house of a man from whom he once purchased some cattle and asked him if he knew which house was Paddy Hearn's. The man knew and started to give directions, then he changed his mind and whilst thinking about the corrected route, confirmed that it was Paddy Hearn that he was after, and Seton added that he drove a blue van. At that he was given precise directions, completely at variance to the first set and Seton impatiently drove off as though time was at a premium.

He waited at a very dangerous cross-roads where the driver coming out of the minor road had to edge his way forward to see if any traffic was coming from either direction. It was known locally as "skid crossroads" due to the number of tyre marks on the road in all directions as those not familiar with the area found immediate peril and panicked. Nobody in living memory had ever seen an accident there but there must have been some faster beating hearts after some near misses.

Beyond the crossroads, two hundred yards up the road to the right, Seton could see a house surrounded by ash trees. An old shed stood behind, on the side of which was stacked lengths of driftwood, there must have been tonnes of it and fair few years' accumulation. He gingerly crossed the road and was still in first gear travelling up the road towards the house when Hearn's blue van pulled out of his driveway going in the same direction as Seton. He followed on a few hundred yards behind and when he had taken a few turns down ever narrowing lanes, Seton stopped in the gateway of one of his own fields as the road into which Hearn had last turned led only to the beach. He would give him ten minutes and then catch him again on the cliff face and threaten him with prosecution unless he handed over the mount.

The blue van was parked in its usual spot and was again on its own. The sea had assumed a grey-green colour as a weakened sun found its way through the streaks of dark blue-grey clouds as they retreated to the south. There was more rain to come, Seton thought, as he got out of his car. He walked up to his fields above Ballingaddy and made his way parallel to the beach so that he would come to the top of the cliff. Fifty yards from the precipice a downpour reduced his visibility to a few hundred yards out to sea and he could just see the other side of the beach. He stood looking down onto the cliff fall and the Cowrie Beach but there was no Paddy Hearn. He walked along the cliff top to the point where he could see all the beach and the route that Hearn would have taken had he gone back to his van but there was no sight of him in that direction either.

The rain got heavier, so heavy that it formed pools of water on the sand across which drifts of rain would shimmer like a veil in wind. Seton knew that there was no shelter below him so sat on the cliff top as though by so doing he wouldn't get as wet. The rain persisted for another ten minutes before abruptly ending with the curtain of cloud parting to permit sunlight to return and give some colour to the sodden landscape.

Seton stood to stretch his legs and there below him was Paddy Hearn, his back towards him scanning the lower slopes of the cliff fall. Seton descended the cliff and called out but Hearn couldn't hear him due to the wind and that he was wearing his earphones. It wasn't until he was closer than ten feet away that Hearn acknowledged his presence but instead of being contrite about being caught yet again on Seton's land he crossly took the headphones off.

'What do ye want?'

'You're on my land again, Paddy,' Seton said.

'I t'ink ye might be takin' liberties there, Mr Nisbet,' Paddy replied, his confidence boosted by Seton's return; he had come to talk business.

'Oh, I don't think so. I think it's time for me to prosecute you, try and recover some of my costs of public indemnity insurance, the premiums of which are artificially raised to cover the likes of you.'

'Have ye come t' talk about my proposition?'

'No, none of that,' Seton said, waving his hand to dismiss the suggestion, 'I've come to collect the sieves and threaten you with prosecution. Another stretch in jail, I shouldn't wonder. Your family will miss you, no doubt.'

'I don't have no family, Mr Nisbet, ye know that. If that is to be the case then I'll see ye there for your part in smugglin' th' art out da country. An' Mr and Mrs Armstrong too.'

'How did you know about them?' Seton asked, dropping all pretence now; the gloves were off.

'Brendan Hassett. I got their address in England as well, all the information for the gards to stop the sale, y' know?'

Seton was instantly deflated.

'Alright. I can offer you the one hundred thousand euros but can only pay you once the goods are sold. I don't have that sort of money, I don't have one tenth of it. We put the fourth corner in a deposit box for which we both have one of two keys necessary to lock it. My bank in Cork has boxes like that. When we get paid, you get paid and I get the fourth piece back.'

Hearn pretended to think for a while.

'Only the price is one hundred and fifty t'ousand, now I have the udder information, ye know? And I'll be keepin' the piece for the duration.'

'No, Paddy! One hundred thousand and a safe place for the corner until you get paid. Otherwise it's all off!' Seton said angrily, although he had suspected that Hearn was never to be trusted. It was alright to know that Seton was involved in the smuggling because he could defend himself but if Jonathan and Tavie's names were involved it would be an easy matter for the police to check against Trotman's vendors list.

'Ah, now then Mr Nisbet, I'm holding all the trump cards y' know. T'would be inadvisable for ye to underestimate me.'

Seton had been told that once before, that time by an older boy at school who had found him smoking by the squash courts and had blackmailed him demanding the remainder of the packet, a valuable commodity to a fifteen year old.

As on that occasion, Seton reacted instinctively and his right fist swung wildly at Hearn's face, connecting between his mouth and chin that sent him spinning to the ground, lying face upwards. Seton was onto him, Hearn's eyes were no longer shaded by their bushy eyebrows but wide open in bewilderment until clenched shut in preparation for the next blow, this time from a flattened piece of slate that Seton's hand had found. The stone, aimed at his left temple, crunched something inside his head and he exhaled heavily as if life had been awaiting the opportunity to escape his form.

Seton's rage vanished as it dawned upon him that the figure at his feet was quite still. He was scared to find out if he had killed him or not and in the end tentatively placed his fingers on his neck to see if he could feel any pulse, checking several positions just in case he had been feeling in the wrong place. He then leant over and placed his ear to his chest but the wind was such that he thought it would have been impossible to hear even if the heart was beating hard and strong.

He sat on the stony beach beside the body and stared at the sea rising like a cobra prior to a strike and crashing down onto the slate's vertical edges. He knew that he had to dump the body in the sea, metal detector and all, as though he had slipped, knocked his head on a rock as he fell and plunged into the surf. He would leave his spade on the beach.

Loathsome as it was, he searched every pocket for the fourth piece but all Hearn had on him was some cash and the keys to his van. The fourth piece could be there, he thought, but could he risk being caught going through his van when a day or so later his dead body was found on the rocks? Should he dash up to the van, have a look and return to put the keys back into Hearn's pocket before hauling him into the sea? There was the risk that somebody could come walking around the headland from the west and discover the body on the beach before he could return to dump it. His finger prints were on the keys now, he might as well search the van in the remaining daylight and then return to dump the body.

Searching the van took only a few minutes as the beach was empty and there were only some documents and a few maps in the glove compartment. Seton had taken the precaution of wearing his thick leather gloves, mindful of fingerprints on the dashboard and other hard surfaces. There was no gold corner in the van unless it was cleverly concealed and Seton didn't have the time to take the vehicle apart.

He returned to the body as yet another shower descended upon him. Paddy Hearn was a slight man, short of stature and not well nourished but shifting his limp form over the twenty feet of rocks was exhausting even to somebody as fit as Seton. By the time he had got him to the water's edge, Hearn's trouser legs were torn and his boots scuffed by the slate. Seton heaved him over the last edge and he rolled down the four feet of slate into the water, his metal detector following him. As his body settled into the sea it turned to be face upwards which Seton thought wasn't right, didn't bodies float face down? There was little he could do about it as the ebbing tide took Hearn further out to sea with every back wash, bobbing like a piece of driftwood.

Seton retraced his steps to make sure that there was no sign of him having dragged the body over the rocks. He got back to the spot where he fell, there hadn't been any blood but Seton kicked a few of the stones about and as a final gesture, picked up the piece of slate that he had used as a club and threw it into the sea, in the other direction to which the body was taken.

He hastened his way back across the beach, knowing that by the next morning his footsteps would be obliterated by the next high tide. It was getting very dark but Seton didn't turn the lights of his car on until he was past the first few houses at least. The curtains were drawn in the Hassett's house and the smell of burning turf told him that they were ensconced for the night.

He drove up to the entrance to Castle Nisbet but instead of going in he drove past and made his way to Skid Crossroads, turned left and drove into the gravelled driveway of Hearn's house.

He waited for a dog to appear in case Hearn kept one at home, he certainly never had one when Seton had met him on the beach and, all being quiet, he donned his fencing gloves again and tried the back door to the house. It was fortunately unlocked, as a good number of permanently lived-in houses in the district were, the contents hardly alluring to your city-bred crook, and Seton walked into what looked like the kitchen from the gloomy light let in from the window. He couldn't make his mind up whether to close the curtains and turn on the lights or fetch his torch from his car. He decided that anybody passing and seeing a torchlight was going to be immediately suspicious. He drew the curtain of the window overlooking the road although Seton couldn't see another light from there and turned on the overhead light.

The kitchen was sparten, a range providing heat, a single table in the middle of the room at which there were only two chairs and an empty glass standing at the end nearest the heat. On the mantelpiece above the range was a row of pewter mugs and some commemorative porcelain vases from various spots around the Irish coast. These contained pencils and old betting slips, rubber bands and paper clips but no gold mount.

He opened the door onto a corridor, across which was Hearn's sitting room obviously not widely used as there were few signs of immediate occupation. Seton walked down the corridor to a bedroom which was used and was presumably Hearn's. There were some sepia photographs of a 1920's and 1930's couple, the later images including a child, Hearn and his parents no doubt, thought Seton. He went through his chest of drawers and then a modest wardrobe, patting each pocket of his suit and jacket and upending each of the three pairs of shoes lined up at the bottom of the cupboard.

The bathroom revealed nothing, nor did a spare room which had only a bed and mattress in it. Beyond the kitchen was a small larder, the floor space of which was taken up with coal. There were two rows of shelves along two of the walls which were largely empty except for a few tins of paint and a pile of tiles left over from his bathroom renovation.

There was no gold mount. Perhaps he had already given it to the gardai - no, that couldn't be as the sale would have been stopped and Seton called in for questioning. Somewhere, somewhere in the life of Paddy Hearn, a miserable life of isolation, there was a piece of gold that was highly incriminating. It wasn't however, within the grasp of the person it incriminated, or if it was, it was doing its damnest to not let itself be known.

Seton turned all the lights off and opened the curtains once more to a pitch black sky. He left the house and groped around for his car in the back yard such was the density of the night. He backed the car down the driveway by the use of the reversing light only and into the road only turning his lights on once past Hearn's house.

He had murdered a man for possibly nothing.

18

The pre-auction publicity gained by Trotman's for the hoard and the general sale was unprecedented for them in New York and Dublin but an auction-weary press in Britain largely ignored the offering after their initial interest. There was an exchange of views in the letter pages about the attribution of the workmanship of the cross although Harry could see that nobody was able to add any more to the discussion that Thornton Bethune hadn't already dismissed on one count or other.

The three days' viewing in London was well attended by private clients and the trade and there were several visits by the academics who argued furiously about the origins of the mounts and cross in front of the cabinet in which they were displayed, thus preventing others from viewing the treasures.

Harry had noticed the absence of interest from British institutions and wondered if the Irish had managed to get to them. Various curators did make their presence known to him but gave the hoard only a cursory glance and had attended Trotman's rooms as a courtesy. They had played these sorts of games with him before, particularly when he had sold a vase by the Berlin painter, which everybody agreed was an exemplary piece of Athenian red-figure ware but was too rich for any museum to buy. In the end, a museum was the underbidder at twice the estimated price.

On that occasion the piece went to Roy Camble, a Scottish businessman, or, more accurately, a crook whose major business was to evade paying tax in each country his activities extended. He had a collection of art and antiques that had one unifying theme; cost. Everything had to be a world record for that particular object and the vase by the Berlin painter didn't disappoint him. It was quite possible that he could wish to own the cross or paten but no-one ever knew of his interest in an item until a cheque from an off-shore company arrived to pay for it, attached to a "With Compliments" slip from his office.

Drew assured Harry that he had sufficient interest in the coins to ensure that they sold. He, hopefully, had Mr McMicking on the paten, as well as any Irish institutional interest, but nothing in writing on the mounts or the cross. The general sale was going to take care of itself with only one major item lacking any known interest. He was desperate not to disappoint Jonathan and Octavia, the latter in particular and had begun to doubt his estimating abilities; perhaps he had gone too far and had given the hoard more importance than it, in fact, had. He couldn't have done a better catalogue, he told himself as he flicked through it the afternoon before the sale.

It was at this time that he wished they had a register of who had attended the viewing, if only to see who hadn't made it. Auctions always sprang up surprises with clients buying items outside their area of interest because they had a bit of cash at the time and because they liked them. There were a few habitual buyers, people who loved to spend money and instead of wasting it on yet another spin around the Caribbean courtesy of the Cunard Line, they bought themselves a trinket in the form of an Assyrian seal or piece of Roman glass. They didn't, however, spend a hundred thousand pounds or four hundred thousand pounds on some speculatively Anglo-Saxon or Celtic trinkets.

'Do answer that phone, Julia,' he asked his secretary although he was closer to the instrument than she was.

She picked up the entire thing and placed it in his lap, unanswered.

'Yes?' he demanded.

'Is that you Mr Knox?'

'Yes.'

'It's Alf at the viewing,' as though Harry didn't recognise the Dublin accent of Trotman's oldest porter.

'Afternoon Alf.'

'Dere's a man t'see you.'

'Down there? Who is he?'

'I'd say he's one of dem rock stars. He didn' give a name.'

'I'll be down right now Alf, you tell him that.'

'Right,' he said before hanging up.

Harry didn't know any rock stars but then to Alf, anybody not in a suit but who looked the slightest bit prosperous had to be a rock star. It was David Reeves, dressed vaguely as would a rock star on his day off.

'What brings you here?' Harry inquired whilst offering a silent prayer to the organiser of good fortune; the patient Sundays had paid off and he had David Reeves in his building. It was a start.

'Thanks for these,' he said waving the two well thumbed catalogues.

'You've read them?' he said.

'Not 'arf. Bloody fantastic reading. Did you write all this stuff?'

'Not all of it. Professor Bethune wrote the three entries for the Viking Hoard, I only wrote the preface. I did most of the entries for the other sale.'

'Yer, triffic stuff. Where's this hoard then?' David asked looking around the room. Harry took him to the cabinet containing the hoard lots, for once not obscured from view by gesticulating geriatrics and got the key from the porter standing to one side.

He took each piece out and explained the more subtle points of design on each lot. It was obvious to Harry that the coins were of no interest to him, just the artefacts. They spent half an hour on those three lots and Harry was again impressed with David's capacity to learn, understand and process that information at such a speed that the questions he asked were more intelligent than a lot of those asked by people who made a living analysing Anglo Saxon metalwork.

Harry showed his enthusiastic client around the lots in the general sale in which he showed a polite interest but before leaving he returned to the hoard cabinet and stared for a few minutes through the glass, declining Harry's offer to get them out again.

'I might give you a call this evening at home,' he said in the foyer.

'Not too late, I've got a long day tomorrow,' Harry replied.

As David left the building a pretty girl entered, clutching the catalogue of the Viking Hoard. She acknowledged Harry by extending her right hand.

'Thank you so much for the catalogue, I've been reading it for two weeks. What a wonderful job you must have,' she said.

Harry must have given away the fact that he hadn't the first clue who she was.

'Rebecca Simon,' she reminded him.

'Of course, I apologise. I've been in three countries in the past three weeks and must have met three thousand people. I'm not usually this obtuse.'

'I'm afraid to say that I am,' she said.

'Harry Knox,' he said.

'Yes, yes, I recall now. Where are the lots being viewed?'

Harry took her to the saleroom and led her to the hoard cabinet. He was again given the key by the porter, who had trouble taking his eyes of his bosses' client, and Harry opened the door.

'I'd really like to see the cross,' Rebecca said.

Harry reached into the cabinet and extracted the cross, placing it in her outstretched hand. He started his spiel on the workmanship and the reasons for attributing it to somebody working in the British Isles but it was obvious that she wasn't listening. All her thoughts and attentions were devoted to the cross, she cared not from whence it came and that it was a Christian symbol, to her it was a fine piece of gold jewellery and as gold was the foundation upon which her family's fortune was built, she considered it apt to purchase the cross for their pension fund. She had met with some opposition within the family to consider investing in such an item but she had won them over, as she was likely to do, by her analysis of the decorative arts market and, in particular, the spectacular rises in price of one-off items when they appeared every fifteen to twenty years.

The cross was as beautiful as she remembered, perhaps more so now that the money to purchase it had been granted by their fund manager. Hopefully, within twenty four hours she would be holding it in the knowledge that she could hold it for the next fifteen years. Fate had brought them together and money was going to ensure that it stayed that way.

'We cross now to Ms Spillane, the National Arts Funding Co-ordinating Director. Good evening.'

'Good evening Padraig.'

'Tell us, Ms Spillane, the so-called Viking Hoard is to be sold tomorrow. When we spoke a fortnight ago, you had no funds available to return the items to Ireland. What is the situation now?'

'We are still well short of the necessary funds to regain the hoard. We might be able to buy a part of it, quite a small part, but certainly do not have enough to consider the hoard as a whole.'

'The hoard is made up of several pieces, is it necessary to purchase it all?'

'Well Padraig, it would be preferable; its interest to historians is its composition but it appears that it will be split up. It is very sad.'

'There was talk of there being a joint effort by the British and Irish governments to purchase the hoard. What has come of that?'

'It never really got off the ground. Such co-operation has never been sought before and the complications were such that time has defeated us. Whoever purchases the hoard may lend it to one of our institutions but it appears that we are not going to be able to have it here on a permanent basis.'

'As you said, Ms Spillane, a sad occasion.'

'Regrettably so.'

'Thank you for your time.'

Rosie took the earpiece out and was helped by an assistant with the television crew to unwire her. They had curiously chosen to film the interview outside her office in Merrion Street with traffic passing behind her back and the close to zero temperature making the wait to the cross to the studio miserable.

The news she had to deliver was no more cheering as the Finance Department had informed her earlier in the day that they couldn't arrange 'a special', a one-off payment for an extraordinary item. Rosie changed 'couldn't' to 'wouldn't' when she passed the news on. They had all done their sums and had come to the conclusion that they had a quarter of a million euros to spend and that it was foolish to throw that money away to buy something that they didn't really want; the only items they could afford being the gold mounts.

She went back into her office to collect her things prior to going home. Most people had left and the sounds of activity were confined to the cleaning staff. The catalogue of the hoard lay on her desk, the pages on which she had concentrated marked with dark pink "Post-it" stickers. She flicked through the illustrations again, convinced that it had been her greatest failure not getting the funding for that particular purpose. Everybody had been determined to make it happen and the submission was as powerful a document that could be conceived, perhaps, in the end, it had been too forceful and the faceless men and women who wrote "No" at the bottom of the page did so because they felt threatened.

'Rosie Spillane,' she said, having picked up the ringing telephone without disturbing her thoughts.

'Ms Spillane? I have the Taoiseach, please hold the line,' the lady the other end said.

'Ms Spillane? We haven't met, I must remedy that soon.'

'Good evening Taoiseach,' she said and was about to remind him that they had sat next door to each other at a dinner a few years ago.

'I've just seen the report on the news about the Viking Hoard,' he said.

'Yes?'

'Presumably you asked for funding through your department?'

'Yes.'

'And Finance turned it down. Why?'

'Usual. No funds available for the arts.'

'Umm. The Finance Minister is in Paris today. How much is needed, in total?'

'One and a quarter million to be safe.'

'Sterling?'

'Sterling.' Rosie confirmed.

There was a silence.

'It's not my field at all Ms Spillane. Are these very important to Ireland?'

'I believe so, as does everybody concerned except the Finance Department.'

'Ah, yes, Finance, we all have problems with them, you are not alone there. The sale is tomorrow?'

'Yes.'

'Who would you get to bid, do you have to pay them a commission as well?'

'We have dealers who buy paintings in London. We pay a five per cent commission.'

'That's a lot of money for a morning's work!'

'I know,' Rosie said, it had been her reaction, too, when first told.

'Could you go?' he asked.

'I can't see why not.'

'Right. You have a maximum of one and a half million pounds to spend. I look forward to seeing the hoard and yourself on your return.'

'Even if I do manage to buy the hoard, Taoiseach, I won't be able to bring it back with me, we will have to apply for an export permit. It is quite possible that a permit will not be given and then the British government or an institution has six months to find the funds to purchase them. That time can be extended if they are well on their way to financing the purchase,' Rosie explained.

'Oh,' the Taoiseach replied, 'well, we'll have to cross that bridge when we come to it. I don't mind bending the ear of the British Prime Minister, we get on very well.'

'It might be a matter of the Prime Minister being tough with his arts minister.'

'Anyway, if the items are Irish how dare they bar their return to Ireland?' the Taoiseach asked.

'Only one item is definitely Irish and the British government are particularly good at stopping the export of items.'

'Let's get the hoard bought first. The very best of luck, that's what I tell the players at Lansdowne Road.'

'I hope I have better fortune,' Rosie replied.

'I'll put this in writing, can you give me your office fax number?'

Rosie gave him the number and he rang off, again wishing her good luck.

When she put the receiver back onto its cradle her first thought was that it was a hoax, probably perpetrated by a Finance Department official. She picked the phone up again and called Seamus Dullea's number but it went unanswered.

She then logged onto the internet to book her flight to London and, as she waited, the promised fax from the Taoiseach's office came through on the machine. There it was, £1.5m available for the items in the "Viking Hoard" to be bid for by Ms Rosie Spillane, National Arts Funding Co-ordinating Director.

She couldn't get on the early flight to Heathrow. Nor the 7.15 a.m. to Stanstead. There was a seat available on the 7.50 a.m. which got into Heathrow just after nine. That gave her plenty of time to get into the West End for the one o'clock start.

She packed up her briefcase throwing the much-stickered catalogue in last and was about to leave when she thought that she ought to take Seamus Dullea's original application because in it were the figures that he and his team had placed on each lot which would be the basis of her bidding the next day. She had only ever attended an auction once before; she accompanied her solicitor when he successfully bid for her on a house in Ballsbridge. It was all very well for her to direct seven figure sums to this or that project but to actually get to spend it and in so short a space of time was going to be a new experience.

Seton heard Janie singing a lullaby to their son, John, as he lay in his cot. As she was occupied he thought it would be a good time to call Jonathan with an update on the situation in Cork.

'The sale's tomorrow, The Ballingaddy Find turns to money,' Jonathan informed him unnecessarily.

'I know, but don't for Christsakes ever call it that,' Seton replied.

'What's happened to our blackmailer?'

'Hang on a minute,' Seton said, 'what do you know?'

'I don't know anything Seton, why so jumpy?'

'We don't have to worry about him any more. He was found drowned off the beach last week.'

'How did it happen?' Jonathan asked.

'It seems he slipped on the rocks, hit his head and fell into the water. His body was found by the lifeboat about a mile out from the shore. His van was parked outside Ballingaddy.'

'Have the gards found the mount, do you think?'

'They haven't mentioned it if they have,' Seton said, maintaining the lie.

'But we've got to get it back!' Jonathan said, 'it could ruin the whole thing.'

'I'll let you out of your misery. He hasn't got the mount or rather didn't have the mount either on him when he drowned, nor is it in his van or house. He had either already handed it in, which I doubt, or has hidden it and hidden it well.'

'Do I want to know how you know this?'

'No.'

'You'd better tell me if it affects the offering of the hoard,' Jonathan said.

Seton paused and strained an ear to work out where Janie was but couldn't hear anything.

'Let's say that I helped him into the water.'

'Oh God, Seton!'

'After I had killed him with a rock.'

'Oh bloody hell.'

'I didn't intend to, but I lost my cool. He upped the price to a hundred and fifty and I knew that it wouldn't be the last of it. We ended up struggling on the beach and I hit him a bit too hard. I searched him, his van and his house, there isn't a trace of the mount at all.'

'So, as far as we know, the gards may have found it?'

'Yes, but that doesn't mean anything. The fourth corner could have been separated from the other three at any time. The gards would only know what it is if they had seen the publicity on the others, but it's unlikely. If they send it to a museum then the story will be different,' Seton said.

His worry, from the time Hearn's body had been found, was that he hadn't searched his pockets thoroughly enough and that it was still on him when he threw him into the sea. He had been tempted to go round to the house once again but had no idea when, or if, the body would be found. He had noticed that the van was parked near the beach for two days before it disappeared and it was a full day before they announced his death, perhaps the gards were lying in wait to see if anybody entered his cottage.

It was then announced that his death wasn't being treated as suspicious, a local garda letting slip that with the absence of any family their investigations were to satisfy themselves only and that point had been reached. The fact that he was unlicensed to use a metal detector and such a machine was attached to his body when found spurred the authority's disinclination to investigate any further.

'I'm very sorry it's come to this,' Jonathan said glibly. 'It's all rather eerie, it's the second person who has died connected with this hoard. How are you?'

'I swing from confidence that they'll not investigate any further to terrible guilt, and dreadful thoughts that he has written everything down and the truth is there for everybody to see, somewhere, anyway.'

'It's over now Seton, we'll reap the benefits of it tomorrow. I spoke to the man in charge of the auction, he's very positive and is expecting some strong bidding. He said that the estimates might look conservative at the end of the day.'

'I'm not greedy, just the half mill. will do me.'

'Does Janie know about Hearn?'

'No, and I think it's unfair for her to have to. Isn't she an accessory or whatever if she does?'

'If Irish law is the same as English. Yes, I agree, best to keep this between us two. Why don't you come over for the sale? I'll pick you up at Heathrow on my way up to London. Is there a flight from Cork early in the morning?'

'It would be tempting fate, wouldn't it? I'm better off here. Call me when it's over, I'll be in for my lunch between one and two.'

'Who was that?' Janie asked, as Seton put the phone down.

'Jonathan, he was ringing with the news from the auctioneer.'

'I didn't hear the phone ring,' she said.

'It didn't much, I was standing next door to it. He says they are expecting a good result. Is John asleep?'

'At last. What are you going to do with the money Seton? How will you explain your sudden wealth?'

'I'll spend it so slowly that nobody will notice. Jonathan has it all sorted out,' Seton said, as he had said on twenty occasions to his wife before.

'Replace a roof tile on this place and it will make the front page of *The Examiner*,' she commented.

Seton knew it to be true, the expenditure on maintenance of Castle Nisbet was a standing joke with the local tradespeople.

'We'll just mention EC grants, nobody can sort all of those out. We're probably due some anyway, I think I'll start investigating.'

'Talking of investigating, the butcher told me that everyone reckons Paddy Hearn was murdered. He had some unpleasant friends in Dublin apparently,' Janie said, picking lint off her shirt.

'It wouldn't surprise me. How on earth would the killers have known where he was?'

'Well, they know where he lived.'

'Yes, but he wasn't at home, he was on the rocks beyond the beach.'

'How do you know that?' she asked.

'His van was parked outside Ballingaddy,' he said, 'it stands to reason that he was along the coast somewhere with his machine.'

'Probably trying to find the rest of your hoard,' she said, concentrating on an unexplained dried smudge on her hem.

Seton guessed that she knew something but wasn't going to push her further. He had weakly told her that his late appearance for tea on that Sunday was because he had trouble with some errant heifers and had to mend the wire in the dark but she took it sceptically, he knew, although it was never mentioned again.

19

Rosie sat at the back of Trotman's saleroom watching the proceedings in the general sale. She followed the catalogue as each item was offered and noted that most people recorded the result alongside each lot number. More often than not the price exceeded the upper estimate on each lot by such a margin that if it occurred during the selling of the hoard then she wouldn't have a hope of buying them.

People came and went, some slipping away quietly, others striding out, whether in disappointment or elation was difficult to tell, but they had their heads down as if to force a passage through the throng around the door at the back of the saleroom. She had to wonder what half the people were doing there as they sat impassively, every now and then craning their necks to have a better view of a particular lot or at somebody bidding, indulging in a curious spectator sport. They didn't record prices, nor did they seem to have the necessary bidding paddle on which their buyer's number was printed. Were these people sellers, hence their interest?

At real estate auctions you were bound to get all the neighbours along so that they could keep tabs on the prices of local houses, but antiquity sales?

She could see very little of the bidding except that received over the telephone as the staff executing those bids were lined up alongside the rostrum facing the room bidders. Every now and then she could see the back of a paddle raised for an instant or a brief nod answering the auctioneer's hand raised in askance.

She wondered if the vendor of the hoard was there. She had been asked by Seamus to "ferret around" to find out who he or she was; whether they were Irish was of particular interest to him. Seamus was emerald green with envy that he couldn't be there, it overshadowed his excitement that they now had a chance to buy the hoard.

Rosie had called him whilst in the cab from Heathrow to give him the news and to agree on the prices to bid to. They also discussed each eventuality: if she failed to get the coins, then was she to continue to pursue the rest, and if she did not get the mounts would she go for the cross and paten, using the unspent portion on the next two lots, and if failing to get the cross, should she then spend everything on the paten? Seamus dared her to do exactly that for the boot was on the other foot now and if he ever did such a thing he would be carpeted by the likes of her and have to write pages in a report explaining himself.

Rosie was torn between exercising restraint, her instinctive answer, or acting for the museum's sake and going all the harder for the paten if she was outbid on the other items.

The first flutter of nerves danced in her stomach and she yawned to relieve them which, at first, worked well, but as the minute hand swung upwards from half past towards the hour they became a constant sensation and started to affect other parts of her body from tingling skin to heartbeats being felt at the back of her throat. Her throat, in turn, started to dry and she stifled a cough, scared that by raising her hand to her mouth she would catch the auctioneer's attention. In the end she rose from her seat to find a glass of water, leaving the saleroom at five to one, but with fifteen lots of the general sale to go.

Harry saw a tall lady stand at the back of the saleroom and make her exit. She was carrying her coat over her arm and a briefcase, and as she got to the aisle he noticed that she was wearing a suit, the skirt of which was of such brevity it revealed a pair of disproportionately long legs that carried her away from him. He wished he had remembered her face but was in the middle of selling Lot 243, a Cypriot iron age amphora with red brown and umber decoration, 7th century B.C., for three thousand pounds, which he knocked down to buyer No. 11.

'Hey, I was bidding,' a call came from before him.

'I was bidding,' a man repeated, holding up his bidding paddle bearing the number 163.

'Oh, I am sorry,' Harry said, unaware that anybody was bidding at all and having knocked it down to his "house number". 'I'll have to reoffer it sir, this gentleman was bidding,' he said to a phantom buyer number 11 who was, in fact, a chairback, 'I'll extend the same facility to you at a later date, no doubt. Thank you very much. Now where were we? Two thousand eight hundred I have.'

Buyer Number 163 sullenly raised his hand.

'Three thousand, another one sir?' he asked the chair, 'three thousand two hundred, thank you.'

He was still shy of the three and a half thousand pound reserve.

'Three thousand, four hundred,' he said, before 163 could raise his hand sufficiently for the auctioneer to recognise it as a bid and then 'three thousand, six hundred,' when he had done so, having exceeded his pre-sale limit by two hundred pounds.

Harry was on a roll, he had carried the sale along at his own, often criticised, rate of a hundred lots per hour. Buyers not used to his canter were often lost and some comments had filtered through to Sam Reid who had tried to slow him down but the first sale he did at only sixty lots per hour fortuitously turned out to be a complete flop and he was allowed to take his whip to the next. If buyers couldn't get organised at a century per hour then they had no hope at all at his speed for coin sales which was twice that, or nearly so; three lots per minute was a comfortable rate for coin sales.

He had failed to sell the vase by the Caeretan painter, his only major failure for the sale and had noticed that virtually all the bids he had received from America were insufficient on the day, most lots selling to people in the room. As he looked at the mosaic of faces in front of him he was pleased to see a few foreign dealers that usually bid through colleagues in London but had chosen to attend this sale in person and who had remained in the saleroom after lots of their particular interest had been sold.

One man wearing a sports jacket had puzzled him as he nodded in acknowledgment when their eyes had met and Harry smiled as if in recognition in return, but it took him several more lots to realise that it was the youthful Detective Inspector Longfield of Scotland Yard.

He noticed that the time was approaching one o'clock and he still had ten lots to get through, the last of which was an important Diorite head of Mut, the consort of the god Amun, for which they hoped to get more than four hundred thousand pounds, the most expensive lot in the general sale. He rather shot through the lots prior to that, if only to give himself some more time to sell her.

In the end he needn't have bothered as he received a call of 'half a million' when he called 'Lot 255'.

'I'm sorry?' he stammered, unused to shouted bids.

'Half a million pounds,' the voice repeated but he failed to see from whom it came.

'Alright. Half a million pounds I'm offered,' he said, 'do I hear five fifty?'

There was a disappointed silence, the crowd had expected a duel, not a single shot.

'At half a million pounds then,' Harry said, similarly disappointed. He wanted a murmur to be going round the room when he introduced the hoard lots. He brought his boxwood gavel down on the rostrum and looked up to see the familiar face of Roy Camble, the Scottish businessman of tax evasion fame, holding a bidding paddle high above his fellow bidders.

Harry duly recorded the number and slyly looked in Camble's direction to see if he was staying for the next part of the sale. It appeared that he was. Harry had never seen him in person, only in the newspapers or on television when one of his companies made a successful, and nearly always hostile, raid on their opposition, or if he sacked yet another member of his board, especially a Peer of the Realm, which he seemed to do with regularity.

'Now, ladies and gentlemen, in a few minutes we will offer the "The Viking Hoard"', Harry announced.

A television crew moved into the back of the room, jostling a few people as they went and set their camera up in the corner.

Jonathan and Octavia Armstrong heard the announcement and entered the saleroom for the first time, having sat outside in the hallway for the past half an hour listening to the smooth delivery of Harry Knox as he coaxed more money out of his audience.

Jonathan held Octavia's hand as they searched for two free seats, finding them three rows from the back on the right hand side, just beneath the television camera. He couldn't remember the last time they had held hands in public, it must have been at Livia's christening, because Octavia hadn't accompanied him when he attended his father's funeral in Christchurch and they only ever held hands when they were in church for christenings, weddings and funerals. The auction had all the facets of a wedding, the vendors there to see off their property, the buyers to unite themselves with new companions and the whole conducted by an auctioneer, there to bring the two together.

Octavia's hand clutched onto Jonathan's even after they had sat down, her long fingers gripping his palm in a rare, for her, admission of expectation and excitement. They had only been fractionally as excited finding the hoard and had somehow got through the two months of waiting for the sale by not mentioning it to each other until the catalogue arrived, which they had had to hide from Livia and the boys, and only talk about when they were in bed or away with friends.

They had explained their journey to London as a business trip and placated their daughter by promising to bring presents back which had imposed upon them a half hour tour of Hatchards to find some books and another half hour in Hamley's looking for yet more furniture for Livia's doll's house, already bursting at the seams.

There were people still milling about the saleroom, mostly looking for a place to sit. Octavia could see Harry take a sip of water, raising a finger to her when he saw them from over his glass. She smiled back, she hadn't flirted for years but her exuberance was such that she permitted herself to bring some joy to the man that was going to bring so much to her and Jonathan, Livia, Augustus, Marcus, Seton, Janie and young John.

Rosie Spillane was instantly calmed by the glass of water given to her by the receptionist in the foyer who, trying to make conversation, asked her if she was buying or selling.

'I'm hopefully trying to buy something. Bit nervous actually,' she replied, holding up the half empty glass as an explanation.

'Oh, it's nerve racking,' the girl replied tactlessly, 'I've bid hundreds of times for clients who can't make it and I'm still a wreck when the lot comes up. Are you going for the Irish things?'

Rosie couldn't imagine how she had known.

'Your accent,' the girl explained.

'Bit of a give away,' Rosie conceded. 'Yes, but I don't think we'll get them.'

'We'll?' the girl asked, looking for a companion.

'The government, I represent the Irish government.'

'Oh goodness, I'm sorry, I didn't mean to pry.'

Rosie had already filled in a registration form under the name of Department of Arts, Culture and Gaeltacht; there could be no pretence now.

'I'd better get back in there,' Rosie said, 'thank you so much for the water.'

'Good luck, I mean it, it gets better once you've done your first bid.'

She did mean it as well, she had seen people rush to the lavatories after failing to buy something and every time she heard a footballer complain of being "sick as a parrot" to express disappointment, she knew exactly what sick parrots looked like.

David Reeves settled himself into a chair sandwiched between two well-dressed ladies whom he had, at first, thought to be companions, but they both shifted themselves to the edges of their seats, away from the vacant spot when he showed interest in it.

They both had their catalogues open on the first lot of the hoard, the Edmund penny, and thick gold mounted pens in their hands ready to record the result. Each wore expensive jewellery, not as well as Tracy, he thought, and were obviously clothed by the same couturier or read the same fashion magazines.

Their haughty expressions of surprise that somebody dressed in jeans, a Marks and Spencer jumper and trainers could possibly be interested in the forthcoming proceedings were hardly disguised and David resorted to his normal ploy of cheekiness in these circumstances.

''Ave I missed anyfing then?'

'I'm sorry?' the lady to his right asked.

''Ave I missed anyfing from the first 'alf, like?'

'The statue of Mut sold for half a million to Roy Camble.'

'What, the 'ead?'

'Yes, of Mut,' the lady replied.

'Gordon Bennett, imagine what it would've sold for if the rest woz there. That Roy Camble needs another 'ead anyway, gawd knows the one 'e hangs around wiv is ugly enough. D'yer get annifink yerself?'

'No, my husband wanted me to record the prices, he's thinking of selling a few things,' the lady replied.

'Wot abaht you, love?' David asked the lady on his left.

'No, unfortunately not today,' she replied and looked to her front as though that was all she was prepared to say on the matter.

'It's like waitin' for the kick off at Wembley ain't it?' David said, but as neither lady had attended Wembley neither thought it fit to comment either way upon the suggestion.

Rebecca Simon had been writing down the prices in the catalogue of the general sale, noting that bids in excess of the estimates were the only successful ones. She had been there from eleven o'clock onwards, standing at the left hand back wall until a gentleman noticed her and generously offered her his seat. She never knew whether to accept such offers; stand up, literally, for women's equality, or graciously accept a chivalrous offer from somebody who only wanted to please, and not test the mettle of the sisterhood.

She thanked him and took his seat, her unease at so doing soon quelled by the departure of somebody two rows in front and the gentleman resuming the vacancy, but only after he had checked that there was nobody more deserving for the place.

Rebecca was not a stranger to auctions but their workings were a mystery. She would record pages of lots selling around the lower estimate, or even failing to sell, until it was her turn and at double the top estimate she would back out and return to being an underbidder. She would then watch the next dozen or so lots receive desultory bidding until the next time she bid and up the price went again as if there was a conspiracy to prevent her from owning anything.

Simon & Simon Co. Pension Fund was now richly endowed with works of art of many nations and many periods, mostly displayed in the offices of their company not frequented by the public. How she was going to display the cross, once purchased, was another matter, but she was determined about one thing, for an occasion, preferably a ball, she would wear it, for although she wasn't in need of adornment, she felt that the cross was in need of a wearer and an appreciative owner.

'Now, ladies and gentlemen, "The Viking Hoard",' Harry said in a louder voice so that it could be heard over the scuffles of chair legs on the wooden floor. He reminded them that they were selling under the terms and conditions as printed in the catalogue, that a buyers' premium was being applied on the knock down price and that all lots had to be paid for and cleared before 4 o'clock in the afternoon of Tuesday, although, he added, in this instance, he wasn't averse to keeping the objects in his office for a little big longer. There was a soft hum of amusement and some smiles, none more radiant than that offered by Octavia. It was good to humanise the mechanics of doing business by auction, a very public consumption like pigeons fighting over a crust in a park.

'Lot 256, the Edmund penny, crowned bust type by Eadgar of Norwich.'

As he read the description, a colour photograph of the obverse of the penny was shown on the screen to his right.

'Do we have the phone bid Julia?' he asked and turned to see his secretary looking at him, phone in hand, as if to say 'get on with it.'

'Right, do I have eight hundred?'

He didn't, but he knew it was there somewhere so he took it.

'Eight hundred, nine hundred, a thousand and eleven hundred,' he said before Julia said 'Yes' firmly.

'Twelve hundred, then, thirteen to the lady on the aisle', he said pointing to Rosie, 'any more Julia?'

Julia shook her head, he knew she was bidding for a dealer in Oslo.

'At thirteen hundred pounds, all done?'

A hand flashed at the back of the room.

'Fourteen hundred.'

Rosie bid once more, her limit was fifteen hundred and the coin, being English, was not of as much interest to her numismatists as the other three. The young man behind her, standing in the doorway, bought the penny for sixteen hundred pounds.

The hoard was now split, she thought.

'Now the first of the raven types of Olaf Guthfrithsson, struck in York by Athelferd, extraordinary for there to be two in the hoard.'

Harry noticed that the illustration was upside down on the large computer screens around the room.

'Ah, a raven headed south for the winter, I see,' he commented dryly.

'Lot 257, do I hear four thousand pounds? Four thousand? No. Three thousand, thank you madam,' he said pointing his gavelled hand at Rosie who had been reluctant to open the bidding, in fact had been instructed by Seamus not to do so, but she was anxious to get it going.

She competed with a tenacious telephone bidder represented by a 'Julia' with whom the auctioneer was enjoying some repartee.

'He doesn't want to better eight thousand Julia?' Harry asked, and Julia confirmed that he had reached his limit, as indeed had Rosie, but the eight thousand was her bid.

'Right, eight thousand, the lady's bid,' he said, 'eight and a half,' he added, as the young man in the doorway stepped into the fray.

'I have eight and a half in the door madam, one more?'

Rosie shook her head and realising that there were many eyes on her, crossed her legs with frustration, the movement of her limbs caught by Harry who now knew the face attached to buyer number 71. He knocked the first raven type penny down to the previous buyer, the young, unrecognised, man in the doorway.

The second raven type penny went for eleven thousand to the same man, pushed to the higher price by Rosie who had a bit more money to spend on the coins and having failed on the third was now armed with more for the triquetra type.

'Lot 259, the triquetra type of Sihtric, only the third known and the second for this moneyer Ascolv, the other being a fragment in the British Museum. As Drew Gatacre, my colleague in the numismatic department says, a once in a lifetime lot. One of the rarest coins in the British series.

Eight thousand pounds?'

Julia bid first, then Rosie, then a man sitting directly in front of Camble, who was still there, his forearms resting on his knees and with head bowed. Harry thought that he was relaying instructions to the man in front of him.

Julia's buyer dropped out at fifteen thousand, Rosie at seventeen and the man in front of Camble at eighteen. At nineteen thousand pounds the hammer went down to the same buyer as the rest of the coins. The hoard wasn't, so far, split up at all, just in the process of changing hands.

Jonathan observed six people get up after the fourth coin sold and leave the room, their interest obviously exhausted. Octavia watched Jonathan total up the result so far on a piece of his firm's letterhead. £40,100 on reserves of £18,500.

Octavia's hand was now gripped onto his right arm, as immovable as her gaze on Harry, her mouth imperceptibly open in amazement at the prices being paid for the small slivers of silver.

'Lot 260,' Harry said, having allowed a little hiatus as the coin enthusiasts left, each passing the unperturbed buyer clutching his catalogue and bidding paddle in one hand and a pen in the other.

Rosie afforded a glance behind her to try to see who it was that had beaten her to the coins and the fact that his bidding number was held between his hand and catalogue told her who buyer number 298 was. His was the highest number called out in the room so far, telephone bidders started with 600 and bids 'on the books' at 700, she had observed. Mr 298, young, spotty, tyro 298, was a late-comer to the sale. He had come to buy the hoard, but, Rosie thought, they had only been playing with the coins, the next three lots were in the big league, too big for the likes of him. He was better off buying the latest Coldplay album and a large quantity of acne cream or the services of a dermatologist, and by the look of the severity of the attack, one in Harley Street.

'The first of the artefacts, three, presumably of four, gold corner book mounts representing Luke, Mark and Matthew. John is regrettably missing,' Harry announced.

'Very regrettably,' Jonathan said under his breath. Octavia pushed his arm in disapproval.

'Lot 260 then, sixty thousand pounds? Sixty thousand? No? Fifty thousand then, thank you sir, fifty thousand it is. And five? I have fifty five in the aisle', Harry scanned the crowd for any movement other than that of the lady with the legs. It had been his fear that nobody would be on the mounts, they didn't seem to inspire anybody. To his left were six telephones, all busy but for the next lot, he knew that there was nobody who had requested a telephone bidding facility for lot 260.

He had a live bidder at fifty five thousand pounds and a reserve of one hundred thousand. Long Legs had exceeded the estimate on every lot of the coins so presumably she would be prepared to do so on the mounts. He had no choice but to take the lot up to the reserve but she was on the wrong rung of the ladder and his final bid would land on the one hundred thousand pounds. He would have to take hers at ninety-five thousand, then invent another bidder who wanted to half the increment, to ninety seven and a half, and then extend the same courtesy to her, a smoother and seemingly altruistic approach.

He took it slowly, it was only himself and she of the legs, he slipped the half bid in at her bid of ninety thousand. She bid ninety-five, he at ninety seven and a half and she firmly held up her paddle at one hundred thousand.

Then the man with the spots started to bid. Why hadn't he started earlier? Harry pleaded.

'One hundred and five thousand,' Harry said, 'in the door' he added, so that she knew who she was up against.

Rosie felt the stares of everybody behind her as she held her hand up ten more times to take the mounts to two hundred thousand pounds, the amount which she and Seamus had agreed was enough to say that they had tried their best.

'Two hundred and ten thousand, is there anybody else?' Harry asked.

There wasn't.

'Two hundred and ten thousand pounds to 298.'

Rebecca Simon adjusted her poise and readied her bidding paddle. She hadn't counted on each lot selling for twice the estimate despite her experiences. She rather doubted her chances of success.

David Reeves hadn't written down the price of each lot unlike his two neighbours and had sunk into his seat so that his straightened body was lying at a forty-five degree angle from the floor in contrast to the ladies either side who were upright from the waist, their legs angled slightly to one side. There was the difference between Lausanne and Leytonstone.

Seton chased the last pea around his plate which had held a generous helping of cottage pie left in the bottom section of the range by Janie, who had taken John into the baby health clinic in town for his weekly check up. However much he tried, Seton's repeated visual reference to the telephone didn't make it ring, despite the clock above the doorway leading to the hall telling him that it was twenty-two minutes past the hour, twelve minutes after the time Jonathan had promised to ring. Perhaps they had been caught out after all and Jonathan was now being questioned about the origin of the hoard, hence no call. He poured himself a glass of beer and resumed his vigil by the phone observing that the skies had darkened outside, presaging the expected southerly gale.

'Lot 261 is the gold cross, probably the work of a goldsmith operating in the British Isles in the sixth or seventh centuries. A remarkable piece of work as I'm sure you'll agree. Do we have the various connections on the phone?'

Six heads nodded in unison.

The television crew switched on their lights, throwing Harry for a few seconds, but his eyes soon adjusted against the glare.

'I have conflicting bids on the books,' Harry continued, 'we will have to start the bidding at ...' he paused as though he was unsure of his opening bid, but had worked it out at nine o'clock that morning, 'three hundred and eighty thousand pounds.'

He looked up at Rosie, expecting her to counter his bid first.

'Yeah, okay Harry,' a Cockney voice sounded to his left.

'Four hundred thousand ... somewhere,' he added to the amusement of his staff behind and alongside him.

A shaky bidding paddle rose towards the back of the room to his right, the identity of its owner obscured to him by a large figure immediately in front of them.

'Four twenty,' he confirmed.

Another paddle broke the surface of heads to his left like a flag over a parapet.

'Four forty.'

Rebecca's shaky paddle made three more appearances but was lowered by an opposing bid of five hundred and sixty thousand pounds.

The battle was joined by the shapely legs until the paddle to his left decided that the six hundred and twenty thousand bid by the lady on the aisle was too rich for him and David Reeves ceased bidding, the two ladies either side embarrassed by their initial summation of his worth.

'I have six hundred and twenty thousand pounds for the cross.'

He noticed the right leg of the bidder, hung over her left, was bouncing with impatience. She deserved a quick result after all her efforts on the six lots so far and he was about to relieve her tension when the young man at the back showed his intent to challenge, with a raised finger as if he was a cricket umpire answering an appeal in the affirmative.

Rosie was growing tired of the spotty man but her limit was seven hundred thousand pounds to allow herself, no, to allow the Irish nation, enough to have a good chance at the paten.

'Seven hundred and twenty thousand pounds then, are we there?' Harry asked, although it was obvious to him that they were, and his gavel descended in a rapid motion, the sharp crack an onomatopoeic reminder of Rebecca Simon's shattered hopes, a tear of disappointment uncontrollably running down her flecked cheek.

It had been hers for a day; that was all.

Harry felt a touch on his left elbow.

'We've got a problem with your man in New York,' Drew told him quietly, 'his phone is engaged.'

'His phone, or all lines to New York?'

'Only his it seems. Can you delay?'

It ruined the atmosphere to have too long a delay but McMicking had seemed to be a genuine contester and he hadn't a clue whether anybody other than Long Legs and 298 would go for the paten. Long Legs, he knew, was Ireland, surely no country could be represented by the young man. Who, then, was he acting for? If it were a longer sale he could send a message to the registration desk and get the details sent up to him but there wasn't the time. Neither of them had bid on anything else and both were prepared to go beyond the odds. Most British institutions were represented by dealers known to Harry and they were all conspicuously quiet.

'Any luck?' he asked Drew Gatacre who was dialling furiously. He waited for the tone that told him the line was still busy, disconnected and shook his head.

'I'm afraid we can't wait, it's the last lot and people want to get in front of their pan-fried Dover sole in a lemon and cream sauce,' he hissed.

He adjusted his sale sheets and looked back up at his audience.

'Lot 262, the paten that probably accompanied the famous Ardagh Chalice, the latter being found in a potato field in Co. Limerick in 1868, with four brooches and a small bronze cup, if I recall correctly.'

'Who'll start me? I'll take half a million, thank you sir.'

Rosie was making a feather pattern along the edge of the catalogue page with her pen. She was aware that there was action in the room, at twenty thousand pound increments, and that the total was rising rapidly like the price wheel on a petrol pump. She wasn't going to bid, there was too much competition, it had exceeded her price limit of eight hundred and fifty thousand pounds that she was to bid to in the event of not getting the rest.

'One million pounds,' Harry announced, 'one point one?' he asked the man in front of Camble. The man cocked his ear backwards as if to get his instructions right. He then bid to one point one million.

Rosie knew that her one and a half million pounds and the ten per cent buyers' premium meant that she could only bid to £1.35 million. She had watched a dealer earlier in the day bid by drawing a horizontal line in the air which had reduced the increment by half.

She repeated the gesture, not at all sure if it would work.

'For you, anything, madam,' Harry said, 'one million, one hundred and fifty thousand pounds, the lady's bid. At one point one five million then,' he gave the spotty young man another glance, he hadn't bid on this particular lot, it had been David Reeves and Camble's stooge until Long Legs got rid of them.

He raised his hand, hamming it up a bit for the television camera, when, from out of the glare somebody shouted 'Yes.'

He saw Long Leg's shoulders collapse in despair, could he not have knocked it down sooner to her?

'One point two million pounds,' he said, and shaded his eyes against the camera light to see who it was that had bid but there was no sign of him.

'At one point two million pounds, then ..', crack, as the gavel struck, 'thank you sir.'

A bidding paddle rose from beneath the camera, number 298, the young man must have given it to an accomplice.

The hoard was intact but who now owned it was a mystery to Harry.

A trickle of applause rose like a small stream running over rocks until it reached a waterfall of appreciation.

'Thank you ladies and gentlemen, the Ardagh paten is the most expensive antiquity of the British Isles to be sold by auction. I thank you for your participation, good afternoon.'

As Harry got down from the rostrum he noticed that the television crew were trying to interview both the young men who had wielded the 298 bidding paddle but they were making for the door without any comment. Staff members were congratulating him on such a successful sale, Julia had totals for him, somebody else had the registration form for buyer 298.

'Who the hell are Mullaghcleevaun Constructions Plc?' he asked, upon reading the form, they had listed their address with a London postcode beginning with SW7, Fulham.

'Great sale Harry, see you Sunday, yeah?' David Reeves said.

'Yes, thanks David, sorry you missed out.'

'Missed out? I wouldn't 'ave missed this for quids. I'll be in the next one, that's for sure.'

'I'll see you on Sunday.'

The saleroom was emptying, the camera crew were packing up and the chatter was beginning to fade away. Harry looked for Jonathan and Octavia but they had gone.

Through the forest of people standing in the aisle he could see the tip of the shoe that adorned a pair of long legs, one still suspended in the air.

'It's just one of those things,' he said to the lady who was scribbling something on a piece of paper. She looked up suddenly when he spoke.

'Yes,' she replied.

'Thank you for your support, I'm just sorry that you have nothing to show for it.'

'No, well, as you said, just one of those things,' it was obvious that she did not want to talk so he moved on out of the saleroom to the large hallway where people were gathered in groups, flicking through their catalogues and expressing their opinions on the prices achieved.

'Will you continue to send me catalogues?' a soft voice asked. He turned to see Rebecca Simon clutching her catalogue between her folded arms and chest, still open at the entry for the cross.

'Of course I will. Please don't be too despondent, it was a very special thing you were after, its like won't come up again.'

'I know, but we all have dreams,' she replied and slid away.

Harry couldn't find the Armstrongs anywhere in the building and Sam Reid couldn't find Mullaghcleevaun Constructions in the telephone book, nor did they leave a contact telephone number, an omission not noticed by the secretary who had taken the registration.

'Mullaghcleevaun sounds awfully Irish,' Drew said unhelpfully.

20

Rosie flew back to Dublin that evening feeling quite wretched about the events of the day. Ever since her first school report, her name and the word "achiever" were never far apart but she had achieved little other than to get 298 to pay well over the odds to own each lot of the hoard.

She called Seamus from the taxi on her way to Heathrow.

'Who bought them?' he demanded.

'How on earth would I know? Number 298, a spotty youth. If you watch the news you'll see him, they filmed the cross and the paten.'

'What was the total again?' he asked.

'With premiums and VAT on that, etc., Mr Acne has spent £2,432,847.62, which is a touch over our limit.'

'Don't sound so bitter about it,' Seamus said, appreciative of her disappointment, 'did you get to meet the vendors?'

'No, nobody with tricolours on their hats and mud on their feet. The only Irish accent was my own. Can you pass all this information on to the relevant people? I can't phone anybody once I'm on the plane.'

During the flight, her mind dwelt on 298 and why he had moved to bid on the last lot and who he was, spending that much money without a flicker of nerves, or so it had seemed to her. He had to be acting for the British government, they could expect to hear the news early the next week, the Irish had been downtrodden by the British yet again.

She arrived at her empty house to find a string of messages on her answerphone, everybody ringing to share her disappointment. Her minister had rung with a message from the Taoiseach commiserating on the result and saying that he would have to find a new way of wishing people good luck in future, it seemed to have a hex on events.

She didn't stir from her house all weekend, she read a book and the papers, watched television, spoke to her mother on the telephone and, uncharacteristically, didn't change out of her nightclothes all day on Sunday. She felt deflated and lethargic, values had been changed, her orderly and precise life invaded by uncertainty and recklessness. She had never experienced disappointment to such a degree before and she wasn't coping at all well.

She arrived late for work on the Monday morning and noticed that she was being avoided by her staff after each had offered their condolences. There were several telephone messages on her desk, left by those that did not have her home telephone or mobile numbers. There were none that she had to return. Seamus called to make an appointment to go through each lot, blow by blow, a meeting she managed to postpone until the next day. She had a small gathering to attend at lunchtime, a progress report on an upcoming event over a plateful of rubber chicken and yesterday's salad, an unnecessary function that could have achieved so much more with a cup of coffee around a conference table.

Her telephone rang once, a signal from her secretary on the other side of her closed door.

'Yes?'

'I've a Liam Kelleher on the telephone, wants to talk to you, he won't give me a subject matter,' her secretary explained.

'I don't know a Liam Kelleher,' she said crossly, 'what does he want?'

'He won't tell me but very specifically wants to talk to you.'

'Oh, alright,' Rosie relented, she always preferred to know what people wanted to talk to her about before they did so. It was an essential part of her ordered life.

'Mr Kelleher, what can I do for you?'

'Are you the lady in charge of the arts funding?'

'Yes, that's right,'

'Ah, finally got through t' the right person,' he said with relief, 'you're a difficult person to track down.'

His voice was deep with the nasal twang of the outer suburbs of Dublin, although there was also an inflection foreign to the capital.

'How can I help you?'

'I'd like to meet you to discuss something that might be of interest to you. Are you free to see me this afternoon? I'm only in town for a short while.'

'Well,' Rosie hesitated. She was free but really wasn't in the mood to discuss funding for anything today, 'can you tell me what it is about?'

'Not on the telephone. I'll be with you in half an hour,' and Mr Kelleher put the phone down before she could say any more.

Exactly half an hour later Rosie's secretary showed him into her office.

Liam Kelleher was every bit as Rosie imagined, large and booming and displayed all the signs of having worked outside most of his life. He was, however, surprisingly well dressed, casual but neat and was carrying a leather briefcase, the kind one paid a lot of money to own.

'Mr Kelleher,' said Rosie politely, 'how can I help you?'

'Y' know the hoard and things, the Celtic bits and bobs from Ireland?' he asked.

'The Viking Hoard?'

'That's the one,' he said, 'I wanted to help you ...'

'That's very generous of you Mr Kelleher, but they were sold on Friday. We didn't manage to get them.'

'I know that. Y'see, I saw you on the telly two weeks ago an' again last week in Dublin. An' you said you hadn't enough money to buy them?'

'That's right. In the event we were given a sum from the Finance Department but we ended up underbidding each lot. If you had come up with some money beforehand then maybe we ...'

'You underbid every lot?' Mr Kelleher interrupted.

'Yes, sadly we have missed out on buying them for the Nation.'

Without a word Mr Kelleher lifted his briefcase and, unlocking the two catches, opened it to reveal the hoard items, covered in bubble wrap but quite discernable through the plastic.

'I bought them for the country. You said you had no money and I sent my two lads in to buy them for you and here they are, all paid for by bank transfer, my gift to Ireland, such a wonderful country although I make my living across the water now. Something I can give back to the country of my birth.'

Rosie stared at the items, the truth dawning on her. Mr Kelleher was buyer number 298.

'But how did you get them here?' she stammered.

'I flew into Dublin this morning,' he replied, puzzled by her question and wondering why she wasn't more grateful for his gift.

'I mean, the export licenses? They would need export licenses.'

'Export licenses?' he asked, 'what export licenses?'

Ballingaddy

Baile an Gadáidhe

The home of the thief

www.ingramcontent.com/pod-product-compliance
Ingram Content Group UK Ltd.
Pitfield, Milton Keynes, MK11 3LW, UK
UKHW041438180426
11947UKWH00007B/508